"I would like to stay, Fiona,"
Rogan said.

"I think it's best that you leave tomorrow. I'm not going to change my mind about the tourists."

"Wait a minute. That subject's off-limits according to the truce. I want to stay another day to see the elephants again. I'd like to stay here with you, Fiona."

She was afraid if Rogan said one more thing, she would give him anything he wanted. The tourists, the campsite, the elephants. The way he held her with his gaze sent a shiver all through her body. His voice held her mesmerized.

Rogan reached across the table and covered her hand with his. "There's some kind of magic out here. I don't know whether it's the dry heat or the birth of the baby elephant. Or maybe it's you, Fiona. I'm not ready to go back. Just give me another day here. Would you do that?"

Dear Reader,

When two people fall in love, the world is suddenly new and exciting, and it's that same excitement we bring to you in Silhouette Intimate Moments. These are stories with scope and grandeur. The characters lead lives we all dream of, and everything they do reflects the wonder of being in love.

Longer and more sensuous than most romances, Silhouette Intimate Moments novels take you away from everyday life and let you share the magic of love. Adventure, glamour, drama, even suspense— these are the passwords that let you into a world where love has a power beyond the ordinary, where the best authors in the field today create stories of love and commitment that will stay with you always.

In coming months, look for novels by your favorite authors: Barbara Faith, Marilyn Pappano, Emilie Richards, Paula Detmer Riggs and Nora Roberts, to name only a few. And whenever—and wherever— you buy books, look for all the Silhouette Intimate Moments, love stories with that extra something, books written especially for you by today's top authors.

Leslie J. Wainger
Senior Editor and Editorial Coordinator

CATHERINE PALMER

Weeping Grass

SILHOUETTE·INTIMATE·MOMENTS®

Published by Silhouette Books New York

America's Publisher of Contemporary Romance

SILHOUETTE BOOKS
300 East 42nd St., New York, N.Y. 10017

WEEPING GRASS

Copyright © 1992 by Catherine Palmer

ISBN: 0-373-07426-3

First Silhouette Books printing April 1992

Printed in the U.S.A.

Books by Catherine Palmer

Silhouette Intimate Moments

Land of Enchantment #367
Forbidden #403
Weeping Grass #426

CATHERINE PALMER

loves creating stories with locales and backgrounds that are as exotic and diverse as the ones she grew up in herself—and as the daughter of missionaries, she's been to quite a few places! One of the most exotic—Kenya, Africa—brings back fond memories of living on a nineteen-thousand-acre cattle ranch and thrilling to the sight of wonderful animals such as gazelles, lions and giraffes.

She now resides in Bolivar, Missouri, with her husband and their young son, and between writing, her membership in the RWA and her interest in art, she is kept very busy. Though her first joys are her family and her writing, she also enjoys crafts, tennis and swimming.

For Janice Owens Duffy

Chapter 1

When elephants fight, it is the grass that weeps.
                                        —*Swahili Proverb*

"She's chillier than the ice on Kilimanjaro," Clive Willetts snorted. The lanky British pilot banked the small aircraft and glanced at his boss, the new owner of the flying safari company. "Not to say I don't like Dr. Thornton, sir. It's just that she can be touchy at times. She doesn't like people intruding."

"And I suppose she'd classify my little visit as an intrusion?"

"More than likely."

Rogan McCullough slid back his starched white cuff and studied his watch for a moment. Three embedded gold dials indicated time zones around the world. Here in East Africa it was ten o'clock in the morning.

His flight from London had been delayed twice, putting him four hours late into Nairobi. He'd sent his suitcases ahead to his hotel with the limousine and boarded one of two Catalina PBY 5As owned by Air-Tours Safaris. Despite the short flight and the clear weather over central Kenya, Rogan knew he hadn't given himself much time to sell a cranky, eccentric scientist on his newest brainstorm.

He gave the watch an absentminded flick as he stared out the side window. Far beneath the plane rolled verdant hills covered in a tangle of vines, eucalyptus and Nandi flame trees. Small villages gathered in clearings, their thatched huts dark against the bright red-orange soil. Then, as though a confectioner had neatly sliced away the middle of a green-iced sheetcake, the fertile highlands stopped. The land fell sharply, and a great barren yellow plain stretched far in the distance until it reached the rise of the distant escarpment.

"The Great Rift Valley," Clive explained, as if sensing his boss's interest in the abrupt change. "It runs from the Mediterranean Sea most of the way along the east coast of Africa. Strangest thing you'll ever see. It's a fault—as though the continent tried to split in two a few million years back. The whole Rift Valley is full of unusual land formations."

Rogan shifted his attention to the British pilot, whose skimpy blond mustache wandered across his upper lip like an uncertain centipede. Despite his preoccupation with business, Rogan had always had a keen interest in natural sciences. As a small boy he had collected rocks and fallen birds' nests. At his boarding school, his room had been littered with pieces of driftwood, feathers and pressed leaves. Even as an adult he'd chosen to include climbing and caving among his pastimes. In a drawer he kept a record of the mountains he'd scaled. Another list noted the ones he hadn't. Through the years he'd checked them off one by one.

"What kinds of formations?" he asked.

"Volcanos," the pilot explained. "Some of them are still active. Lakes full of pink flamingos. Caves lined with thousands of bats. Craggy black lava flows. Soda-rimmed marshes. Snowcapped mountains. And escarpments."

He let the plane drop and glide along the sheer edge of the valley.

"Can anything live down there?" Rogan asked as his gaze traced the razor-sharp cliffs and the wide plain between.

"The place is a regular Garden of Eden, sir. Zebras. Gazelles. Antelopes. Cheetahs. Elephants."

"People?"

"Unsociable sorts. The Maasai have the run of the place. They're a fierce, primitive lot who still carry spears and don't think too highly of modern civilization. And, of course, there's Dr. Fiona Thornton."

"Ah, yes." Rogan closed his eyes and conjured up the image he'd formed of the woman who ran the Rift Valley Elephant Project. He pictured her as a mixture of his high school English teacher and his great-aunt Rose.

In the weeks he'd been planning his trip, he'd come to imagine Dr. Thornton as a short, buxom woman with steel gray hair and a thunderous voice. She would wear a khaki dress left over from some World War II women's corps, thick support stockings in a pale shade that skin had never considered turning and heavy black lace-up boots. Her stern face would wither him from the shade of a pith helmet as her pinched lips formed the answer she would snap at his request. *Absolutely not.*

The trace of a grin formed a subtle dimple beside his mouth. Sorry, Dr. Thornton, he thought, but I'm afraid you've met your match.

He leaned against the headrest and closed his eyes. As a matter of fact, he was looking forward to the challenge of outwitting the old battle-ax with as much anticipation as he felt for a boardroom confrontation at McCullough Enterprises. His persuasive style and bullheaded stubbornness had built the company into a multimillion-dollar operation, after all. And he intended to reverse the sagging revenues of Air-Tours by applying the same determination.

"If you'll excuse my frankness sir," Clive said, "you look exhausted. Jet lag will catch up with a man, no matter how strong he is. I'd suggest you get a little rest. When your father owned Air-Tours, he used to stretch out in the lounge back there and take a good long catnap. We've got a well-stocked bar, a library of old maps and books and a clean rest room. Your father always said the rumble of the engines did him more good than a hundred-dollar massage."

"I'm fine. Really."

The pilot smiled, showing a set of uneven teeth beneath the wispy mustache. "Your father learned the hard way, too.

But after he'd been coming to Kenya for a few years, he once told me that Africa was the only place where he could really rest. Africa was where he could let go. He said it was the only place he knew of where he was really himself—"

"If you don't mind," Rogan interrupted, "I'd rather not talk right now, Clive. I need to review some figures."

"Yes, sir." The pilot gave him a sideways glance and clamped his mouth shut.

Rogan flipped the gold clasps on his leather briefcase and extracted a file. Air-Tours. The company had shown a steep decline in the past five years. He intended to rectify that. In many ways, resolving financial difficulties was his specialty. Oh, he enjoyed the media aspect of McCullough Enterprises, and he liked working with the journalists and admen he employed. Their bright-eyed enthusiasm kept him pushing for innovation long after his own fiscal goals had been met.

But it was in the resurrection of companies on the brink of financial extinction that Rogan excelled. It was how he'd gotten his start. And the prospect of bringing some of his father's small businesses back to life helped ease the sting of the pitiful legacy he'd inherited. Rogan was well aware that the collection of flagging industries and the small lump sum—only a tiny percentage of John McCullough's vast estate—were little more than conscience money. They were his father's way of acknowledging to the world that once, among all his other accomplishments, he'd produced a son.

The rest of the estate had been parceled out among ex-wives, financial institutions and charities bearing the McCullough name. Rogan didn't really care that he'd been left the financially weak companies, he told himself. He looked on them as a challenge. Something to keep him going.

From his offices in New York, he'd examined the books and records of Air-Tours and the others. He'd made calls. Set up contacts. Investigated and instigated programs. In just three months, the pizza chain was showing a spark and the hotels were preparing for face-lifts. Now he had his sights set on the tiny flying safari company.

Rows of neat figures swam before his eyes as Rogan stared at his father's signature scrawled across a balance sheet. John McCullough. The ink flourishes personified the man. He had personified extravagance. Wealth. Show. Pomp. Scandal. Clive Willetts's recounting of talks with the tycoon didn't fit the picture his son held of him. Rogan rubbed a finger across his temples.

He didn't really want to think about his father. When he did, he felt six years old again. Six years old and hiding behind the stair rail watching his parents hurl accusations and Ming Dynasty vases at each other. Six years old and trembling as his mother screeched and wept and hung on to his father's coattails. Six years old and frozen inside as he stood at the iron gate of an ivy-covered boarding school and stared at the settling puff of dust from his father's Mercedes.

Rogan slammed down the briefcase lid. Clive lifted one eyebrow.

"About Dr. Thornton," Rogan said irritably. "What's she most likely to respond to? Money? Publicity?"

Clive snorted. "Well, Dr. Thornton isn't your average sort of person, if you know what I mean. She's more than a little eccentric. Not the kind of woman who'll give you the time of day... unless you're an elephant."

"Surely she's in need of funding or new supplies. I've heard these research projects are always in the hole."

"Could be. I wouldn't doubt it."

"You told me she gives you tips on where the elephants are so you can fly tourists over them. You must know something about her. How does she operate? What drives her?"

"She's never said a word to me about herself, mind you. Just talks about elephants. She grew up in Kenya just like I did. But we didn't know each other in those days. My father was a farmer down near the coast, and we stayed fairly isolated. I heard she was born in Nairobi to an American father and an English mother. Her father's a professor of anthropology at the University of Nairobi. Her mother was a painter, but she died a long time ago."

"How?"

Clive shrugged. "No idea. Anyway, Fiona Thornton came back to Kenya and met a woman studying lions in the Amboseli Game Park. Dr. Howard sponsored her, saw that she was educated and helped her get research grants from scientific societies. Since then, Dr. Thornton has studied elephants. Elephants are her passion. It's like I've tried to tell you, sir, she doesn't have much interest in humans. When she does actually decide to say something, it might be only two or three words...if you're lucky. Odd thing about Dr. Thornton, though. The Africans who work with her call her Matalai Shamsi. It means Princess Sunrise."

Rogan shook his head, declining to respond as the plane banked steeply and began its descent into the Great Rift Valley.

Fiona Thornton stared at the neat row of figures for a full minute. She lifted her head. "Three calves this month," she said.

Sentero eyed her, his face impassive.

She tapped her pen on the metal folding table. "I want to find the M family this afternoon. Moira was in estrus in—" she scanned the papers in her hand "—in April '90. During the long rains, I saw her in consort with the old bull, James. At the time, he was definitely in musth. Moira's had the full twenty-two-month gestation, and I've noticed her breasts seem fuller than usual."

"Yesterday she was restless." Sentero's voice was deep, his English enunciation clear.

"She seemed out of sync with the others, don't you think?"

The African nodded, then stiffened and lifted his eyes, as if he could see through the tent's olive canvas roof.

"What is it?" Fiona had come to rely on her Maasai assistant's keen senses. He often heard and saw things much sooner than she did.

"Airplane."

"It won't land here. It's probably going to one of the Mara lodges."

Sentero shrugged. "It will come here."

At that moment Fiona heard the distinct rumble of the plane's engines. She chewed the inside of her lip for a moment, then brushed a hand across her forehead. Standing, she replaced her records in a metal file box and locked it.

"I didn't order any supplies from Nairobi. Did you?" she asked.

Sentero shook his head. Framed in the opening of the tent flap, his tall, sinewy body stood dark against the brilliant African sunshine. He was a sinister-looking man with a face chiseled by time into sharp angles and harsh planes. His eyes, small and almost black, glittered with a canny sparkle.

Fiona had rarely seen Sentero wear anything but draped layers of bloodred cloths, some plaid, some checked, all smelling of wood smoke. Three bead necklaces circled his throat, one a choker with a central button of mother-of-pearl, the other two dangling at his bare chest. His ears, each lobe pierced and stretched to form a two-inch hole, sported beaded bands of red, yellow, white and blue. Occasionally Sentero plugged the hole of one earlobe with an old black plastic film canister filled with tobacco. Chewing tobacco was his only vice.

"Sentero, start the Land Rover," Fiona said calmly as the plane's engines roared over her camp. The tent trembled. Vervet monkeys shrieked in the acacia trees overhead. Her cat leapt down from his perch on the wardrobe and darted under the bed. She grabbed her jacket and camera. "I'll tell Nguyo to ward them off, whoever they are."

Sentero flashed his only smile of the morning, snatched his iron-tipped spear from beside the tent pole and strode out. Fiona knelt at the foot of the small camp cot. Flicking on her flashlight, she swept its beam through the dust until she caught the cat's green eyes.

"Oh, Sukari, are you afraid?" With small kissing noises, she gently patted the tent's canvas floor. She snapped off the light. "Come on, sweet one. That was just an old airplane. I won't let it hurt you."

Sukari crept forward until he butted Fiona's cheek. She stroked beneath his chin, smiling at the deep, satisfied purr. The spotless white cat was nearly blind, the casualty of a close encounter with a spitting cobra. Fiona stroked between his ears and nestled her nose against his furry neck.

"Now, be a good boy," she whispered. "Sentero and I are going to see if Moira's had her calf. I'll zip you into the tent, so mind your manners and don't chew on my philodendron."

The airplane slipped over the tops of yellow-trunked acacia trees. Like great green umbrellas, their canopies provided a measure of shade in the otherwise scorching heat. Rogan took in the pitiful little camp scattered at the edge of a nearly dry streambed. Several scraggly, patched and faded tents, olive in color and nearly camouflaged, rested in the shadows like bedraggled bag ladies. A thatch-roofed shed of some sort emitted a thin wisp of blue smoke. Like an aging, rusty King Pelinor, a Land Rover with a dented fender guarded the camp's entrance.

He quickly made mental notes about the needed upgrade. New tents, of course. At least ten of them—the deluxe model, with room for two beds and a table. An expanded campfire area. A dining room with a connecting kitchen. Bath and shower rooms.

The plane glided toward a humped dark mountain shaped like an elephant's sloping back. Then it swung around, touched down and taxied across a stretch of barren ground.

"I know you're a pilot yourself, sir," Clive commented. "In Africa you want to watch out for ant bear holes when you're landing. Damn things can ruin an airplane. Your wheel goes in and *boom*, that's it."

"What's going on over there?" Rogan grabbed the chrome door handle before the plane had come to a stop. Just across the riverbed he could see a tall figure striding across the clearing. "Who is that?"

"That's Dr. Thornton, sir. And it looks like she's making for her car. She's leaving."

"Not if I can help it." Rogan flung open the door and swung down from the plane. Loosening his tie, he set off through thigh-high golden grass. Behind him the plane's propellers wound down with a deep, air-cutting thunk-thunk. A rich smell of heat and soil and fragrant grasses hung thick in the air. It clung to him as he walked, filtered through his hair and onto his skin as if alive and seeking.

He scrambled down the stream bank and splashed through the trickle of water, a damp sediment seeping into his shoes and filtering through his socks. He strode on, irritation making inroads into his careful composure. The woman ignored him, marching toward the Land Rover as if she'd never even heard the plane come in.

"Dr. Thornton," he demanded.

She stopped. For a moment she seemed to disappear, her body camouflaged among the slender acacia trunks. Her clothing, a pale green shirt and tan slacks, melted into the surroundings. She made no sound. And then she turned her head.

Rogan's first realization was that Dr. Fiona Thornton was no battle-ax. Great-Aunt Rose and his high school English teacher vanished into thin air.

This woman had hair the color of a flaming sunset. Redgold. Rippling over her shoulders in a tangled swath. A pair of hazel eyes, thick lashed and as cold as ice, scrutinized him. Accustomed to painted lips and powdered cheeks, he was startled to realize that her face was bare. Yet color infused it with life—cheeks and nose blushed by the sun, faint freckles beneath a ruddy tan and lips almost too full.

He cleared his throat. With one hand extended, he walked toward her. "Dr. Thornton, I presume?" He smiled, hoping to melt her a little.

"Yes?" She spoke only the single word, but her voice had a husky quality that resonated in the marrow of his bones. She made no move to grasp his hand. Coolly she assessed him. With an unpainted fingernail, she tapped the camera that dangled against one curved hip.

"Dr. Thornton, my name is Rogan McCullough. I'm sure you've heard of McCullough Enterprises. New York." When she didn't respond, he leaned toward her and coaxed her fingers from the camera strap. He expected a cold-fish handshake. He was wrong.

Their hands were clasped as if they had silently agreed to engage in a battle of elemental arm wrestling. He stared into her eyes. Camouflage eyes. Green and brown, mottled with bits of gray and yellow. He sensed that she hid inside them, as if they could protect her merely by their color.

"I have a proposal for you, Dr. Thornton," he continued. "It's one I think you'll like very much. May we talk?"

"I'm listening," she said. The man's hand felt warm and hard, slightly callused, unyielding, with the sort of power she had sensed often in animals but rarely in humans. As always when it had been months—or even years—since she had engaged in the greeting ritual, she was struck by the sensation of human touch. A part of her rebelled against the contact. Another part, some deep inner recess, responded.

The man was holding her, willing her with the grip of his hand. His eyes, blue as the African morning, probed. She wanted to turn away from them. They beckoned, as if searching for some hidden weakness, an Achilles' heel she had learned to protect.

She studied his face, an even face. This Rogan McCullough was handsome, though he looked nothing like the Greek statues she'd studied in college or the male models who posed in clothing magazines. Piercing blue eyes, their irises white-flecked and rimmed in navy, were set beneath a brow faintly etched with two parallel lines. Battle scars from the pressures of big business, she supposed. His nose was straight, classic. High cheekbones, sheer planes of shaved skin and a strong chin balanced his face.

His hair couldn't seem to decide how to behave. Light brown with hints of gold on top, it had been willed into place, combed off his forehead and parted on the side. But in the slight breeze, the careful side part was quickly mussed, the strands sifting this way and that. From there his hair disobediently tumbled over the tops of his ears and down his neck. As though the man had forgotten he even had hair in back, it had grown long and thick, an unkempt ruffle that spilled over his collar.

All this Fiona could accept. It was his mouth that tilted her off balance. Rogan McCullough was tall, and when she stared straight ahead, her eyes met his mouth. She wanted that mouth to be grim, rigid perhaps. But instead he had lips that were dangerous with masculine sensuality. The crooked lift of his smile formed a shallow dimple in his right cheek.

His teeth were strong, white, even. And his mouth seemed to summon her, even when it said nothing.

"Sentero," she snapped suddenly, jerking away her gaze—and her hand. She spoke in Swahili. *"Ngoja kidogo, tafadhali."*

The African cut the Land Rover's engine and emerged from the vehicle. He moved leopardlike across the clearing, his spear held against one bare brown thigh, pointing at the intruder.

Rogan swung around and stared at the Maasai. The heart rate he thought of as so carefully under control suddenly doubled. It occurred to him that this was no New York boardroom. This was Africa. This was an eccentric woman and her savage guard. A man with dangling earlobes and snakelike black eyes was advancing on him, weapon menacing. Here the rules were different.

"Excuse me, but what does he have in mind with that spear?" Rogan asked.

Dr. Thornton's lips twitched. Her mouth formed a wry smile. "Don't worry," she said as the African's path took him safely to one side. "I've told Sentero to wait a bit until we're finished."

"Does he really need the spear? I'd think guns are a lot more efficient these days."

She glanced at Sentero, seeing him through another's eyes. The Maasai had settled under an acacia. His hooded gaze revealed nothing, but she knew he was thoroughly alert. She stepped back and ran her eyes down Rogan McCullough.

"You, on the other hand, are perfectly equipped for the African bush?" she asked. "A gray business suit? A navy tie?"

"My plane into Nairobi was late. I didn't have time to change."

"Wool?"

"It's February. Winter in New York." Retaking the offensive, he gestured toward a pair of faded wooden folding chairs beside the cold camp fire. "Could we sit down, Dr. Thornton? I'd really like to—"

"What is it you want, Mr. McCullough?" She felt impatient suddenly. This man had disturbed her. He had interrupted her routine.

"May we?" He held out a hand to indicate the chairs as he gently cupped her elbow. This second touch—the warmth of his hand on her bare skin—sent a shiver deep inside her. If only to escape him, she obeyed his request and walked across to the chairs.

"Now, Dr. Thornton," he began, sitting beside her. He leaned forward, blue eyes focused on her face as he spoke. "As the new owner of Air-Tours Safaris, I've been studying ways to make my company viable. When I was in New York inspecting the records of the business, I spoke with Clive Willetts by phone. He mentioned that you'd been a big help to him. He told me all about your fine camp and your elephant research projects. And that was when I began to see a future for this place."

"I have no trouble seeing the future, Mr. McCullough. I've worked with the Rift Valley elephants for more than ten years, and I intend to continue working with them for the rest of my life. I have only one goal, and that's to ensure the continuation of the African elephant."

"Exactly my point. And that's where Air-Tours comes in. I have the resources that can enable you to accomplish your goal."

"What resources are those?"

"As you may know, Air-Tours caters to very wealthy individuals. We work with highly influential people. People who make a difference in this world. I'm proposing to bring them here, Dr. Thornton. To the Rift Valley. You can show them what you're doing. Show them the life of the African elephant and why that life deserves preservation. You're a brilliant woman. You have a lot of creative energy. People will flock to learn from you. Think about it. You could hold seminars. You could touch people with the stories of your elephants."

"What on *earth* are you talking about?"

Bemused, Rogan studied her. This woman showed none of the enthusiasm he'd seen in potential clients, who usually swallowed his speeches as though they were strawberry ice cream. In fact, she looked as if she'd just eaten a dill pickle.

"I'm suggesting," he said, "that I can introduce you to the kinds of wealthy, influential people who are just looking for charitable foundations to support. With the cooperation of Air-Tours Safaris, you could have a major impact on wildlife awareness."

"Mr. McCullough, I appreciate your interest in the elephants, but we really have nothing to discuss." Annoyed at him, she crossed her arms.

The action tugged her green shirt tight against her full breasts. He could see their peaks, taut with the tension of conflict. It occurred to him that she wasn't wearing a bra. That thought, in turn, made him wonder why he was staring at this woman's breasts and imagining what it would be like to stroke them.

He lifted his head and rubbed his palm behind his neck. "What?" he asked lamely.

"I said we have nothing to discuss, Mr. McCullough. I'm not interested in your plan. Air-Tours is failing, so you think you can lure rich tourists with promises of 'getting close to the animals.' You want to bring planeloads of loud, trash-littering, gum-chewing people here to complain about the poor roads and the lack of hot water and electricity. They'll squeal over the lions and scream at the sight of a snake. They'll try to pet the vervet monkeys and feed bananas to my elephants."

"*Your* elephants?"

"*My* elephants. And if you think I intend to allow—"

"Dr. Thornton, please. I'm genuinely puzzled by your lack of understanding here. These are the people who can support your project. These are the people who have the money to make the difference between a healthy budget and a skimpy one. They matter to your elephants. I have a vision here, Dr. Thornton."

"*I* have a vision here, too."

"Don't you see what I'm offering you? I propose to bring in a fleet of new, comfortable tents. I'll expand the camp area, chop down some of those trees—"

"My acacias? You'll do nothing of the sort." She heard her own voice, near the point of shaking. How odd it felt to be so moved, so affected, by another human being. She felt a little giddy with the emotion.

"I'll build you a brand-new water pump," he was saying, his face intent, that intriguing mouth forming words of strong persuasion. "Don't you understand? I'll bring in generators. You'll be able to see at night. You'll be able to work and study as late as you want."

"I don't want generators. They smell. They belch diesel smoke."

"New Land Rovers, Dr. Thornton. Think about that. I'll buy you three or four of them if you want. And how about a water hole? I could build a big concrete water hole for you. The elephants would be able to come right up to the camp and drink."

"And what's going to keep them from walking straight in here, knocking your tents flat and smashing your generators? Elephants have no interest in human boundaries, Mr. McCullough."

"I'll hire guards. This could be a completely self-contained enterprise. I'd put in a kitchen and hire cooks. You'd have free food every day of your life."

"With a big trash pile for the elephants to sample, no doubt. Look, Mr. McCullough, I've found plastic bags, gloves, medicine bottles, pieces of metal and all sorts of wrappings and containers in elephant droppings. And it's all due to the rubbish the tourists leave behind."

"I'd build a fence."

"Nothing can keep elephants away but an electric fence. They walk straight through iron and wood and even concrete without the slightest hesitation. My elephants have died after eating shards of broken glass from human garbage pits. *Died.*"

Her face went soft all of a sudden. The veil over her eyes seemed to lift, and he saw a deep, unbearable pain there. She lowered her head and sagged just a little in the chair. He stared at the top of her head, at the wild red-gold tumble that smelled of rainwater and fresh air. She was breathing deeply, and with each breath came the slightest tremble.

"I'm sorry," he said. "About your elephants. About . . . about the glass."

For a long time she didn't look at him. And it wasn't because she didn't want to. She couldn't. At his words, his quiet, deep-voiced expression of sympathy, something inside her had escaped. She struggled to shut it away again, but it refused, filling her instead. Threatening her with its power. She couldn't even identify the feeling—something foreign, alien, and evocative in its strength.

"I didn't know elephants would eat trash," he said, almost under his breath.

"We've had a drought," she whispered. "The December rains failed. The grass is almost all dead or eaten away. But even in the rainy season the elephants raid the lodge garbage pits. Once they acquire a taste for bananas, mangos, pineapples—"

"Forbidden fruit."

She lifted her head and met the steady blue light of his eyes. "Elephants don't know what's good for them and what isn't. They're not like humans."

"Not all humans know what's good for them, either."

"I know what's good for *me,* Mr. McCullough. The Rift Valley Elephant Project is my life. I don't want changes. I won't allow anything different, anything disturbing."

"Change can be a good thing," he countered. "Change is what keeps me alive. Keeps me going. I'm always looking for something new. I stay ahead of the crowd, on the cutting edge. That's why I'm where I am today. That's why people listen to me. I have a certain measure of influence to accomplish the things I feel are important in life. There's a sense of satisfaction in that power."

"I don't need power. I have peace."

"But you *do* need it. You need power to earn financial support, and you need people to provide that support."

"The last things I'll ever need are people and money. I have the elephants. I have my camp, my research, my assistants. We're all we need."

"You need what I have to offer, Dr. Thornton. And so do your elephants."

She wanted to run from his intensity. His blue eyes cut into her, and she suddenly understood what he was trying to do. He was trying to touch her. He wanted to reach inside her and change her.

"I don't need you," she said, standing. "I don't *need* you, and I don't *want* you."

"Let me outline my proposal, Dr. Thornton. On paper. Let me explain in detail what I can do for you. Why don't you let me bring in a group of tourists? We'll show them your work. Just a test run. A trial."

"Absolutely not," she snapped. "Absolutely not!"

Before his invasion was complete, she pivoted and motioned to Sentero. The African was on his feet instantly. He loped toward the Land Rover, spear glinting in the noon sun.

Fiona fixed her eyes on the large dent that Margaret, the old elephant matriarch, had made in the front fender. She wouldn't think about Rogan McCullough. She wouldn't listen to him. She would go away, and then he would go, too. And her peace would return.

"How did it turn out, Mr. McCullough?" Clive Willetts asked, coming up beside Rogan. "Did you talk her into it?"

Rogan smiled. "Not exactly."

"Well, I warned you. She doesn't like to talk. I've never seen anyone who could stand up to Dr. Thornton."

Rogan unbuttoned the collar of his shirt as he studied the vanishing Land Rover.

"Let's start back to Nairobi," the pilot said. "There's no shame in being beaten by someone as stubborn as Dr. Thornton."

"Beaten? Hardly, Clive. In fact, I'd say the battle has only just begun."

Slinging his suit coat over one shoulder, Rogan set out across the grassland toward the airplane.

Chapter 2

Like a slow and silent periscope, Fiona rose through the Land Rover's roof hatch. Binoculars to her eyes, she scanned the group of great gray animals near the water hole. A huge female with large curved tusks scooped dry, red dirt into the tip of her trunk and blew it over her head. The dust settled on her back and ears in a fine, talcumlike powder.

A smaller female with a deep slit in her left ear rubbed her head against the larger animal. A young male calf lay stretched out on his side in the stubbly grass. A second calf slumped beside the first. Beside the babies, a half-grown female hung her head, her trunk flaccid and almost touching the ground.

The dust-bathed matriarch of the herd eyed Fiona for a moment. Then she draped her trunk over one tusk. Her eyes shut. Her breathing deepened.

"They're napping," Fiona whispered.

"Is Moira there?" Pen in hand, Sentero flipped through a notebook. "I don't see her."

Fiona studied the forest of wrinkled gray legs and, above them, the muted landscape of sloping gray backs. One of the elephants stirred and swished her trunk at a fly. "She's behind Margaret."

"Has she had her calf?"

"No, I don't think so. She's restless again this afternoon, though. She keeps waving her trunk and swinging her front foot. Look at Madeline! She's so fat. Could she be pregnant? She's awfully young—only thirteen."

"You show no record of her estrus on this chart."

"It's possible I might have missed it. She was hardly more than a calf, and she was always acting so silly during that rainy season. Once that year I lost the M group for two weeks. They vanished altogether."

Sentero rose through the hatch and lifted his own binoculars. "Yes, Madeline is very fat. Her breasts are larger, too. I think she *is* pregnant."

Fiona studied the small, dark eyes of her assistant. He regarded her gravely. In silence, they communicated their fears. Then Fiona sighed.

"Why did the rains have to fail?" she breathed. "Why *now?*"

Sentero shrugged. *"Shauri la Mungu,"* he said. "The will of God."

Fiona let the binoculars dangle. She propped her elbows on the warm metal roof and studied the sleeping elephants. A fly landed on her arm. She watched it for a moment as it cleaned its long front legs, rubbing them together over and over. Its bulbous red eyes gazed blankly. The fly uncurled its proboscis and tested Fiona's skin. Finding nothing of interest, it buzzed away.

A white egret skimmed the surface of the pathetic water hole. Landing on skinny legs, it picked a path across the geometrically cracked and dried mud. Then, with a quick hop, it settled on Moira's back. She shook her head, her ears rustling with irritation. The egret lifted its long neck for a moment, but when Moira slumped again, the bird tiptoed up the elephant's neck and began to peck for ticks.

The long grass, almost silver it was so dry, ruffled in a small breeze. In the distance a faint rumble shimmered across the sky. Fiona lifted her head. A plane?

Her thoughts lurched along a path she had forbidden her mind to take. Rogan McCullough.

What a strange name. Rogan. Rogue. Like an angry rogue bull whose tusk had broken off and left an unbearably painful raw stump. Like a bull in musth, when the sexual drive was so strong the elephant plunged through his territory dominating every other male for the right to mate. Like Jesse James and his gang of militant elephant bulls, who must have experienced something so excruciating, so terrifying, in their young lives that they hated the sight and smell of humans. When she came upon one or another of them, they tore up bushes and trumpeted their fury at her. One, Billy the Kid, had gouged a big hole in her Land Rover door. Another had trampled a village outside the park. Though hunting was illegal in Kenya, the Maasai had speared the elephant to death.

Fiona shook her head. But Rogan McCullough wasn't like that, was he? He was no rogue. He wore a silly wool suit in the middle of Africa. He proposed ridiculous ideas like building concrete water holes and chopping down the acacia trees.

After all, where did he live? New York. And he'd come from London that morning. She pictured him in his antiseptic world, surrounded by a clutter of clean-shaven executives with shiny black shoes and pasty white hands, soft from the lack of manual labor. He probably had one of those sleek apartments filled with chrome and glass. Sanitary. Efficient.

At the water hole a small herd of Thomson's gazelles emerged through the grass. Glancing warily about, they tiptoed to the shore. Some kept watch, black noses lifted to the wind and white tails flicking anxiously. Others spread spindly legs and lowered their heads to drink. The elephants took no notice.

Rogan McCullough, Fiona decided, had absolutely no sense of her world. He thought he could bring his herd of noisy tourists and expect her to show them the real Africa. This Africa. This quiet, sleepy, dangerous, burning land. These magnificent beasts who strode the plains, whose family units, bond groups and clans were so complex she had struggled for years to sort them out.

How wrong Rogan was. He knew nothing. He understood nothing. She crossed her arms and hugged herself, trying to shed the memory of the man. How fiercely his blazing blue eyes had held her, never wavering. She thought of Sentero and Nguyo and the other Africans she knew. They rarely met her gaze. It wasn't polite to stare.

But Rogan McCullough stared. He forced her to feel emotions she didn't like to acknowledge. She was a scientist, after all. She was detached about her life and work. And yet, at the man's badgering she had spouted off about "her" elephants and "her" acacias. As if Africa could ever belong to any human. She had come close to tears telling him about the elephant who had died from eating glass. And she had sensed things . . . feelings . . . she didn't want.

Though she knew it was ridiculous, she couldn't seem to stop thinking about him. The memory of his rich light brown hair, his tall, solid body and his blue eyes had stayed with her far too long. It was his mouth, that persuasive, sensual mouth, that annoyed her the most. If only he'd had hard, pencil-thin lips, she could have forgotten him at once. If only he hadn't said some plausible things, his mouth moving over the words like a caress . . .

She slapped the roof of the Land Rover. "Sentero, let's move on."

The Thomson's gazelles bolted from the water hole, their brown bodies vanishing into the grass with a flash of black stripes and white tails. The elephants stirred and shook their heads. Their great wrinkled eyelids slid apart, and they stared at her like irritable great-aunts awoken before times from their afternoon naps.

"Dr. Thornton." Sentero glanced at the digital watch on his left arm. "You've woken the elephants and frightened away the Tommies. Now our reading of their sleeping time will be inaccurate."

"Oh, skip it for today," she snapped. "Let's go and find the R group. I want to see how Rosamond is handling that bullet wound."

As she slumped into the seat, a puff of dust clouded around her legs, then settled to the floor. She shooed a fly and blew at the glass on her binoculars. "Rain," she said. "Why won't it rain?"

Rogan ran one finger down the sleek mounted ivory tusks on the foyer table. "Yes." He spoke into the black telephone receiver. "Dr. John Thornton of the University of Nairobi. The anthropology department. This is the third time I've been transferred. Is Dr. Thornton there?"

"Are you his student?" a starchy voice returned.

"No, I'm not his student. I'm a visitor from the United States, and I'd like to talk to him."

"Dr. Thornton has requested that he be contacted only by students in his advanced classes. He's working on a very important project."

Rogan jammed a thumb onto the tip of one tusk. "Madam, I'm afraid I'm becoming impatient here. I need to speak to Dr. Thornton about his daughter and the Rift Valley Elephant Project."

"I'm sorry, sir. Dr. Thornton does not like to be disturbed."

At the click on the other end of the line, Rogan thunked down the receiver. "How the hell is a man supposed to get any information around here?"

He jerked aside the heavy gray silk curtains behind the tusks and stared out at the city of Nairobi. A few skyscrapers dominated the center of the metropolis. Two of them were round towers, one topped by a strange, upside-down rotating cone. Others were tall, glass-windowed office buildings, hotels and apartments. A few older structures left over from the days of British colonization elbowed for space, their half-timbered or stone facades oddly quaint among the modern monuments to progress.

On the streets below Rogan's luxury apartment cum office, cars honked as they sped around bougainvillea-covered roundabouts. Traffic lights flashed green, yellow, red. People stopped at street corners to chat or buy a newspaper. Indian women in bright silk saris...African businessmen in sleek polyester suits...an elderly British couple tottering arm in arm toward a sidewalk cafe.

Rogan dropped the curtain into place and picked up his list. Sliding a gold pen from his breast pocket, he drew a black line across "Call Dr. John Thornton. Find out Fiona's background and what might influence her."

He raked a hand through his hair. In the two days he'd been in Nairobi, he'd had no luck at all. He couldn't contact Dr. Thornton. The daughter had obviously inherited her reticence from her father. The wildlife federation's director had told him nothing new. He couldn't reveal her financial status, he informed Rogan. The Ministry of Tourism had been no help at all.

He knew he should forget her. He had the names of three other researchers. But their work wasn't nearly as appealing. One was studying rock hyraxes—little rodentlike animals that resembled prairie dogs and were almost as reticent. Another was into termites. And the third studied crocodiles in Lake Turkana in the blistering desert heat of the Northern Frontier District.

Tossing the notebook on the table, he jammed his intercom button.

"Yes, Mr. McCullough?"

"Ginger, come in here, please."

"Yes, Mr. McCullough."

In a moment the huge, brass-studded carved door of the room opened. A thin, buxom blonde in a tight yellow suit and high heels clattered into the room. Her hair, trimmed close around her head, was spiky stiff with mousse and spray. She always reminded Rogan of an old photograph, sepia toned, with the lip and eye color painted on but the true dull brown-gray tints showing through.

"Ginger, where's Clive? Clive Willetts?"

His secretary flipped through the notebook in her hand. Her inch-and-a-half fingernails traced a line down the page. They were crimson today, he noticed. One had a diamond stud in a hole drilled through the nail. It always made him feel a little sick to look at that nail.

"He said he'd be at the airport this morning inspecting the planes," she said, her voice nasal. "He has a group of tourists flying out tomorrow."

"Call him, please. Tell him I'm taking him to lunch." He tugged a suit coat onto his shoulders. Ginger sped to assist, her red nails scrabbling at the fabric. He shooed her away. "On second thought, never mind. Cancel that. I'd rather not talk to him this morning after all. Anything from Megamedia?"

"No, sir. I'll let you know the minute they phone. I'm expecting a call any moment."

"Ginger, please. I need your attention here. I've tried to explain this. It's *night* in New York. The middle of the night. Nobody's going to phone until this evening at the earliest."

"Yes, Mr. McCullough. I'm sorry, sir." She gnawed on one red lip.

Immediately he felt bad. He sighed. "What's happening with the interview with Jackson Ayodo? That idea I had to promote Air-Tours in cooperation with the national museum. Have you set up a meeting?"

"Mr. Ayodo isn't available this morning, sir. I've been trying to contact him since eight-thirty."

"All right, never mind." He turned away. "You can go back to your desk now, Ginger. I have some things to take care of here."

"Yes, sir."

He watched her clatter across the inlaid wood floor, her high heels clicking and her ankles looking as if they might collapse at any moment. Why had he been so short with her? She was obviously doing her best, and he knew it had been hard for her to agree to leave New York for two weeks.

But the sight of those long nails and that spiky hair had made him think of the contrast with Fiona. And the thought of Fiona irritated him. He had to admit, it wasn't just the fact that she'd turned down his offer cold. Nor the fact that nobody would give him the time of day about her.

It was Fiona herself.

He thought about the women he knew. How elegant and sleek they were compared with her. The women in his circle knew how to dress. They wore suits of linen, silk or wool in shades of taupe and beige. Necklaces of pure gold circled their necks. Shimmering stockings covered their legs. And beneath . . . beneath they wore frilly, lacy things with little bows that came easily untied. Their breasts overfilled small demibras. Their thin, exercise-honed bodies teased and flirted, daring a man to touch.

On the other hand, there was Fiona. From an objective standpoint, the woman was frankly unappealing. Wasn't she? Her eyes were strange. Camouflaged eyes, haunting him. And she had freckles. Freckles! The women he knew would have covered them with a thick coating of makeup and powder. Not to mention that mass of fiery hair. Fiona didn't even seem aware that she *had* hair. Uncombed, un-parted, unpermed, undyed, unfrosted, unsprayed, un-anythinged hair. Masses and masses of thick, coarse, red hair. Hair he'd wanted to touch so badly he could hardly stand it.

He slammed his fist onto the table, strode into his bed-room and grabbed his briefcase. He had to forget her. Had to forget Fiona Thornton and her ridiculous elephants. She was impossible.

Hell, she didn't know what she had turned down. He could have brought her fame, recognition, in-depth articles in national magazines and spots on late-night talk shows. He'd been willing to spend his money to equip her with brand-new Land Rovers, tents, a complete staff. She was crazy, that was all. Completely nuts.

He would talk to the crocodile man. And the termite man.

He hurled the briefcase onto the bed again. He didn't want crocodiles or termites. He wanted elephants. He wanted Fiona Thornton. And she needed him, whether she knew it or not. Even if she didn't need the recognition and the supplies he was offering, she needed something else. She needed his money.

"Ginger!" he bellowed.

The carved door flew open. "Yes, Mr. McCullough!"

"Ginger, come here, please." He pulled out his wallet and thumbed off a wad of bills. "Take this. I want you to get me some clothes."

"Yes, sir. A new suit? Something in a navy blue? A . . . a striped tie?"

He stared at her, struck by how little she understood him. No one understood him. He wasn't sure he understood himself.

"Never mind, Ginger. I'm sorry I bothered you." He took the bills from her pale fingers and headed for the door.

"Mr. McCullough, Mr. McCullough!" She hobbled after him. "Where are you going? What if someone calls? What shall I tell them, Mr. McCullough?"

"Tell them I've gone shopping."

Fiona shifted the Land Rover into first gear and ground up the steep slope of the ravine. Dust spun a fine red cloud. Pebbles pinged against the metal chassis. Sentero grabbed the dash.

"I want you to contact the wildlife federation in Nairobi," she shouted over the roar of the engine. "Tell Mr. Ngozi the situation looks critical."

"Shall I phone the Ministry of Wildlife?"

"Yes. I want them to know that this park is up against a severe drought, and the impact on the animals is awful."

As the Land Rover topped the hill, a low thornbush scraped the undercarriage. Fiona struggled with the unwieldy stick shift, and when the vehicle leapt forward, she sat back and relaxed. A tingle of satisfaction at what she had observed tickled deep inside her. But it was satisfaction tinged with fear.

Madeline, one of the lovely young females in the M group, had given birth the day before. Her calf, a floppy, pink-eared male, had been nursing avidly all that afternoon. This was Madeline's first baby, and she seemed a little unsure of herself. But her older sister, Mallory, and her mother, Megan, along with Matilda and even Margaret, the *grande dame,* had fawned on the tiny elephant.

If the baby stumbled, Mallory rushed to lift him, her trunk gingerly nudging his backside. Margaret, huge and matronly, made certain the calf always stayed in the cool shade of someone's shadow. And if he wandered out of the inner circle of protective legs, she rumbled until someone went to fetch him.

It had been a happy scene, Fiona thought as she steered the Land Rover onto the rutted track that led to camp. Happy, but oh, so tenuous. The elephants were thinner than they should be at this time of year. Their shoulders and hipbones showed beneath the skin, and they had begun to look a bit like sagging gray tents that had been left out in the weather too long. Their behavior was becoming listless. Testing the brittle grass with their trunks, they kicked at dry roots in frustration. Newly weaned calves, already looking weak and lethargic, foraged beneath their mothers for bits of dropped grass.

Fiona had thought about traveling to Nairobi herself to speak to the authorities. But she liked neither the long drive nor the city. In fact, she couldn't remember the last time she'd been there.

It was strange that she had even considered it. And all the more strange because her nagging thoughts of Rogan McCullough had suddenly filtered into a new shape. She would go to Nairobi, she began to imagine, and she would see him.

Rogan.

She pictured herself strolling down Kimathi Avenue. He would notice her from a distance and lift a hand in greeting. "Well, hello, Fiona. What a pleasant surprise."

Fiona shook her head. This was ridiculous. The chances of running into Rogan McCullough in a city the size of Nairobi were almost nonexistent. Even more ludicrous was the idea that he would greet her with any sort of enthusiasm. In fact, he would probably turn and head the other way.

She wasn't going to Nairobi. Sentero had planned his trip for weeks, and he could take care of official business just as efficiently as she could. Better, perhaps.

"Look," he was saying, his long sinewy arm pointing to the sky. "The plane returns."

"Which plane?" Fiona almost drove the Land Rover straight into an ant bear hole. She swerved and fought to regain control of the wheel. Then she craned her neck to study the gray-blue sky.

Sentero glanced at her, the tiniest of smiles lighting his face. "You are driving badly today, Dr. Thornton."

"Sorry. I'm . . . I'm thinking about the drought."

"Yes, of course." He lifted his face to the sky for a moment. "It's one of the planes of Bwana Willetts. But perhaps he's flying to the Mara Lodge."

"Do you think so?" She couldn't yet see the plane, and it annoyed her to think it might speed past before she had a chance to look. That, in turn, annoyed her further. She had never given much thought to Clive Willetts and his airplanes. Now here she was, studying the sky with as much interest as she had scrutinized Madeline's newborn calf.

Sentero remained silent. He didn't look at her, but she guessed what he was thinking. It bothered her to be so readable. She had worked hard to level her emotions, to make herself inscrutable. And yet the Africans she knew had no trouble discerning her every humor.

"Here is a plate of mango, *memsahib*," Nguyo, their camp cook and worker, would say. "Perhaps it will cheer you." Or, "I have ironed the red shirt today, *memsahib*. You always enjoy it when you are happy." Or, "Sukari is hiding under the bed, *memsahib*, where he always hides when you are angry."

How did Nguyo and Sentero know? She studied the Maasai for a moment. His small dark eyes scanned the horizon, darting like a pair of hummingbirds up and down, side to side. She knew his thin nose sensed smells with more accuracy than hers. His dark ears with their beaded, elongated lobes heard at levels she couldn't hear. He was more a child of this raw land than she could ever be. Did that give him the right to see into her heart and mind?

"Tell me, Sentero, what did *you* think of the *bwana mkubwa*, Mr. McCullough?" she asked, using the phrase of esteem he had given Rogan.

The Maasai never looked at her. "That man walks where he pleases and takes no notice of the world. He moves always straight ahead."

"That's for sure. Well, I guess he's moved straight off to London or New York by now."

"Perhaps," Sentero said. "Or perhaps not."

* * *

A smile flickered around Fiona Thornton's lips as she emerged from the Land Rover. Rogan took it as a good sign. But then the tall African with the spear and the dangly earlobes started toward him, his red cloths fluttering in the breeze, revealing a stretch of bare black thigh.

Rogan lifted his shoulders and cleared his throat. "Dr. Thornton," he began.

"Mr. McCullough." She couldn't keep the surprised lilt out of her voice. "I didn't expect to see you again."

"I've come with a new proposal for you."

Her smile faded. "I'm not the least bit interested in—"

"I think you'll find—"

"Really, I don't—"

"Dr. Thornton." Sentero interrupted with such command that Fiona clamped her mouth shut. The Maasai had jammed his spear shaft into the ground. His eyes, small and very black, glittered.

"Yes, Sentero?" she asked.

He spoke in the cultured, schoolbook Swahili he used only to communicate matters of great import. *"Wapiganapo tembo, nyasi huumia."*

Fiona's eyes darted from the African to the businessman. She thought for a moment, weighing the words he had spoken. *"Ndiyo,"* she whispered finally. "Yes. I understand."

"What did he say?" Rogan asked as Sentero walked away.

"He reminded me of an old Swahili proverb. When elephants fight, it is the grass that weeps."

Rogan's blue eyes followed the African until he disappeared behind the thatched kitchen. "I guess in this case you and I are the fighting elephants. But what did he mean about the grass? What suffers if you and I happen to have a few differences of opinion?"

"Sentero thinks the African elephants are the weeping grass. So tell me what you have to say, Mr. McCullough. I'll listen to your proposal. For my elephants' sake."

Their eyes met and locked. Fiona studied the blue depths of his, wondering whether Rogan McCullough would ever be able to look beyond his safari company and see the real needs of the wildlife.

At least he'd made some changes in one respect. The navy tie and wool business suit had vanished. The starched white shirt and shiny leather shoes were nowhere in sight. Even the carefully shaven jaw now sported the shadow of a dark beard.

In place of the New York uniform, Rogan had donned a cotton khaki safari suit. Epaulet tabs on the shoulders. Large, square, pleated pockets on the chest. A D-ring belt. Trousers with knife-sharp creases down the front. And suede, crepe-soled safari boots. Though it was true that he had purchased the finest in tourist-style safari wear, Fiona couldn't deny that he looked much more comfortable than he had the first time she'd met him. In a way he had become more visible, as if he had shed one of his impenetrable layers.

She noted with some surprise that Rogan's shoulders were broad, massive even. Dark, crisp hair curled from the V neck of the safari jacket. More dark hair brushed down his arms. He looked more earthy, more masculine, to her. And yet the outfit, with its muted color and gentle lines, had also softened him somehow.

"May I call you Fiona?" he asked. "It's very unusual. Fiona."

The sound of her name spoken in his deep voice slid into her belly and nestled there. Her mouth went dry. She nodded.

For a moment she considered the camp chairs around the cold fireplace. If she offered him a seat, she knew he would start in on her again about wanting his tourists to overrun her tidy world. But if she turned him away, he would leave.

"Would you like a seat?" she asked.

"Thanks."

Settling into a camp chair, she decided she might like to study this Rogan McCullough a little longer. Perhaps one day she would write a thesis on human beings. New York businessmen, maybe.

She imagined herself sitting for hours in a bustling Manhattan office, notebook propped on her knees. "Mc-

Cullough reviews morning agenda with secretary," she would pen. "47 minutes. Blue eyes sharp and focused. McCullough plans strategic attack on next business conquest. 23.8 minutes. Deliberate tone of voice. Face set with determination. Straightens tie." Perhaps she would even put a little monitor on him to record his blood pressure and heart rate. Or a radio collar, so she could track him through the concrete jungles.

"Fiona?" Rogan was asking. From the large leather attaché beside him, a file had emerged.

"Yes?"

"Would you like to hear my proposal?"

"All right."

He flipped open the file and scanned through sheets of typed pages with careful rows of figures marching down them.

"I sense, Fiona," he began, "that, like myself, you're a well-organized, efficient, logical person. I sense that you maintain an orderly existence. That you have a deep devotion to your chosen pursuit. That you would do anything to prevent its demise."

"Go on," she said, wondering what he was getting at.

"I also sense that you're a woman of foresight. You see potential for the future. You have ambition. Goals. Dreams, we might call them."

"And if I do?" She felt more hesitant now.

He held his breath for a moment, ready to plunge, to take a stab in the dark. He had nothing to base his argument on. No one had given him any data. But a lack of information had never held him back in the past. He had arrived at a series of logical guesses, and now his surmises would be put to the test.

"Fiona," he said, studying her eyes for the first sign of reaction, "the Rift Valley Elephant Project is in financial difficulty. Your funding has always been inadequate to accomplish the purposes you have in mind. And now, with the fiscal year only half over, the Rift Valley Elephant Project is in trouble. Donations have slacked off due to national recession, economic hardships, worldwide tensions. Kenya is in a period of severe drought. Your dreams are turning to ashes. Your hopes for the future of the African elephant are growing dim. Am I right, Fiona?''

Mesmerized by the intensity of his blue eyes, the sensual movement of his mouth and the charisma of his deep voice, she shrugged slightly. ''Go on.''

''I'm here to present you with the solution. It's not an easy solution. Problems of this magnitude are never resolved simply. Sacrifice is often required. I trust you are aware of that, Fiona. But because I believe in the Rift Valley Elephant Project, because I'm committed to the future of the African elephant, I'm prepared to supplement your funding to the tune of a half-million dollars.''

A gasp hung in the back of Fiona's throat.

''Examine these figures, if you will.'' Sensing he had the upper hand, Rogan moved in. He spread the sheet of numerical data. ''McCullough Enterprises, which is primarily a publishing industry, has always contributed magnanimously to various charities. You'll see here the yearly donations we've made. And you'll find that we're broad in our support of worthy projects such as yours. I'm willing to divert some of our funds to the Rift Valley Elephant Project. Now, Fiona, I'm a businessman. And though you don't like to see yourself as one, you're a businesswoman. We're in this world to make enough money to keep our dreams alive. Am I right on this, Fiona?''

''Well . . .''

''Dreams can't come true without financial support. Your dream is to keep the Rift Valley Elephant Project alive, to keep the African elephant vibrant and safe from extinction. My dream is to run a profitable flying safari business. Why don't we compromise, Fiona? I've flown to your camp today, alone, to speak frankly with you. I've come to make you an offer. An offer of half a million dollars.''

Fiona moistened her lips. She glanced anxiously at Nguyo, who was setting out dinner. He worked silently, his bare feet noiseless in the dust. She wondered what the African was thinking.

''I'll draw up papers,'' Rogan went on, ''papers solidifying the pledge of McCullough Communications in support of the Rift Valley Elephant Project. And I ask your cooperation in this."

"What kind of cooperation?"

"I've realized maybe I was hasty when we talked the other day. You have a better understanding of your camp and the needs of the elephants than I do, of course. I'm prepared to incorporate your suggestions into the revitalization of this project, Fiona. I'm prepared to listen to your needs. I see us as a team. You need me, and I need you. If we work together, our efforts will bear fruit. My safari company will grow. The elephants will benefit from increased exposure to concerned visitors. The visitors will benefit by expanding their world view. What do you say, Fiona? Do we have a package here? Do we have an understanding?"

Fiona studied the orange fingers of sunset that wove across the pink sky. The acacia trees, black in silhouette, stretched thorny arms heavenward. Monkeys settled on branches, their tails draping down and swaying in the slight breeze. A dove cooed. A cricket began to chirp.

Somewhere in the distance an elephant rumbled. It was a low, vibrating sound, almost inaudible. Margaret, perhaps, calling the others to gather near her for safety. The new baby would suckle in contentment. Moira would grunt and rub her chin on Megan's back. Madeline would drape her trunk across her tusks, and her head would droop. Great, wrinkled eyelids would shut.

"No, Mr. McCullough," Fiona said softly. "We don't have an understanding. But perhaps you would like to stay for dinner?"

Chapter 3

Rogan stared at Fiona. He couldn't believe what had just transpired. This woman, sitting here in a broken-down, faded camp chair, preparing to eat heaven-knew-what for supper, had just turned down half a million dollars. It was unthinkable.

"So you aren't going to go along with my proposal," he stated.

"I said we didn't have an *understanding*," Fiona answered. "You haven't understood from the very beginning. You don't know who I am. You don't know what I do. You don't know why I do it."

"I think I understand you perfectly." Angry now, he stood and faced her. His voice was calm, lethal. "You drive that junk pile of a Land Rover out into the middle of the African bush and sit around watching elephants all day, that's what you do. And do you know why? Because you'd rather stay hidden out here with your elephants than face reality. You're afraid of people who might be a little different from you. As a matter of fact, I think you're afraid of people *period*. You prefer your elephants to people. You're afraid to let my tourists come, aren't you? You're afraid of them, just like you're afraid of me."

"I'm not afraid of you, Rogan McCullough." She faced him. "Africa's my home. The elephants are my life. *This* is the real world, not some artificial megalopolis of steel and concrete and glass. Here I can be myself. I don't have to walk around trying to balance on high heels or slather lipstick all over my mouth just to impress people."

"No, you don't need lipstick, Fiona. You're right about that." He touched her chin, lifted her face with one fingertip. She moved her head as if she wanted to break the contact but couldn't. "The fact is, you have beautiful lips. You have beautiful hair. Fantastic hair. But you wear these faded T-shirts and ragged jeans every day, don't you? Maybe you're right after all. Maybe I really don't understand you. You're tall, you're striking. You have a sharp mind that would let you hold your own anywhere. And yet you live out here in the boondocks talking to natives and elephants, for heaven's sake."

She regarded him, her mouth dry, her stomach quivering with something she couldn't explain. She had the most awful feeling inside. It was as though she were about to explode. But not in anger. Some crazy combination of fear, joy, sorrow, pain and elation was bubbling up, threatening to froth over.

Even worse, she found she couldn't look away from Rogan's blue eyes. A flame, hot and almost painful, flickered between them. It licked the edges of her mouth and skittered down her chest. She couldn't think. Couldn't reason. The small patch of skin where his finger was touching her chin felt more alive at this moment than any other part of her body.

As they stared at each other, neither speaking, she watched as his face seemed to transform. The traces of anger vanished. Fascination took their place. The blue in his eyes softened. Their dark pupils widened, opening to her. His breathing sounded heavy, as if the air were thick and had to be forced into his chest.

Neither moved.

His hand lifted her face a little more. She held her breath. The flame between them crackled and seared the tips of her breasts. His lips parted. Her gaze fell to the line of his mouth.

She breathed in. "What are you trying to say? What are you . . . doing?"

He stayed as he was, not releasing her, not moving.

"I'm trying to get through to you, Fiona. I'm trying to tell you—" He stopped speaking. It was as if he suddenly drew back from himself, as if a part of him slipped a mile away to study the situation. His body felt light, floating. He saw the tall man and the slender woman. He saw the way he had spoken to her. He heard echoes of the unfamiliar sound of anger in his voice. And he saw from the way he was touching her that he wanted her.

"I'm trying to . . . to tell you," he said again, stumbling uncharacteristically.

"Yes," she breathed.

"What I'm trying to say is that . . . that I will stay for dinner."

Fiona and Rogan sat under the stars sipping the last of their coffee. They had been silent through most of the meal, yet Fiona knew that if she continued to say nothing, Rogan would never understand why she had taken such a determined position against his proposals. He would continue to see her as a reclusive eccentric and not as she really was.

She cleared her throat. "I want you to understand, Mr. McCullough, that I'm not completely isolated here in the Rift Valley. Sentero, my research assistant is wonderful company. Our camp worker, Nguyo, is as fine a friend as I could ever hope for. I have a close relationship with the Maasai who make their homes in the area surrounding the park. I've been known to dine in the lodge at Lake Naivasha. I do most of my shopping in the towns of Naivasha or Narok. Over the years I've had several foreign research assistants who have lived right in this camp with me. I have an extra tent down by the stream. It's not as though I'm a hermit."

Rogan surveyed her from across the expanse of the white-clothed wooden table. At this moment her words were making a bit too much sense to him. He supposed it was the way she spoke, in that half-British, half-American accent. Mesmerizing. A tendril of hair lifted and floated across her mouth. She hooked it with a fingertip and swept it away.

"I have a wireless radio I can switch on when I want the news from Nairobi," she was saying. "I have a transmitter to call for help if I need it. Not that I ever have. Once a month or so, the wildlife federation packages my mail and sends it to the lodge."

"Who writes to you?" He had a hard time imagining her writing chatty letters to friends. Or sending perfume-scented envelopes to a man somewhere.

"I'm a researcher, Mr. McCullough. I correspond with my university supporters. I write papers for the foundations that fund the elephant project. I subscribe to various scholarly journals."

"I wish you'd call me Rogan."

She looked away.

"I mean, it *is* my name," he finished.

"A group of ladies from a church in Tennessee has been writing to me for years," she said as if she hadn't heard him. "They have craft bazaars and bake sales, and then they send their proceeds to support my work. They see it as a kind of mission—their part in protecting the Creation, so to speak. In return, I mail them photographs of the elephants. One woman sends me magazines when she's finished with them. *Good Housekeeping. Vogue.*"

Rogan's eyebrows lifted. *"Good Housekeeping?"*

She settled her coffee cup in its saucer. "It's not as though I've never considered living in a normal house. I grew up in one. I once lived with gardens and flowers and goldfish and bicycles. When I was very young, I used to dream that my life would go on the same way forever. I thought I'd live with my mother and father...."

She trailed off, staring at her cup.

"What happened?"

She lifted her head, feeling the pain of things she couldn't speak about. "I suppose you've noticed that not *all* our dreams come true in life. Circumstances change. We change. I've made a different life for myself. And I'm happy."

"Are you?"

"Yes, I am." She felt that she'd said it a bit too defensively.

Rogan cleared his throat. "If you're such a normal, average woman, why is it the people around here call you Princess Sunrise? That sounds a little ethereal to me."

She felt taken aback by his blunt questioning. "Where did you hear about that name?"

"Clive Willetts."

This topic of conversation could lead into an area she didn't want to cover, so she decided to simplify. "It's my hair. The Africans say it's the color of sunrise. I like to wear blue or green clothes, so I can sort of blend into the landscape and not startle the elephants. One or two of the men have mentioned that from a distance I look like the sun just coming up over the land. You have to understand, Africans are an imaginative people."

He mused on that for a moment. "Well, they are different. I'll have to backtrack on what I'd been thinking about your eating arrangements. You've got quite a cook there. Where'd you find him? I didn't realize a native could—"

"Listen," she interrupted, once again reminded of how far he was from understanding her world. "Nguyo's a native in the sense that he's indigenous to Kenya. He's not a 'native' in the sense of being primitive, uncivilized or in any way some stereotypical savage out of a Tarzan movie. Nguyo belongs to the Kamba tribe. He's intelligent, witty and insightful. For years he worked for a missionary family in Machakos. When they retired, he came to me, bringing excellent references. His cooking is superb. He has run this camp loyally for years. I'd trust him with my life."

As though the sound of his name had evoked the little cook, Nguyo stepped out of the darkness and began to clear the table. His dark hands worked swiftly, scooping up knives, forks and spoons, stacking plates, scraping food into a small tin. Fiona could see that he was smiling.

"*Memsahib,* what will you be wishing for dinner tomorrow?" he asked in perfect English.

"Perhaps a roast," she suggested. "Potatoes in a cheese sauce. A salad with vinaigrette dressing."

"A soup, *memsahib?*"

"Chicken, please."

"And for dessert?"

"A pie will do. Chocolate, I think."

"Very good, *memsahib*. And now will you take tea beside the fire?"

"Perhaps not tonight, thank you. Mr. McCullough will be going soon."

Nguyo marched away, loaded with clinking plates. Rogan stared after him. "Vinaigrette dressing? Chocolate pie? Maybe I'll stay."

"Oh, he never cooks what I suggest," she said, waving away the notion as if it were ludicrous. "Every evening we progress through the same ritual, and the following night Nguyo has cooked something entirely different. 'You requested chicken,' he'll say, serving up a marvelous coq au vin. 'And an oxtail soup.' Dessert is always a surprise. If I suggest pie, I'm just as likely to get pudding."

"Doesn't he know? Doesn't he understand?"

"Of course he understands. But he's extremely creative. Once he settles into his kitchen, his imagination runs wild. I was warned of it in his references. It's been a delightful problem."

Rogan nodded. The thought of one of *his* cooks making up his own menu was unpalatable. His secretary kept a computer file of dinners he'd given, lists of guests and the meals served. He liked to juggle it and never have the same food or combination of people twice. But with this little gray-haired cook, you would never be sure.

"It's getting dark," Fiona said. "You won't be able to see the ant bear holes in the airstrip much longer."

"I suppose that means you want me to leave."

"No, no," she said, wanting to be polite. Then she realized how it sounded. "Of course, I . . . well, you said you'd be going."

"You mentioned that you have a radio. Mind if I listen to the weather report before I take off?"

Fiona left him sitting in the camp chair and walked to her tent. She lifted the wireless from the desk where her cat lay sleeping. Stroking the top of his head, she whispered reassurances that she would return soon.

As she made her way across the dark clearing, she saw Nguyo piling brush and firewood in the center of the ring of stones. Rogan was talking, his voice too deep for her to make out words from a distance. The small African smiled and nodded, as though he were pleased at the conversation.

Fiona stopped a few feet behind the camp chairs. Hugging the radio against her chest, she studied the back of Rogan McCullough's head. The brown hair falling over the edge of his collar gave him a look of gentleness. She could hardly imagine he was the same man who lived in a huge city full of noisy traffic, a man who negotiated hard-nosed business deals and could casually drop half a million dollars on this charity or that.

From this view he didn't seem driven or forceful at all. His big shoulders stretched far beyond the confining width of the canvas chair back. He had relaxed one elbow on the armrest, his weight shifting the flimsy chair to a precarious angle. It didn't occur to Fiona to worry that the chair might collapse and send him sprawling. He was solid as a rock. Immovable. It seemed, in fact, that the man was supporting the chair rather than the other way around. If the chair suddenly crumbled, Rogan would simply remain, one elbow poised as if still resting on the invisible arm.

"So why do you live out here?" Rogan was asking Nguyo. "If you've got a wife and seven children, seems like they'd need you around. Don't you want to live in your village?"

"Please try to understand the way of my people, *bwana*. I am the youngest son of fourteen children. When my father died, his *shamba*, his farm, was divided among the sons. Now, you can see that my *shamba* is very small. My wife can grow only a few beans and some maize. From the days when I was a young man, I have worked for money to send my wife. Once every month I go on the bus from Naivasha to visit her and our children. Because I can work for Dr. Thornton, I have paid for my three sons to go to school. Two are shopkeepers in Nairobi, and the third is studying at the university. And you see, I am a very good cook."

"I can't argue with that. But don't you get lonely out here? This place is so far away from everything."

"You don't understand, *bwana*. This place is in the middle of everything. Here we have our camp. We have our very fine kitchen. Here we have the stream, the Land Rover, the monkeys, the elephants. Here we have the quiet nights and the warm days. This is all we need."

Rogan lapsed into silence. This camp was in the middle of everything? He listened to the night sounds, the hum of an insect, the rustle of leaves in the acacias, the grunt of a lion far out on the plain.

He had always imagined New York was the center of life, trucks honking, sirens wailing, music pulsing from open windows until the early hours of morning. In the city decisions were made, deals drawn up, money exchanged. Ideas became reality. Movers moved. Shakers shook. The earth trembled beneath the heavy, progressive footsteps of industry and business.

How could one little ragtag camp in the middle of nowhere be the center of anything?

"The radio," Fiona said, setting the metal box in Rogan's lap. "Your world is ready to speak."

Rogan glanced up, surprised that she had read his thoughts so clearly. The African had melted away into the night, leaving a blazing fire that licked the edges of the white stones. Fiona's face glowed in the red light. Her hair came alive, flickering and dancing with gold. She sat staring into the flames, her hands folded in her lap, her eyes lost.

"In world news tonight, tension continues in the Middle East," a voice announced as soon as Rogan flipped on the radio. "A speaker for the United States Pentagon stated that the U.S. will not tolerate terrorism.... The British prime minister has refused to comment on the crisis in Northern Ireland.... South Africa today was the scene of more bloodshed.... Another attempted coup in Bolivia has left hundreds dead and perhaps as many as three thousand homeless in fires.... Experts on global warming have warned that the situation is..."

Rogan shifted. His chair sagged in the opposite direction. He'd always listened to the news. His publishing business dealt in news. Sometimes he even created news, for heaven's sake. But tonight, here in the desolate silence, the announcer sounded like an angel of doom.

"And in local news, the murder of a woman in the Shauri Moyo area of Nairobi..."

"Affair of the heart," Fiona whispered.

Rogan turned the volume down. "What?"

"Shauri Moyo. The name of that section of Nairobi where the woman was murdered means 'affair of the heart.'"

They both fell silent as the radio blared on. "A fire broke out in a downtown section of Thika this morning. Police believe arson is the cause.... In the Muthaiga district, a child was struck and killed by a passing motorist...."

Rogan rolled the station dial. "Don't they have a weather report somewhere?"

Fiona said nothing. She picked up a stick and prodded the fire, and a shower of sparks shot into the black sky. The radio crackled as Rogan searched the airwaves. A pop tune faded in, its beat artificial and raucous in the night. It quickly died. The monotones of a talk show intensified, then ebbed. Another spot of music. Rogan left it on.

"Mind if I spend the night in your extra tent?" he asked. "I've decided I'd rather fly out in the morning."

She considered for a moment. "I suppose so."

Neither of them moved for a long time. The fire began to die, the logs mellowing into glowing orange bars. The music continued, something soft and classical. A chill crept around Fiona's arms and slid up the insides of her sleeves. She shut her eyes.

Margaret walked across the dark stage. Not Margaret the old elephant matriarch. This was Fiona's other Margaret— she of the soft skin the color of coffee and bright brown eyes crinkled at the corners. Margaret who wore the wonderful faded yellow dress with a blue belt tied at her waist. A patterned nylon scarf tied over her head with a small knot at her neck hid tight black curls scattered with white. Somehow Margaret had freckles, too. Very black freckles peppering her dark brown skin. She and Fiona often sat in front of the mirror where they would compare. And laugh.

"Come, *toto*," Margaret was saying. "We'll sing our song. 'Two fingers, two thumbs, two arms, two legs, one head, stand up, turn 'round, sit down, keep moving...' Dance, *toto*. Dance, Fiona..."

"Fiona?"

She jumped at the touch. One warm hand covering her arm, Rogan leaned over her, his dark form blocking the firelight.

"I asked if you'd like to dance."

He asked, but he didn't wait for her answer. He lifted her out of the camp chair as if she weighed no more than a feather and drew her against him, his warm arms coming around her, one large hand covering her back, the other surrounding her hand.

She felt as if she were still in her dreamworld, half asleep and half awake. Somehow her nose had gotten pressed against this man's neck. His collar crumpled under her cheek. He smelled of...of what? Not Africa, surely. No, this was the scent of spice and something else, something unbearably compelling.

She felt as if she had suddenly developed an extraordinary sense of smell. The crisp starch in his new shirt drifted into her nose and mingled with the gentle scent of red dust that had settled in his hair during the afternoon. And there was shampoo, something masculine. Soap. Shaving cream. And skin. Male skin.

His hand slipped up her back. She could feel her shirt bunching beneath the movement. And then his fingers went into her hair, gathering and crushing it again and again. As swiftly as her sense of smell had been granted, it vanished. Now there was nothing but the touch of Rogan's hand in her hair. Her legs moved between his, and she could feel the hard outline of his thighs against hers.

She couldn't hear the music. The chill of the night evaporated. Her line of vision held only one thing. The V where his collar came together. One round brass button. And the crisp curling of his dark hair.

His fingers slid to her neck, his thumb and fingers rotating over the slender cords at the base of her skull. His other hand slipped free of her palm and came up to cradle her head. Like a puppet, she moved with him, completely controlled. His hands held her head so that she had no choice but to look into his face. His legs moved her around the dying fire. And his eyes caressed her lips.

"You can touch me, Fiona," he murmured. "I won't crumble into a hundred pieces."

She realized she was swaying against him with both her arms dangling loose at her sides. But how could she bring herself to actually place her hands on this man? This stranger with his hypnotic blue eyes? She hadn't touched another person since... since Margaret, perhaps. And then it was with tears and sobs and holding on for dear life as they were pried apart.

"Your hair is brighter than the fire," he was murmuring. "I've never seen hair like this."

"My mother," she whispered. "She gave it to me."

"Every woman should be so lucky." He smiled, and she thought she would be the one to crumble into a hundred pieces. He caught a handful of her hair and lifted it slowly. Then, like a silk waterfall, it slid and tumbled down her back. "It's very soft."

"My father used to tell me it was as coarse as a horse's tail."

"I breed Arabians, Fiona. This is no horse's tail."

"I should... I should be going. I'm usually at breakfast at dawn, and it's getting very... late."

"Stay."

"Really, I—"

"Stay with me, Fiona. I'm enjoying this. You feel soft and warm in my arms. And very, very beautiful."

As he held her and looked into her face, he realized that what he was saying was God's truth. He did enjoy this woman. She was, at this moment, the most gorgeous woman he'd ever seen. Her face and hair were full of glowing pink light. Her lips, moist and full, beckoned him with a lure more tempting than words.

He could feel her breasts against his chest, swollen beneath her flimsy shirt. She wore no bra, and he sensed their crests tight and aching for a man's touch. She was all woman, from her keen mind to the delicate tips of her pink toes.

He took one of her hands and laid it on his shoulder. He took the other and settled it at his back. She felt loose and melting against him. Her breath was ragged, and her head was tilted up toward his face. She parted her lips, her tongue slipping out to moisten the pink flesh.

He drew her close and bent his head, his lips brushing lightly, so lightly, across hers.

She stiffened. "Well," she said, stopping suddenly and shoving his shoulders away. "It certainly has gotten late, and I do believe the fire's out. Your tent's down by the stream. But don't worry—the animals have all finished drinking for the evening. If you hear thumps and bumps in the morning, its just the monkeys playing on your roof. You'll find blankets in the metal trunk at the foot of the cot. Good night, Mr. McCullough."

She swung away, her hair flaming like molten lava down her shoulders. Her legs ate up the distance to her tent so fast he barely knew what had happened. And then he realized that he was standing in the middle of Africa.

Alone. Cold. And very much disturbed by the sudden absence of one enigmatic redhead.

Fiona curled into a ball on her cot and covered her head with a blanket. Sukari draped himself over her feet and began giving himself a bath. The whole bed trembled at his ministrations. She was tempted to spill the cat over the side and send him to his basket. She would never get any sleep at this rate.

Pressing her fingertips against her lips, she tasted them. How they burned. When she closed her eyes, she saw Rogan's face moving closer, his breath warm on her skin, his mouth touching hers. She felt his hands in her hair, squeezing and lifting. His words slipped through her bones like hot syrup. "Very beautiful . . . beautiful . . ."

She sat up and nudged the cat. "Sukari, please. Haven't you finished by now?"

The cat licked the back of her hand, his rough tongue dryly scraping her skin. Sorry she'd been short with him, she bent and nuzzled her nose in his rich fur. Now, this cat was real. This cat understood her. He didn't send her world into chaos. This cat could be relied on.

Rogan McCullough could not.

The man understood nothing. Perhaps he had simply danced her around the fire and kissed her in order to get her to change her mind about his tourists. It was possible, wasn't it? She had learned long ago that, unlike cats, people could not be trusted.

Rogan was probably even married, with two or three children. At the least he would have a girlfriend in New York. Maybe he'd been married and divorced any number of times. Perhaps he had a mistress in every city. Wasn't that the sort of thing high-powered businessmen did?

Fiona pictured Rogan with someone chic and ultramodern. She would have short hair and smoke cigarettes and negotiate her own megadeals. Fiona thought of the ads she'd seen in the magazines from America. No doubt Rogan wanted a woman who might have stepped from the pages of *Vogue.*

She flopped backward onto the pillow and let out her breath in a rush. Why should she care what Rogan McCullough wanted in a woman? She was thirty-one years old, for heaven's sake. She had established herself educationally and professionally as a single-minded, highly intellectual scientific researcher. She did not need any man to come along and dance her around a fire for any reason.

Throwing back the blanket, she buried Sukari in a tumble of wool. Then she lifted the hem of her white gown and slid her feet into her boots. Grabbing a flashlight from the file cabinet, she unzipped her tent door and stepped outside.

The cat meowed, but she didn't hear him.

"Mr. McCullough," she called, rapping the flashlight on a tent pole. "Mr. McCullough, this is Dr. Thornton. May I speak with you, please?"

She waited for a moment, but heard nothing from the inside of the tent. Standing on tiptoe, she peered through a tiny tear in the canvas fabric. The interior of the tent was completely dark.

"Mr. McCullough—are you in there? Rogan?"

The door flap swung back. Rogan stepped out into the moonlight, wearing nothing but a pair of pale blue boxer shorts.

"You called?" he said.

Fiona nearly dropped the flashlight. She didn't know why she'd expected to find him in pajamas. Her father had always worn a nice set of plaid flannels. But then she really hadn't stopped to consider what Rogan might be wearing, had she? She hadn't even planned exactly what she would say to him. She had merely acted on impulse, something she never did unless faced with a charging elephant or some other life-threatening situation.

"I guess you realize it's after midnight, Fiona," Rogan was saying. "I thought you needed your sleep. Breakfast at dawn and all?"

"Well, I just . . . I . . ."

Amusement twitching his lips, he raised one arm, cocking it on the tent pole. She could see the swath of dark male hair the movement revealed. His chest, too, wore a large diamond of curls.

"I'll have to admit," he said when she was unable to continue, "I'm glad to see you here tonight. I was lying in there thinking about you—"

"Mr. McCullough, please." She found her breath. "I came to tell you that I'm not the least bit interested in . . . well, in anything you have to offer. I was trying to tell you at dinner that I'm content with the life I've made for myself out here, and I don't want anything to complicate that. You might as well know up front that I will not be swayed from my position. You made a very generous offer to the elephant project, and I thank you for that. But I just can't go along with having tourists here. I'm content with a solitary life. And, as I said, I really don't think you understand what I'm trying to accomplish here in the—"

"Is that what you sleep in?"

"I beg your pardon?"

"This." He lifted a handful of her gown.

"Yes." She could feel her hem swaying around her bare ankles. They were the only part of her that was uncovered, but for some reason she suddenly felt naked, exposed.

"It's very Victorian, isn't it? Tucks and tiny white buttons and lace. You look a little like an angel."

"Oh, please."

He grinned, enjoying the flush that rose to her cheeks. She was delightful tonight, her hair all a tumble around her shoulders, her cotton gown brushing against her ankles. She was so upright, so utterly proper.

"Come here," he said, taking her arm. "There's something I think I should tell you."

"I'm the one who came here to talk to you."

He bent and tucked a ribbon of red-gold hair behind her ear. "When you cross your arms like that," he whispered, "I can see right through your gown."

Her hands shot to her sides. He smiled again, the corner of his mouth tilting up. "What did you really come here for?" he murmured. "This is the middle of the night. Or couldn't your speech about how happy you are as a single woman wait until morning?"

"But I came here to tell you—"

"Because tonight, when I was lying there in my tent, I got to thinking about the way it felt when I put my arms around you just like this." He drew her into an embrace. "And I was wondering if maybe you'd gotten to thinking about it, too."

Yes, she thought. But she shook her head. "No. Of course not."

"Are you sure, Fiona?" He pulled her closer, and his mouth stroked across her lips, once, twice. His lips drew a damp line up her cheek, and his tongue flicked her earlobe. "How long has it been?" he whispered.

"Really, please, I—"

"How long since a man tasted the soft skin of your neck?" he asked, demonstrating. "How long since you let a man hold you close and touch you?"

Forever! she wanted to shout. It's been forever. I've never felt this, never known that a man could make me feel so warm, so tingling, so melting with hunger deep inside. But she couldn't speak. Her breath wouldn't come as his fingertips stroked over the rise of her cheekbones, under her jawline and down her neck.

"Rogan," she tried to say. It came out as a sigh.

He let the palm of one hand slide down the front of her gown. "Fiona," he whispered. "I've decided you're right about how little I understand. So I think I'll stay a few more days. Then you can teach me everything about you that I don't know. How does that sound?"

She opened her mouth, but his lips covered it. His tongue stroked over her lips, testing, probing. And then he was straightening, setting her away from him.

"Until tomorrow," he said with a smile. "Good night, Fiona."

Chapter 4

Fiona sat on the edge of her camp cot and stared down at the wool socks on her feet. She wiggled her toes and watched the socks lump up and down. At least she had control of her limbs. Now.

What had happened? She'd made up her mind to tell Rogan McCullough one thing: that she wasn't the least bit interested in anything he had to offer. Not his offer of new Land Rovers. Not his money. Not his warm dances around the campfire.

Instead, he'd told her that he would be staying at her camp for several days. Worse, he'd held her in his arms, kissed her, whispered in her ear and stroked his hand down her breast. And she'd liked it! Liked it? She couldn't stop thinking about the way his lips had felt against hers. About the way his tongue had slid into her mouth in a sensual, tantalizing dance. About the feel of his hot palm grazing her body through the fabric of her nightgown.

No man had ever touched her breasts. Now she leaned forward and cupped them in her hands, aware of their heaviness, their swollen tips, the tingle that slid from each nipple into the pit of her stomach and back again. Her scientific mind, normally so absorbed with data and statistics, reeled with unstoppable thoughts that zinged back and forth like ricocheting bullets.

Had Rogan liked her breasts? Were they acceptable? Why hadn't she ever noticed this unbearably delicious feeling before? Heaven knew she'd washed her body enough times, scrubbing her breasts down with a bar of soap and a rough washcloth. They might just as well have been a pair of feet for all the attention she'd paid them.

Not that she hadn't ever thought about men. Oh, there had been a time when she'd dreamed of a large house with a garden full of roses and a husband coming home for tea. She'd imagined plump pink babies and tiny fingers sticky with jam. She'd pictured herself in someone's arms. He would hold her as gently as a china cup; he would treasure her and protect her. Like a handsome prince in a fairy tale, he would rise to her defense and make certain they lived happily ever after.

But, of course, these things hadn't happened to her. And she had learned they didn't really happen to anyone. Rogan McCullough, with his persuasive arguments and big-city life-style, was certainly no prince.

On the other hand, a gentleman who treasured her like a teacup would never have penetrated the high stone wall she'd built around herself. It would take someone bold, someone as determined to get in as she was determined to keep him out. It would take a stubborn, single-minded, driven sort of a man....

She jumped off the edge of the cot and grabbed a pencil from her desk. With a flick of her wrist, the propane lantern hissed into a bright blue glow. She tugged on her chair and sat. Jerking open a file drawer, she dumped a manila envelope full of photographs over the desktop.

Now, she thought. Enough of princes and teacups. Back to the real me. Rogan might hold her and kiss her, but she knew who she was. She'd withstood charging bull elephants; surely she could withstand one blue-eyed man.

She began sifting through the pile of photos. There was only one thing to do about the situation—show Rogan that she was right and he was wrong. And the M family would help her do just that. First thing in the morning, she would drive Rogan out in search of Margaret and the others. In the space of two or three hours, she would explain her work. As logically as a thesis, she would outline why his plan would never work. Then she would point him in the direction of his airplane and send him away for good.

She began to write, jotting down the points of her argument. The tumult of emotions inside her settled as she flipped through card files of analytical data. She searched notebooks, careful mosaics of her ten years of research. She reread her articles. She extracted series of figures on the evolvement of the M family unit, their bond groups and their clan.

She wrote and outlined. This was who she was. This was what she did. Her head sagged onto the desktop, but still she wrote. And when at last she collapsed onto her cot and her eyelids dropped shut, she dreamed of elephants and wide-open plains and the African sunrise tangled in her hair.

When Rogan appeared for breakfast, Fiona began to wish in earnest for the return of that stiff wool business suit. His rumpled bush shirt hanging unbuttoned and untucked revealed the diamond of dark hair she had noticed in the night. His jaw was shadowed with unshaven beard. The hair on his head was rumpled from sleep, and she caught herself imagining what it would feel like to slide her fingers through it.

He sat in the chair at the opposite end of the table from her and stared. His eyes, framed by the tangle of dark hair, glittered like ice.

Fiona took a swallow of tea, regarding him. "Do you always dress so elegantly for breakfast, Mr. Mc—"

"Please. It's Rogan. And, no, normally I shower, shave and dress before breakfast. But then I'm usually not sleeping in a tent with growling lions outside keeping me awake half the night. And I don't usually have a little African man shaking my shoulder at dawn. And I don't often find myself in deep conversation with a nightgown-clad woman at midnight."

"I assume the women you normally converse with in the middle of the night are *unclad?*"

The corner of his mouth tipped up as he leaned forward and spoke in a low voice across the table. "The women I'm with in the middle of the night are not interested in conversing, Fiona."

Nguyo wandered out of the thatched kitchen with plates full of scrambled eggs and bacon and a neat arrangement of fresh pineapple. Like a waiter in a fine restaurant, he served his steaming dishes with an elegant flourish. His bare feet pattering in the dust and the clink of silver against china were the only sounds in the clearing.

"I don't usually eat breakfast," Rogan said as the cook reentered the kitchen.

"You'll offend Nguyo if you don't. He takes things like that personally. And by the way keep an eye out for the vervet monkeys," Fiona cautioned. "They like fruit. They'll jump on the table and steal your breakfast before you know what's happened."

Roger glanced into the pink-lit branches of the acacias. As Fiona had predicted, the small gray-furred creatures had gathered to inspect the humans' buffet. A group of them sat on the ground only a few yards away from the table. As the meal progressed, they inched closer.

Eating in silence, Rogan realized how out of place he felt in this wilderness. In his New York suite he normally read the morning newspaper at the long table in his formal dining room. Next he scanned his agenda for the day, then flipped through several briefing files. Hardly aware of his surroundings, he downed several cups of dark black coffee. Two or three telephone calls interrupted every meal. In fact, he had installed a speaker phone in the dining room. It sat on the table along with the salt and pepper, as though it were another of the dining accoutrements.

But here in the middle of Africa there was no telephone jangling. No secretary buzzing. No windows being washed or vacuum cleaners roaring. The sound of traffic—tires screeching, horns blaring, radios pumping music—was so far away as to be nonexistent.

As Rogan ate, he noticed that the only sounds were soft ones. Sounds nature had invented. The stream gurgling. Doves cooing. Monkeys making quick movements. Breezes rustling the acacia leaves. The smells came softly, too. Not smog and exhaust fumes and artificial pine-fragrance room deodorizers, but the scent of fresh air, eggs and bacon, wood smoke, sun mingling with dust.

He speared a bite of egg and twirled it slowly, watching Fiona over the tines of the fork. "You look good this morning," he said.

She glanced up, one rust-colored eyebrow arching. "I'm afraid you look terrible."

"Thank you."

Actually Fiona had decided she felt very uncomfortable with the way Rogan looked. Keeping her eyes on her breakfast was simpler than facing that broad chest with its swath of dark hair. The more she thought about it, the more she realized she'd preferred Rogan in his suit and tie—silly as they had seemed—to this uncombed, bare-chested savage at her breakfast table. The wool suit had toned him down a little. It had contained him.

Finishing his breakfast, he stood and stretched. Muscles bunched in his arms and rippled down the flat plane of his stomach. "Guess I'd better take a shower," he said.

Thankful that he was finally making himself decent, Fiona led him across the clearing to the small, canvas-enclosed shower stall. A nearby tree with branches carved into hooks held a collection of bath towels and white robes.

"Nguyo lit the fire an hour ago, but you'll still have hot water," she explained.

Rogan's brows narrowed as he studied the large tank insulated with mud held in place by chicken wire. Beneath it glowed the remains of a fire. A narrow pipe ran from the tank to the shower head.

"It's called a Tanganyika boiler," Fiona said. "It dates back to the days when East Africa was colonized by England and Germany. And it's still very efficient. Just turn on the tap and *voilà*, hot water."

"What if Nguyo builds the fire too hot?"

"Then steam comes out the tap, and you have to wait awhile. Or you can just have a cold shower. They're really very refreshing in the morning."

"Yeah, sure. Just the thing to start the day."

"Go easy on the shampoo," she said, slapping a heavy bottle in his palm. "I don't like to alter the environment."

"Got a washing machine around here?" He began to peel out of his shirt. "These are all the clothes I brought along."

She averted her head, pretending to inventory the towels and soap. "It won't hurt you to wear what you have on for a few more hours. You can put on your suit when you get back to Nairobi this afternoon."

"I told you I'd like to stay for a few days."

"That won't be necessary. Within a couple of hours I'll have you convinced your ideas won't work. You'll see."

She turned to go, but he caught her arm. "I said I want to stay here. In this camp."

"And I've asked you to leave this afternoon." Her hazel eyes flashed as she spoke.

"Are you going to buck me every step of the way, Fiona?"

"If at all possible."

"Is there something you don't like about me? Because if there is, I'd really like to know about it."

"You're just a completely different kind of person than I am. You see the world from a different angle. Take people, for example. You've accused me of preferring elephants to people. And you have a point. But your relationships with people aren't the kind I'd want to have anyway."

"What do you mean by that?"

"Based on what you've told me about your background, I suspect you're used to controlling people. I imagine you've always had the power to manipulate and move people around like chess pieces. You've always gotten exactly what you wanted. You've been fawned on and showered with everything you could possibly need. Am I right?"

"As a matter of fact, you're wrong. I've worked damn hard to get where I am today. And the reason I worked so hard is because I *didn't* have the things I wanted or needed. I forced the world to sit up and take notice."

"Well, you won't force me into anything."

"Watch me."

He stared at her. She stared back. Her eyes, reflecting the dark green shirt she wore, looked daggers. Her nostrils quivered slightly. He noticed out of the corner of his eyes that her jaw had clamped shut and her tiny neck muscles were flickering with tension. Her red hair tumbled down her shoulders like an erupting volcano.

By heaven, he liked this woman. He liked her shy; he liked her obstinate; he liked her angry; he liked her warm and trembling in his arms.

"Fiona," he said, lowering his voice. "*Please* will you ask Nguyo to launder my shirt? And if you don't mind, I'd appreciate it if you could find me something else to wear."

She didn't move. She didn't blink. As he finished stripping off the wrinkled shirt, he saw it was all she could do to keep her eyes focused on his face. He folded the shirt into a neat square, lifted one of her hands and set it in her palm.

"Please?" he repeated.

Not waiting for an answer, he stepped behind the canvas curtain and left her standing alone in the clearing.

When Rogan emerged from the shower, he saw Fiona and Sentero talking earnestly beside the Land Rover. Heads together, they were conferring at a level of intensity Rogan had come to recognize as normal for Fiona. Under one arm she carried a large packet of papers, and as she talked she jabbed the packet to punctuate her sentences.

Sentero nodded, said a few words, nodded again. Fiona shook her head and pointed one long arm in the direction of the humpback mountain. Then she swept her hand across the horizon. But when she got to Rogan, she stopped, lowered her arm and turned abruptly.

For some odd reason it pleased Rogan to disconcert her. Maybe it was the fact that she was so damn complacent about every single area of her life. He'd never met a woman like her. Oh, he'd known confident women, of course. As he shrugged into the clean T-shirt Fiona had draped over a bush for him, rows of self-assured, aggressive businesswomen filed through his mind like so many automatons.

But Fiona's confidence wasn't born of clambering over others on the way up the corporate ladder. Nor was it a product of wealth and power. Fiona knew who she was. And she liked herself.

That, Rogan realized, was the true reason he enjoyed throwing her off balance. He sensed that Fiona was attracted to him—and this *didn't* fit her carefully plotted plan. He liked the way a blush had crept up her neck when he'd stepped out of the tent the night before. He liked feeling her melt a little in his arms. And he liked the way she averted her eyes every time she saw him bare chested.

Not that he'd lacked female attention. But it certainly was interesting to watch someone fight it so hard.

Pushing his fingers through his wet hair, he attempted to comb it into order. A tiny mirror hung on the trunk of the acacia, and he peered into it, scrutinizing himself. The shave had done him a world of good, but he still looked like hell. His hair stuck out on one side. The T-shirt, obviously left behind by an assistant, was several sizes too small. It cut into his biceps and stretched across his shoulders like an elastic bandage. The wrinkles in his trousers would have done an elephant proud.

"Are you coming?" Fiona called across the clearing.

It was true, Rogan realized as he walked toward her—she did look like the sunrise. Her thick hair fairly glowed with an orange-red light. Her dark green shirt and matching pants were the color of the distant escarpment. Dusted with red African soil, her boots blended into the earth as if she had grown roots.

"Great shower," he commented, approaching. "That boiler idea ought to be patented."

"Why don't you go ahead? Maybe you'd make yourself another million dollars. You could invest it in Air-Tours. Then you'd be happy and leave me alone."

"I wouldn't leave you alone for a million dollars, Fiona."

She glanced at him, hesitant and uncomfortable. "I hope you remember our conversation last night."

He smiled. "I remember a lot of things about last night."

"And you'd better buy some aspirin," she said, turning to Sentero. "I think I'm going to need it."

"Yes, Dr. Thornton." Unsmiling, the African eyed Rogan. "Shall I convey a message for you, Bwana McCullough? I'm going to Nairobi now."

"You speak English?" Rogan ran his eyes down the Maasai. The plaid cloths rustled idly in the breeze. One beaded earlobe held a small black film canister. A pair of bare feet with thick toenails emerged from worn leather sandals.

"Of course I speak English," Sentero replied. "How else would it be possible that I have received my master's degree in wildlife management from the University of Texas?"

"Texas? But you're—"

"I am a Maasai, *bwana*. I've taken the knowledge of your country, but I have chosen the ways of my people."

"Sentero's taking a bus to Nairobi from the lodge at Lake Naivasha," Fiona interjected. "Do you want him to telephone your associates?"

"That's all right. I'll call Clive on the radio later."

Sentero accepted the packet of papers from Fiona. "Very well, Dr. Thornton. I'll return in one week."

"Give my greetings to Dr. Patel and Mr. Ngozi. And say hello to Ian for me."

"Yes, Dr. Thornton." He switched into Swahili, his face serious and his eyes devoid of sparkle. *"Kumbuka—hasira hasara."* Without a further word, he set off, his long legs loping across the plains.

"What was that all about?" Rogan asked, his eyes following the Maasai.

"Just another proverb he wants me to remember."

"Well, what is it?"

"Hasira hasara. It means 'anger destroys.'"

She opened the Land Rover door and climbed into the driver's seat. Rogan just had time to slide in before the engine roared to life and the vehicle blasted out of camp in a cloud of red dust.

"We could have driven him to the lodge," he shouted over the deafening rattle. "It's not that far."

"He wanted to run. He says it clears out his lungs before he hits Nairobi. He dislikes the city as much as I do."

She worked the sticky gear shift as the Land Rover plunged down a ravine. Following the dry riverbed, she skirted huge gray boulders and patches of damp sand.

Things were bad enough, she mused, without Sentero and his proverbs. Not only did she have to lose a morning's serious research, but she had to play chauffeur to this great hulk of a man with damp hair that lay dark against his neck, a pair of indecently brawny arms and a set of shoulders that threatened to burst the seams of the borrowed T-shirt.

"Where are we going?" he was shouting over the rumble.

Never mind about the hair and the arms and the shoulders, she thought—this man's entire body nearly filled the front of her Land Rover. His long legs were jammed into the dashboard. His head threatened to smash into the roof. She began to wish he would roll down his window. She was suffocating.

"I said where are we going?" he repeated.

"I'm taking you to find the M family. I need to check on a new calf."

"Why do you call them that? Does the *M* stand for something?"

She tried to put her mind to matters at hand. Perhaps she was just used to having Sentero in the front seat with her. The African was so lanky, so loose limbed and lithe. His body was like a gazelle's compared with Rogan's massive elephantlike physique. Rogan wasn't fat, of course. But then neither were elephants, contrary to popular opinion.

Fiona knew that if she were to survive the morning, she had to focus. There was her well-constructed argument to review. And there were the elephants to study. That seemed like more than enough to keep her thoughts away from Rogan McCullough and the blunt-fingered hand resting on his thigh as his blue eyes flicked across the landscape, his carved chin jutting forward.

"I've assigned each elephant group in the park a letter of the alphabet," she said, interrupting her own train of thought. She drove the Land Rover out of the ravine and headed across a stretch of grassland. "In each group, the elephants' names begin with that letter. It's a way of coding them."

"So they're kind of like people to you, with names and personalities?"

"No. I'm a scientist. I stay detached so I can study them objectively. If I started to feel sentimental about them, I wouldn't see them clearly."

"So you're telling me they're just a herd of data? Just a bunch of carefully organized letters of the alphabet."

"Well..." She felt he'd pushed her into a corner. "I've worked with the Rift Valley elephants for years. Even though I'm a scientist and I do keep my distance, I've gotten to know them. It was sort of inevitable. Each of them has certain...mannerisms, you know? They have habits and temperaments. They like and dislike certain things. They tend to behave in specific, almost predictable, ways."

"Do they know you?"

"They know my scent and my presence. They show an awareness of me, and they're not afraid of me. At least, most of them aren't. Several bulls near the Suswa area are wary of any humans. They avoid me, or they threaten when I approach."

Rogan watched her drive across the plain, her slender arms shuddering with the rattle of the steering wheel, her eyes scanning the land for thornbushes and ant bear holes. She brushed a wisp of hair from the corner of her mouth, and the binoculars around her neck bounced against her breasts, their strap cutting into the rise of soft flesh.

"Can you walk around with the elephants?" he asked. "Do they know you that well?"

"They're wild," she said. "Wild, untamed, free. *They* rule this land, not me. I keep a respectful distance. I'm not afraid of them, though. One or two—especially the calves— like to come right up to the Land Rover to inspect it. But I stay away. I don't interfere. I let them live their lives the way they want."

She looked at him, eyes piercing, before continuing. "It's the only way to handle wild creatures. You have to leave them alone."

He understood what she was telling him. She, like the elephants, needed space. She needed to be left wild and free and untouched.

"Then how can you be sure you really know them?" he asked. "How can you truly understand them?"

"I don't truly understand them," she answered. "I don't think I'm meant to."

They drove along without speaking for several minutes. Fiona scrutinized the golden plains for any sign of gray, ponderous monoliths. The Land Rover bumped past herds of zebras, their black-and-white stripes brilliant in the early-morning sun. Thomson's gazelles lifted startled heads and then bounded away. Giraffes sauntered among the tall acacias bordering the streams. Their brown-and-tan-mottled hides blended so well with the shadows that only their long necks, peering like periscopes over the treetops, gave them away.

"Margaret was feeding in this area yesterday," Fiona said. "I suspect she and the other Ms slept in that clearing. And then they probably wandered toward Longonot early this morning."

She stopped the Land Rover and lowered the window. A cloud of dust rolled in, settling on humans and metal alike. She flipped back the overhead canopy. In distinct gold-and-brown bars, sun streamed through the dust motes. Standing, she lifted her binoculars and ran them over the horizon.

"See anything?" Rogan emerged beside her, his shoulders taking up more than half the space.

She wedged herself against her side of the opening. "Not the M group. Old James and Nick are over by that large baobab."

He peered in the direction she was pointing. Sure enough, a pair of gray shapes materialized out of the grass beneath a gigantic, bare-limbed tree.

"Which family do James and Nick belong to?" he asked.

"Mature bulls don't belong with any herd. Elephant families are matriarchal. They're composed entirely of females, young and old, with a few male calves mixed in."

"And the bulls?"

"They wander around doing whatever they want. Once in a while they come along and test the females to see if any are in estrus—ready for mating. Then they mate and go on their way."

"Sounds like fun."

She lowered the binoculars. "It's an efficient way to pro-create the species. Which is, after all, one of the primary motivations of these animals. They want to survive, and they want to reproduce. It's an internal drive, the need to pass along their genes and biological imprints. Having *fun* isn't part of the program."

"Too bad for elephants."

She let out a breath. "You don't ever give up, do you?"

"Nope. It's part of my genes and biological imprints."

She watched him speaking, his sensual mouth forming the words, his lips tilting at one corner to form a smile that punctuated each sentence. Strands of drying hair began to lift and brush against his collar. Sun danced off the gold that spilled over his forehead. The shirt strained with every breath he took.

"So, Fiona," he said, "why don't you start explaining all these things I don't understand about you? Like how the sunlight turns your eyes from brown to green . . . and what your hair feels like when it's wet . . . and what you were thinking about last night when you went back to your bed, alone."

His arms, resting on the edges of the sunroof's metal opening, slid toward her. One fingertip traced a line down her bare forearm.

"Because," he went on, "I lay awake for a long time wondering about all those things. I lay on my bed looking at the shadows and thinking about you."

She tore her gaze away and looked over his shoulder. It was one thing for her to toss and turn, remembering him and the way he had looked in the moonlight. But the idea that he had actually lain awake thinking about her was something new. She'd never imagined anyone wondering anything about her. She never thought Fiona Thornton crossed anyone's mind—other than perhaps as "that scientist in Africa who studies elephants."

She glanced at Rogan again, imagining him imagining her. What had he thought in the middle of the night? What had his mind invented between them?

This wasn't happening to her. She couldn't actually be wanting this man to kiss her again. Not after all her hard work, all her resolutions. Maybe it was simply a biological reaction. The mating instinct. She'd read in scientific journals that women in their early thirties had strong sexual drives. Maybe hers had suddenly come to life, like a light bulb that had been waiting for someone to flip the switch.

But she was no animal, driven by uncontrollable instinctual drives. She was a trained, educated scientist. She would simply have to take herself in hand and set the matter straight.

"I think what you should know—" she began, then for some reason faltered.

"What is it I should know, Fiona?"

His chest was barely two inches from hers. Again she felt that strange tingling sensation that started in the tips of her breasts and spread to the pit of her stomach. The metal edge of the roof cut into her back.

"I want you to understand," she tried again, "that I really—"

"I'm waiting."

"You see, if I step back and analyze myself and this situation, everything is clear."

He nodded and took a step toward her. His thighs brushed hers. One hand began playing with her hair. "Why don't you go ahead and analyze things for me, then? I like hearing the sound of your voice."

She clamped her mouth shut. She felt panicky, like a cornered doe staring at the barrel of a gun. But she wasn't afraid Rogan might shoot her; she was afraid he might kiss her again. And she was even more afraid she wanted him to.

"Here's *my* analysis," he was saying. "After a great deal of scientific observation, I find that you, the intrepid researcher, have been living all alone in the middle of Africa with very little human contact. Now, that's completely unnatural. The human species was made for interaction. We're social animals. We need a certain amount of communication. We rely on interplay, collaboration, fellowship. Intercourse."

"Oh, thank God!" She gave him a quick smile. "I've found the elephants. Come on, let's go."

She slid between his arms and landed with a plop on the seat. Rogan was still standing as the Land Rover sputtered to life and started across the plains. He loosened a strand of her red-gold hair that had gotten hooked on one of the sun-roof latches. He examined it for a moment, sifting it between his fingers.

Yes, he decided, Fiona Thornton was indeed an interesting and challenging example of the human species. As he dropped the strand of her hair and watched it settle on her shoulder, he smiled.

"That's Margaret," Fiona whispered, pointing out a lumbering gray female who was eyeing the Land Rover and flapping her ears. "She's never pleased to see me at first. Poachers killed one of her daughters and two sons. She's always very wary."

Through the roof hatch Rogan watched the elephants feeding on tufts of brittle yellow grass. They all looked the same to him. Big, gray, wrinkled animals with huge ears that swayed slowly back and forth. The only differences he could discern were tusk sizes and shapes. Some of the elephants had large tusks, some had small ones and others had none at all. The tusks were either uptilted or straight. Some had grown askew, like teeth in need of braces.

Beside him, Fiona leaned across the roof, chin resting on her knuckles. "Margaret's the matriarch, the mother of the larger females. She leads the M family. Megan and Moira are her daughters. Can you see Megan there? She's the one with the tear in her ear. Look, she's just picked up some dirt and blown it across her back."

Rogan watched the elephant, trying to memorize her characteristics. Size, ear shape, tusk configuration. "Where's Moira?"

"I don't see her just yet. They're all clumped together. Oh, look!" She touched his arm. "See the baby. That's Madeline's calf. He's just three days old. Watch how he nurses."

The tiny gray calf lifted his trunk and tested his mother's skin. Then he put his mouth to the full breasts between his front legs and began to suckle. As the baby drank contentedly, his mother ran her trunk over his little body, touching and reassuring him.

"Oh, you fine little boy," Fiona whispered.

"Who's that?" Rogan asked, pointing out a large elephant some distance from the others. She was swinging her head and kicking out with one front foot.

Fiona peered through the tangle of thorn scrub that nearly concealed the elephant. "That's . . . oh, Rogan—it's Moira! I think she may be in labor."

She slid down into the seat and fumbled for her camera. Rogan joined her. "Shall we try to drive closer?"

"I don't want to disturb her. She's been having such difficulty lately. I thought she might be preparing to give birth."

"Here, let me do this. It'll save you time." He took the camera from her and began to load film. "Go on up. I'll have this for you in a second."

Grateful for the help, Fiona climbed onto the metal roof and studied the elephant. From this vantage, she had a clear view across the thorn scrub. The large female kept backing up and shaking her head. Just under her tail, a bulge began to appear.

Fiona reached through the hatch and grabbed Rogan's T-shirt, half hauling him up. "She's going to give birth! I've only seen this once in all my years of study. Come on— you've got to watch."

He seated himself beside her and handed her the camera. "What's she doing? What's going on?"

"See beneath her tail? That lump? Oh, heavens, where's my notebook?"

Rogan grabbed the small pad and pen. "You talk—I'll write."

"Nine thirty-seven a.m.," she dictated, as though he were Sentero and not the unwelcome intruder she had labeled him. "Moira's vulva is enlarged and hanging very low. Much lower than usual. Liquid is dripping from it. Her breasts are full."

Rogan realized that he had to take care to form legible words on the paper. He studied the elephant. Then he watched Fiona. Her eyes shone. Her breath was shallow, and a smile lit her face.

"Nine-forty," she said, snapping a photo. "Moira is lying down. She's resting, I think. The others are totally ignoring her."

"She's up, Fiona! Look at that bulge now. It's moved down about a foot or more. It's slipping farther down."

"She's moving. She's coming toward us. She's turning. Oh, Rogan!"

At that moment, with only the slightest push, Moira gave birth. A baby elephant completely enclosed in a fetal sac slipped to the ground. The mother rested for less than a minute before touching the sac with her foot. Fiona and Rogan sat breathless, watching for movement. Moira bent and punctured the sac with her tusks.

The calf began to jerk its legs.

"The others are coming over," Fiona whispered. "See how their temporal glands are streaming."

The elephant family filed toward the new mother. Long wet streams ran down their cheeks from pores on either side of their eyes. Moira had finally freed the baby and was attempting to lift it with her front foot.

"It's going to stand," Rogan murmured. "Uh-oh. It just fell down."

"They're very wobbly at first. Can you see the baby's ears? They're pink in the back. Look, it's a female, a little girl. She's up again, Rogan. She's searching for milk. Oh, no, she's fallen."

The other elephants surrounded the mother and new baby. Margaret rubbed her head against Moira's backside. Mallory rumbled, and Moira answered. Matilda picked up the fetal sac and swung it around for a few minutes. Finally she tossed it over her head.

"Look," Rogan said, his hand covering Fiona's knee. "Moira's got the baby on her feet again. See the two of them, right there between those other elephants? The baby's rooting around between Moira's legs."

"Has she found the breasts? I can't see from this angle, Rogan."

"Yes," he said, pumping one fist in the air as if he'd just witnessed a touchdown pass. "She's up. She's nursing. We did it!"

He turned and pulled Fiona into his arms. Her camera clicked an involuntary picture as he drew her close and kissed her lips.

Chapter 5

Rogan and Fiona spent the rest of the day watching elephants. The M family, new addition included, inched toward the shadows of Mount Longonot. The sloping dormant volcano beckoned with the possibility of untouched vegetation and flowing streams. Overhead the sun rose to its zenith, scorching the metal roof of the Land Rover and turning the bridge of Rogan's nose a bright pink.

Neither he nor Fiona mentioned the impulsive kiss of the early morning. Instead, they fell into a routine in which she spoke her observations and he wrote them in the little notebook. The fact of the matter was, Rogan realized over a lunch of peanut butter sandwiches and hard-boiled eggs, he'd been just as disturbed by the kiss as Fiona had.

When she'd come to him in the night, responding to his touch and his kiss like a woman who wanted more, he'd begun to imagine playing out a sort of mating dance with her here on the African plains. They would tease and play, he would win her over, and finally the game might culminate with them exploring each other's passion beneath the stars of the Southern Cross.

But as this day wore on, it became clear to Rogan that Fiona hadn't been playing—not the night before, nor that morning in the Land Rover. As much trouble as she had breathing every time he came near, and as deeply as she responded when he held her, it was apparent that she really had no inkling of the woman's traditional role in the mating game. Which he had to admit was refreshing.

She averted her eyes from his face and wedged herself into a corner of the open hatch every time he stood to join her. When his hand brushed hers, she jerked away from the touch. Her communication consisted entirely of scientific observations about elephants.

And yet for all that, he knew she wasn't just an emotionless researcher. He'd seen her eyes sparkle at the birth of the baby elephant. He'd watched her laugh aloud as the calf suckled. More important somehow, she had responded to *him*. But it wasn't the sort of response he'd expected.

She acted more like a skittish colt. Melting into his embrace, then shoving him away. Breathless at his kiss, then turning her head. Gazing into his eyes, then quickly diverting her attention to stare far into the distance. The realization that this was not a game had dawned when he'd kissed her that morning. Fiona Thornton didn't play games. Her every move was deliberate. Every response was honest. Every glance held a world of meaning.

It occurred to him that he ought to back away. He ought to steer clear of such a woman. He ought to watch his step.

It also occurred to him that he didn't want to.

The orange sun hung just over the horizon when Fiona pressed on the brake and the Land Rover rolled to a halt under the spreading, yellow-trunked acacia tree. The next instant Nguyo hurried out of the kitchen, a butcher knife in one hand and a frying pan in the other. His white cook's hat slid to the back of his head as he pattered to a stop.

"*Bwana, bwana!* Many calls for you. All day long." His dark eyes were wide with worry. "The radio calls fifteen times. Maybe twenty."

Fiona stepped out of the Land Rover. "Who called, Nguyo?"

"The people of Bwana McCullough. A lady named Memsahib Ginger. 'Where is Bwana McCullough?' she asked me. I told her he is away on safari. She wanted to send a plane to find him. I said no. She said everyone from America is looking for Bwana McCullough. Everyone!''

Fiona turned to Rogan. ''You must be a popular man.''

''Immensely. I'll call Ginger. Nguyo, where's the radio?''

Rogan followed the anxious African into the kitchen, where the transmitter was housed. Fiona studied him as his broad shoulders pushed through the sagging door and disappeared.

It was odd how things had turned out. She'd expected a day of relentless if subtle pressure to come around to his way of thinking. Instead, he'd gone straight to work as though this were some new business project he was eager to tackle. All morning he'd taken down her observations—and he'd even made a few of his own. When lunchtime came and she expected to start urging him back to the camp and his airplane, she found herself avoiding the subject. He never mentioned wanting to leave. So she dropped it, deciding his assistance was worth putting up with the man a few more hours.

Now, wandering into her tent, she rubbed the back of her neck. Her thoughts, so regulated with carefully timed observations and details, lurched into unfamiliar territory.

Who was this persistent woman named Ginger? Could she be Rogan's wife? Maybe she'd been calling because he'd left her all alone in Nairobi. Perhaps she wanted to return to the States.

Fiona pictured this Ginger—a sandy-haired beauty with a full bosom and a tiny waist. Unlike Fiona, Ginger wore a lovely shade of lipstick and groomed her nails with tasteful matching polish. She brushed her hair more than once a day. She knew how to flirt and tease. And her lips belonged to Rogan.

Wiping a hand across her mouth, Fiona slumped onto the cot. Sukari meowed and crawled into her lap. As Fiona rubbed the cat's ears, she decided enough was enough. She'd spent a full day struggling to concentrate on her work. The night before had been even worse. The dancing, the midnight conversation, the lack of sleep—all had robbed her of

the sense of security and normalcy she coveted. This had to
stop. It was time for Rogan McCullough to go.

"Hey, Fiona. You in there?" His deep voice on the other
side of her tent wall made her sit up. "Just wanted to let you
know I've decided to stick around a couple more days.
Ginger's going to man the fort for me."

Fiona curled her toes inside her boots.

"Fiona? Did you hear me?"

When she still didn't answer, he pushed back the door flap
and stepped in. She was sitting on a narrow bed, a fluffy
white cat in a purring ball on her lap. Red-gold hair spilled
around her shoulders and down her back. Wide hazel eyes
stared at him.

"I'm staying," he repeated.

"Rogan," she said evenly, "you may not stay. You really
aren't needed and, to be honest, you aren't welcome.
There's enough daylight to fly your plane. I want you to go
now."

"No," he said.

"Yes."

"No. I've decided to stay. I'll help you out tomorrow."

"Why? I told you I don't need you."

"You do need me. Besides, I'm only just beginning to see
the possibilities for this place."

"Possibilities?" She rose to her feet, and the cat rolled off
her lap to land neatly on the floor.

"Possibilities for the future. Air-Tours Safaris. I'm finally beginning to understand the impact my company can
have here. The elephants are a wonderful drawing card.
That birth this morning—now that was a real coup. People
will flock for things like that. The photographic opportu-
nities out here are endless. If I can improve that little airstrip of yours—"

"Stop! Just stop right now, Rogan McCullough. I've
spent this entire day trying to show you that your plan *won't*
work. That birth was a once-in-a-lifetime thing. A fluke.
I've only seen one other myself, and I've been out here every
day for years. It just so happens that the abundant rainy
season we had two years ago led most of the mature females into estrus and they conceived. Now their babies are

being born. It's not like this happens all year long. It's not like I can stage dramatic elephant births for your tourists. Besides, every elephant birth requires that much more record keeping from me. I barely managed with you along in the Land Rover, and only because you were willing to take notes. Can you imagine if I had to guide a pack of tourists around every day?''

"I'll provide the guides. You can schedule and plan the tours.''

"No!'' She shoved his chest. "Just get out of my tent. I don't want you here. You're interfering.''

He took her wrists and held her hands in place against him. "You're being unreasonably stubborn. You won't even look at my suggestion.''

"I've looked at it. And I've decided it's nothing but a load of bunk.''

"What's bunk is that you imagine yourself completely isolated from the world and totally self-sufficient. You think you don't need anybody, Fiona. You think you can just carry on for years and years until you turn gray and shrivel up and die out here with your elephants.''

"Yes, I do! That's exactly what I think, and that's exactly what I want.''

"Fine. I'll take my half-million dollars and my ideas for improvement and everything I have to offer you and the elephants. I'll just leave you out here to wither into a dried-up old stump of a human being who never knew what it was like to laugh and cry and love and be a part of the family of man.''

"And good riddance!'' she shouted behind him as he stormed out of the tent.

Dust puffed around Rogan's boots as he stalked across the clearing and ripped back the door of his tent. The hell with her, he thought. He could just see her years from now. Her hair would all be white. She would be bent over and hobbling to her Land Rover. She would spend day after day watching those damn elephants until one afternoon some game warden would find her, dead as a doornail with a lap full of notes.

And good riddance to you, too, Fiona Thornton.

He stuffed all his written ideas and proposals into his briefcase and fumbled with the gold latch. Maybe he should just sell Air-Tours. It had been his father's company, anyway, and it certainly had nothing to do with publishing. The only reason he'd considered messing with it was for the business challenge and the possibility of adventure it represented. It was something a little different. Something he could look forward to as a getaway from McCullough Enterprises.

Of course, if the deal with Megamedia came through, he would pretty much let McCullough Enterprises go. And then what would he do? He certainly wouldn't need money. He'd spent years struggling to make his organization a viable contender in the industry. Maybe it was time to relax. Time to spend a little of that money. Maybe he could buy an island somewhere. Or build a house in New Mexico. Maybe he would just sell off everything his father had left him and use that money to start some brand-new business. Something on the cutting edge. Something risky and improbable.

He liked a challenge. He enjoyed fighting against long odds. The battles and the struggles were what kept him going and made him feel alive.

"Bwana McCullough?" Nguyo's voice sounded outside the tent. "*Hodi,* may I come inside? I have brought your shirt."

Rogan swept back the tent flap, and the small African man stepped in. He laid the pressed and folded safari shirt on the bed and then, like a fluttering moth, he began lighting lamps and unfolding blankets.

"It will be a cold night, *bwana.* In Kenya hot days can bring cold nights."

"Nguyo, I won't be staying the night."

"No?" The African straightened. "But I have prepared a roasted chicken with peas and new potatoes."

"Sounds good, but—"

"Oh, very delicious. And a large spice cake with marzipan frosting."

"Well . . ."

"This cake is the favorite of Matalai Shamsi. This morning, when I saw that she would be very angry today, I decided to bake her the spice cake. Then she will smile. You will see."

He puffed a pillow and settled it on the cot. Humming a small tune, he took Rogan's briefcase from his hand and wedged it beside the tent wall. Then he turned back the corner of the bedding, revealing a snowy white sheet beneath the blanket.

"Perhaps you will stay for this one night, *bwana*. Just for my spice cake and roasted chicken. Perhaps you will not shout at the Matalai Shamsi. Perhaps you will sit beside the fire with her and eat. And then, perhaps you will dance again. If you wish to make her smile, you will dance."

Rogan cleared his throat and scratched the rough stubble on his chin. "She's a difficult woman. Always angry."

"She is angry only with you. And this is good."

"Good?"

"We don't see her smile or shout or speak. She is always alone. Always very quiet. For Matalai Shamsi, anger is good."

It was odd to think that anger could be a positive emotion for Fiona. Especially odd, Rogan realized, because at this moment he felt strangely alive. Arguing with her had made his blood roar and his body surge with adrenaline. She certainly was a challenge. A battle. One he would like to win.

"Sometimes," Nguyo confided, "we think among ourselves that the Matalai Shamsi will one day become an elephant herself. She will forget how to speak. She will forget to return to the camp. Her food will be the long grasses, and at night she will sleep among the elephants."

Rogan smiled. Interesting concept. He'd just been picturing Fiona as gray and wrinkled himself. "Tell me why you call her Matalai Shamsi, Nguyo. What does that name really mean?"

"For that story, you must ask her yourself."

"I did ask her. She gave me some nonsense about her red hair and green clothes looking like the sunrise."

"It is true. She is a woman of sunrise. But you must learn the whole legend if you wish to understand Fiona Thornton."

Nguyo gave the tent one last inspection before he started through the door. At the last moment Rogan touched his shoulder.

"Nguyo," he said, "you told me you made the spice cake because you knew Fiona would be angry when she came back to camp. How did you know this morning that she would be angry tonight?"

For a moment the African stared up at a corner of the tent. "A sleeping woman who lives in the pleasant land of dreams does not like to be awakened," he said. Then he turned and vanished into the twilight.

Fiona sat in her tent and listened for the rumble of the airplane's propellers. Surely after such an argument, after such clear instructions to leave, Rogan McCullough wouldn't consider staying in the camp another night. Surely he would know he wasn't welcome. Surely he would comprehend that she wasn't going to change her mind about the tourists.

She slipped on a navy blue cotton sweater and worked her hair into a loose braid. Evening shadows crept around the tent, enclosing it in a comfortable green warmth. The philodendron leaves drooped a little. The cat settled into his basket. A cricket began to chirp just outside the tent flap.

Fiona tied her small mesh window shut against the crisp breeze that filtered through the acacias. She turned up her propane lamp and settled at her desk. There would be time for a few minutes of study before Nguyo rang for dinner. Leafing through her files, she added Moira's new baby to the M family list.

Another little female. Would this one survive the drought? Would Moira have enough milk to sustain the baby? Would the milk have enough nutritional richness for the tiny calf to develop into a strong and healthy member of the family?

Flipping open her notebook, Fiona scanned the list of the day's observations. Bold black pen strokes recorded each moment of Moira's labor and the calf's birth. Rogan's writing. Strong down strokes. Evenly spaced letters. Punctuation that could never be mistaken for accidental ink blots.

Fiona turned the page. Rogan had missed nothing. Every word she had spoken had been set in his dark regular print. He'd even added a few things she hadn't said. She scanned the writing. "ll:05 a.m. Margaret moves northwest toward crest one mile past birth site. New calf struggling to keep up. Moira lagging just a little. Mallory watchful. Family stops to feed on twigs and barks of *Acacia xanthophloea* trees and dried clumps of *Sporobolus consimilis.*"

Fiona frowned and reread the last sentence. She didn't remember telling Rogan the scientific names of the trees and grass that formed the primary food for the elephant population.

She skipped a few more notes she *did* remember dictating. Then her eyes fell on another notation in Rogan's hand. "Madeline searches out a patch of *Cynodon dactylon* beside dried streambed. The grass is only a rough stubble."

Fiona stared at the page and its careful script. She tried to picture Rogan writing these words, but she saw only the man himself and not his work. A whimsical smile crossed her lips at the memory of the pair of them seated on the Land Rover roof conferring about the elephants' progress toward Mount Longonot.

Rogan's hair had dried quickly in the heat of the day. Each time he'd bent his head to write, the breeze drew a random part down his scalp. She wondered if his neck had burned in the intense sunlight. His nose certainly had. She should have mentioned the name of a good healing ointment before he left.

Lifting her head, she listened again for the sound of his airplane. She heard instead the gentle melody of Nguyo's bamboo xylophone calling out the evening supper song.

For a moment she studied the notebook again. She slipped her fingertips across the writing, feeling the lumps and bubbles that Rogan's heavy-handed penstrokes had embossed on the thin paper. Shutting her eyes, she held her fingers to her nose and breathed in. Then she closed the notebook and walked to dinner.

The deserted campsite, completely dark now save for the glowing campfire and the flickering kitchen lantern, beckoned. Far across the plains she recognized the rumbling calls of elephants, communication almost too low for human ears. She sat at the white-clothed table and unfolded her napkin across her lap.

"Roast chicken for *madame?*"

She swung toward the familiar sound of the deep male voice. Rogan emerged from the thatched kitchen bearing a tray of steaming food. Nguyo marched immediately behind him with an armload of plates and silverware. Still wearing the tight T-shirt, Rogan had topped it with one of Nguyo's jackets. The gray corduroy sleeves hit him midarm, and the front didn't have a hope of buttoning.

He presented a fragrant roast chicken, still sizzling and popping. He uncorked a bottle of white wine and poured Fiona's glass more than half-full. While Rogan arranged a bowl of peas beside a basket of snowy dinner rolls, Nguyo set the table for two.

"Mr. McCullough," Fiona began, feeling as if the world had tilted on its axis just a little. "You're certainly the most—"

"First of all, my name's Rogan. And you did make it clear that you wanted me to leave. But the fact is, I decided it was too late to fly out." He sat in the opposite chair and eyed her. "I've also decided we'll have a truce."

"The word 'truce' implies mutual agreement, *Rogan,*" Fiona said, deliberately emphasizing his name. "One person can't make that decision alone."

"Wrong. If one of the warring parties elects to stop fighting, you have an automatic truce."

"Or a massacre."

He laughed. "Massacre at will, Fiona. But I'm no longer in the battle."

She spooned a helping of peas and a slab of chicken breast onto her plate. Taking a sip of wine, she swirled it in her mouth and then swallowed. She *could* destroy Rogan, she realized. Massacre would be so simple. The easy way out. She could refuse to have anything to do with him. She could shout at him, run him out of the camp, send him away in his plane.

She sensed that Rogan McCullough was not a man who often called a truce. Like the determined warrior he was, he won his battles. But this time, with him so clearly in submission, she could win. He would be taken off guard if she refused to back down, if she banned him from the camp. She knew that he *would* go away then. And that would be the end of the strife.

"All right, you can stay," she said suddenly, not allowing herself time to weigh the consequences.

Rogan looked at her, a forkful of chicken poised at his mouth. "Truce?"

"Truce."

He chewed, mulling something. Then he glanced up a second time, his blue eyes as bright as the stars above him in the night sky. "Tell me the legend of Matalai Shamsi."

She stiffened. "I told you what the Africans think. It's just my red hair—"

"This isn't about you. I want to hear the legend of Matalai Shamsi. Tell me the story."

"It's just a fairy tale."

"I'm in the mood for fairy tales. Come on, Fiona. Indulge me."

Smoothing out the folds of her napkin, she kept her eyes on her plate. "The legend of Matalai Shamsi is an old Swahili folktale," she said. Her voice drifted. She lifted her eyes to the fire, and the flames flickered in them.

"Once upon a time," she began, "a king had six sons. The youngest was named Shamsudini. The king and his sons were sitting in the garden one afternoon when a beautiful bird flew overhead. The king wanted the bird and told his sons to catch it for him. 'The one who loves me truly will bring me the bird,' the king told them."

"I bet the youngest son caught it."

"Don't interrupt, Rogan. It's rude." Her eyes flashed with warning, and he grinned. "All the sons were given money, a horse and servants. But Shamsudini's brothers were jealous of him, and they tried to kill him on the way.

He chose not to fight. Instead, he gave up his possessions and set out alone to find the bird. Soon he met a gigantic spirit, who threatened to eat him and pick his teeth with the prince's bones. Shamsudini told the spirit that whatever God willed would happen.''

"I bet the spirit didn't eat him, did he?'' Rogan was leaning halfway across the table, his face animated.

"No, the spirit offered to set Shamsudini free in exchange for food. So the prince prayed, and forty pots of food appeared. After eating, the spirit offered to help the prince find the bird. They traveled to a castle, where the prince found the special bird. But the lord of this castle wouldn't set the bird free. He wanted a thunder sword in exchange.''

"So the spirit took him to find the thunder sword,'' Rogan interrupted.

"Why don't *you* tell the story?''

"Sorry, it's just that when I was a little kid I...'' He stopped and looked at the fire. "I like stories. Go on.''

"In the castle where the thunder sword hung, Shamsudini faced another king. This king wanted the prince to bring him Matalai Shamsi in exchange for the sword. So the spirit and the prince built a ship and sailed away in search of the Princess Sunrise. Finally they arrived at the palace where the princess's father, the sultan, lived. Shamsudini pretended to be a powerful medicine man. When the sultan asked the prince to cure his sick daughter, Matalai Shamsi, Shamsudini insisted she'd have to be brought on board his ship for the cure to work.''

"What was wrong with her?''

"I don't know. The legend isn't specific. It just says she was sick. Some people think she had a sort of sleeping sickness—she walked around in a dreamland from which she couldn't be awakened.''

Rogan's eyebrows lifted. "And so the prince cured her and stole her away,'' he said.

"That's right. Shamsudini had fallen in love with Princess Sunrise. But then he had to face all the other trials again. He tricked the thunder sword king by giving him Matalai Shamsi's maid instead. He tricked the king who

owned the beautiful bird by giving him a false sword that
had been crafted to look like the thunder sword. Finally,
when the spirit and the prince parted ways, the spirit gave
Shamsudini one of his feathers. The prince could summon
the spirit at any time by throwing the feather into the fire.''

''What about the brothers? I bet Shamsudini really let
them have it.''

''Actually the brothers captured the prince on his way
back to the castle. They strangled him until he was almost
dead and tossed him in a heap. Then they stole the princess, the sword and the bird, and they went to find their father the king. When the king asked about Shamsudini, the
brothers told him that the prince had gone off on his own.
The king was furious. He planned a wedding for the oldest
boy and Princess Sunrise.''

''Wait a minute now!'' Rogan took a swig of wine and
thunked his glass on the table. ''The prince deserves better
than that. He's smart and brave. He triumphed over all the
odds. He fought hard to win the princess. You can't let his
brothers strangle him just like that, Fiona.''

''Do you want to hear the ending or not?''

''This story better end right.''

''How would you end it, then?''

''If I were the prince, I'd come to. Then I'd break into the
palace and challenge the brothers to a duel. I wouldn't let
them get away with that. I'd win the sword and the bird and
the princess back. Any man knows he's got to fight for the
things that are rightfully his. He's got to climb to the top of
the heap. He's got to win over adversity.''

''All by himself?''

''Well, who's going to help him?''

''*You're* the one who's so sure people can't exist all alone,
Rogan. People need each other, remember? People have to
communicate, share ideas—''

''Okay, okay.''

''What the prince did was throw the feather into the fire,''
Fiona continued, ''and the spirit appeared. Together they
went into the king's hall, where they found everybody ready
for the oldest brother's wedding. Shamsudini talked with his
father and told him the whole story. Then the prince called

the princess by name. She ran to him and spoke for the first time, calling him her prince. Then the spirit's voice boomed out, 'It is true.' The king ordered the five bad brothers sewn into sacks and thrown in the ocean. Shamsudini married Princess Sunrise, and their wedding lasted many days.''

"And they lived happily ever after?"

"That's not part of the original tale. In Swahili it ends with them eating rice and cakes until they could eat no more."

Rogan pondered this. "I want a happily-ever-after ending."

"Why not?" she said. *"And they lived happily ever after."*

They sat in silence, both staring at the fire. Fiona was remembering Margaret and the long evenings in the oak rocking chair. She could almost feel the warm curve of her *ayah's* breast and see her dark cradling arms. How many times had Fiona asked her for the legend of Matalai Shamsi, over and over again? Margaret would tell the story until her head nodded and fell against Fiona's. Then the little girl would listen to her *ayah's* deep breathing and would imagine herself a beautiful princess who would one day be woken from sleep by a handsome, brave and very wise prince.

"Would you care to dance, Fiona?"

She focused on the man across the table. His face was open, beckoning. "Well...the radio is in the tent and...no, I don't think..."

"We don't need the radio. Come on." He rose and pulled her to her feet.

And then she was in his arms again, circling the fire to the music of silence. She closed her eyes and rested her cheek against his shoulder. The smells of dust and smoke mingled around him. The sun's heat radiated from the skin of his neck, carrying in its warmth the essence of his male scent. She breathed deeply.

"When I was a little girl," she whispered into the corduroy, "my *ayah* used to tell me stories. She's the one who taught me the legend of Matalai Shamsi."

He held her, one hand caressing the waves of her braid. "I sat in my mother's lap for hours listening to stories," he said. She could feel the vibrations of his voice against her forehead. "But that was a long time ago."

"I don't remember my mother's stories."

"You were young when she died?"

Fiona's breathing went shallow as she nodded.

"Well, I guess everyone knows about the great McCullough scandal," he said. "So that's what happened to my mom. Didn't see her much after the breakup. She never married well, you know."

His laugh held no humor. Fiona wanted to take her hand away. He was squeezing so hard the blood in her fingers had stopped.

"I don't," she said. "I don't know the story of the great McCullough scandal."

Rogan stopped. He drew her away from him just enough to read her face. And he saw in her eyes that she was telling the truth. She knew nothing about him. She didn't know about his past—his parents, the scandal, his own rise above it all. She was a fresh slate. Unbiased.

What a strange revelation. He took her again and moved her around the fire. Never—not in all the long years of his life—had he met someone who didn't know his past. National gossip magazines had spread the word, it seemed, to every household in the United States. His mother had appeared on talk shows; his father had been interviewed by the press. The story of young Rogan McCullough had been covered throughout the years from the day he was left outside the iron gate of the boarding school until he rose to the pinnacle of McCullough Enterprises.

He weighed the idea of Fiona's innocence back and forth. If he told her everything, he could observe how the story affected her. He could see if she somehow changed toward him the way women did when they learned his name and realized who he was. Or he could keep it all from her—he could keep her pristine and honest.

"Well," he said finally, "it's not important."

She could feel the tension emanating from him, the unspoken emotion that he held bridled. Barely.

"There is one thing about you I want to know," she said, meeting his eyes.

"And what might that be?"

"I'm curious about the notes you made this morning."

"What about them?"

"The grasses. The trees. Did I tell you their scientific names? I don't remember that."

"Oh." He smiled for the first time since dinner. "Crazy, huh? I know you're not going to believe this, but in college I majored in biology. I'd been interested in that kind of thing since I was a kid. I took a course or two in plant identification. Took pictures of wildflowers. Went on camping trips. The whole nine yards. So when I was out there in the Land Rover today, the plant names suddenly came back to me out of the blue."

"You spelled them right."

"Photographic memory, you know?"

His body had relaxed against hers, and she was beginning to decide she preferred him stiff and uncomfortable. His mouth moved close to her ear, his breath heating her hair. His hand began to slide up and down her braid again.

"I thought you mentioned publishing as a career," she remarked.

"Sure, publishing. That's what I do now, of course. You know," he said, forgetting again that she didn't, "during college a buddy and I started this small on-campus student guide. Then a German pharmaceutical company asked us if we could produce a single-sponsor magazine for them. So we did. Then we bought *Manor,* the men's magazine."

"Manor?"

"You never heard of *Manor?* It's a very popular American magazine. But in those days it was foundering. My partner and I bought it and brought it back to life. Three years later we split our interests. He took *Manor,* and I took the smaller publication."

"And then what?"

Rogan stopped moving but kept her close. "After the split I started McCullough Enterprises. Right now I have over a thousand employees and a fifty-million-dollar headquarters in New York. I run the thing. It's my life."

"I thought you owned Air-Tours."

"I do. My father died three months ago and left it to me, along with about six other companies—most of which are in better shape. Air-Tours is just a . . . a sideline. A diversion. What I really do is publish advertising-sponsored magazines that are supplied to doctors and dentists and businesses. All kinds of professional groups. I do television. Video. I have homes in New York and Florida and Monte Carlo. I own a yacht and three planes. I collect cars. You sure you weren't aware of any of this?"

"Of course not."

"It just seems so strange to me." His eyes studied the ground between them. "All my life, everywhere I've gone, people thought they already knew all about me. They always made assumptions. I've been pigeonholed. I've been expected to follow a certain set of prearranged rules."

He looked up and saw that she was smiling. "So who are you supposed to be?"

"I'm this . . . this mover and shaker. This guy who rocked the publishing industry. I'm the man who climbed higher than anybody else. High enough to eclipse even my own father."

"But who are you really, Rogan?"

"I'm . . . well, I'm . . . Hell, I'm just me."

"And this is what I know about you." She took his hands from her shoulders and settled his arms at his sides. "I know that you're intelligent and bold and very stubborn. I know that once, long ago, you looked at plants and took their pictures and memorized their names. I know that this morning you understood the elephants. And that, Rogan McCullough, is quite enough for me."

Chapter 6

Before Rogan could respond, Fiona spotted the arrival of Nguyo's famous spice cake. With an uncharacteristic laugh of delight, she detached herself and hurried around the fire to the table.

During the dessert course—which Rogan decided was, indeed, the best cake he'd ever tasted—Nguyo and Fiona went through their nightly meal-planning routine. Rogan listened half in amusement as Fiona requested fillet of Lake Turkana tilapia, a green salad and potato soup.

"I wonder what we're really going to get," he said as the African paraded off, arms loaded with dinnerware. "Maybe spaghetti?"

"Oh, I doubt that," Fiona responded with a laugh. "Nguyo has never been fond of Italian foods. There's no telling what we'll be eating. If he prepares his roast beef, you'll love it. He makes a wonderful tartar sauce. And he has this casserole that you—" She stopped speaking and stared across the table.

"I *would* like to stay, Fiona," Rogan said.

"I think it's best that you leave tomorrow. I really have so much work to do."

"I'll take Sentero's place. I'll write the notes."

"No, Rogan. Please. I'm not going to change my mind about the tourists."

"Wait a minute now. That subject's off-limits according to the truce. I want to stay another day just to... to be out here. I want to see the elephants again. I'd like to stay with you, Fiona."

She was afraid that if he said one more thing, she would give him anything he wanted. The tourists, the campsite, the elephants. The way he held her with his gaze sent a shiver of weakness all through her body. The way he spoke, his lips moving sensually and his mouth caressing each word, made her completely forget to listen to what he was talking about. His voice held her mesmerized, like a swinging watch in the hands of a wizard.

"Well..." she said in a blank tone. "Well, I..."

"The thing is, Fiona." He reached across the table and covered her hand with his. "There's some kind of magic out here. I don't know whether it's the plains and the animals, or the dry heat, or the birth of the baby elephant. Or maybe it's you. I don't know what it is. But I'm not ready to go yet."

"But Ginger said—"

"No. I don't want that right now. I don't want that world. I'm not ready to go back. Just give me another day here. Would you do that? No arguing. No anger. Just a quiet day watching the elephants."

"All right." The words barely sounded in her throat. "One more day. Now, if you'll excuse me..."

Before she could tumble into the pool of his blue eyes and drown there, she pushed her chair away from the table and walked across the clearing to her tent. Fighting for breath, she zipped her door flap shut and tore out of her shirt. This was not good. The feelings she was having were not sane. She stripped her trousers down her legs and fumbled under her pillow for the folded white nightgown. Everything in her life was coming unraveled. Things were out of control.

On a normal night she would have sat by the campfire for another hour. She would have drunk two cups of tea with milk and sugar. She might have dozed a little. Then she would have returned to her tent and worked for several

hours on her notes. Finally turning down the lamp, she
would have crawled under her covers with her cat and—

"Fiona," Rogan said just outside the tent.

She grabbed her nightgown and shook out the folds.
Where was the opening in the hem? She searched frantically through the voluminous swath of white fabric.

"Fiona, I just wanted to say good night."

"Good night," she called. "Sleep tight."

"Fiona—"

"Don't let the bedbugs bite."

"Fiona, could I talk to you a second?"

She finally found the hem and began peeling it apart. Oh,
why did Nguyo have to be so conscientious about his iron-
ing? The zipper on her tent door started moving slowly up,
metal mumbling in the night.

"Rogan," she warned. "I'm not quite—"

He walked into the tent. She jerked the nightgown to her
chin and tried to spread the fabric around her bare legs.

"Sorry to interrupt, Fiona," he said, amusement glitter-
ing in his eyes. "Glad I got to see those shoulders, though."

"So, what did you want?"

"About today. I wanted to thank you. I enjoyed myself."

"I'm glad. Well . . . good night, Rogan."

She had backed against the edge of her desk chair. The
knuckles clutching her nightgown were white.

"You know," he said, "I'm beginning to understand
what the Africans mean about that sunrise comparison. It's
the strangest thing, but in the lamplight your hair begins to
glow. Yours is not just average shiny hair. It's luminescent.
The orange and gold inside the red light up. And then there's
the way it all spills down your shoulders. Did you know you
have freckles on your shoulders, Fiona?"

He had moved to within a foot of her now, wanting to
touch her once more tonight. His fingers sifted through her
hair and began to move across her shoulders.

"My mother," she whispered. "She had freckles."

"They're muted. Almost invisible. But I can see them. Do
you have freckles on your arms? There they are, sprinkled
like fine powdered sugar.

By now his hand had slipped down her arms and then back up. With one fingertip he touched her lower lip. "Fiona, something has occurred to me."

She cast a glance at the cat, who was having another bath, oblivious to the peril of his mistress.

"I suddenly realized," Rogan went on when she didn't respond, "that if you don't know anything about *me,* then maybe there are a lot of other things you don't know. Things that are common knowledge to most people."

"I don't think that's true. Just because I never heard of you or McCullough Enterprises, I'm not ignorant. I'm not stupid."

"I'm well aware of that. It's just . . . there may be some things you're innocent about. I mean, has anyone ever told you that you have the most amazing mouth? There's something about the way your lower lip kind of pouts. And your upper lip is bowed on the top, like two smooth hills with a gentle valley between them. It's remarkable."

She brushed his hand away. "Rogan, really. I have lips just like anyone else's. *Labia.* The outer and inner margins of the mouth aperture, usually regarded as the source of speech."

"Speech *and* kissing." He traced the line of her upper lip. "You know, everything on the human body has a double function. I mean, true, there's this hair of yours—"

"Cylindrical filaments composed of protein and growing out of the epidermis."

"Yes, but yours smells of flowers and lemons and sunshine."

"It's just my shampoo. Lemon is the only kind they sell at the *duka* in Naivasha."

"Feels like silk." He moved closer and lifted a mass of her hair. "Looks like fire. It's a halo. See what I mean? And anyone could say, sure, we all have eyes. But your eyes are unusual. They tilt up at the outer corners. And the color . . . reminds me of tortoiseshell. Strange, magic eyes. Always changing."

He touched her eyelid and then ran his finger around the tender skin as her lashes fluttered against his touch.

"Oculus," she said quickly. "Eyes are merely the organs of sight. A pair of spherical bodies contained in the orbits of the skull."

"And speaking of bodies... Now, scientifically, what we have here is just a mass of bone and muscle and nerve endings and such. But what I've found is that if I run my hand down your neck like this, you'll suddenly forget about all the web of *ossius, musculus* and *nervus.*"

His hands stroked the sides of her neck and slipped over her bare shoulders. His mouth trailed a damp line across her forehead. Brushing aside the thick tresses of wavy hair, he drew a row of kisses down one shoulder and across the fragile bone at the base of her throat.

"Rogan," she whispered, "please keep Ginger in mind."

"Ginger?" He lifted his head.

"The woman in Nairobi who keeps calling. Is she...well, I've thought she might be your wife."

"She might be, but she isn't. Nobody is, for that matter. So, if you don't care, I'd rather keep *you* in mind."

"Well, yes, as a matter of fact, I do..."

"Good. I do, too." He drew her to him, his hands on her back pressing her to his chest. His mouth found hers, and with a gentleness that belied the surging rush through his body, he stroked his lips across hers. Through the thin T-shirt, he could feel her heart hammering as he caressed the sensitive inner lining of her mouth and ran his tongue across her teeth. Her clenched fists, holding up the nightgown, formed a barrier that kept his body slightly distant.

"Fiona," he murmured in her ear, "If you were to put just one of your arms around me, I think you might find you liked it."

"Actually the thing is, Rogan..."

"Like this, see? Now, if I run my hand down your back, you can feel my fingers on your skin. And if you were to stroke my back...like that...then I might find that I wanted to kiss your neck... and your cheek... and your ear."

She thought she was going to melt into a puddle all over the floor like the Wicked Witch of the West. If she did, maybe Rogan would go back to Kansas where he belonged. But if she kept touching the hard muscles that ran down his back, and if he continued wetting her ear with his tongue and tracing circles between her shoulder blades, she honestly believed she might turn into a liquid pool. Everything about her felt wispy and ethereal. Shivers slipped up her neck and down her spine. The tips of her breasts had begun to throb. The pit of her stomach pulsed with a rhythmic beat that coursed down her thighs. She felt dewy and shivering all over.

"I've noticed that you don't wear many underthings," Rogan was whispering.

"There's never been much point out here."

"But I see a point..." A smile tilted one corner of his mouth as he smoothed the wrinkled nightgown over the tips of her taut breasts.

At his touch she sucked in her breath and backed harder against the desk chair. Trails of fire shot through her nipples as his fingers grazed the white fabric over them. He stroked around one jutting crest and then the other. Her lips parted as she tried to take in air. His mouth covered hers, and he gently touched her tongue.

"Oh, Rogan, really," she gasped, turning her head at the shock of his gesture. How intimate it had been, how possessive. She felt invaded and horrified and deliciously intoxicated. Like a tippler after the first morning taste of liquor, she was drawn to him again. She lifted her head and met his mouth, this time testing the secret herself.

Oh, his mouth was warm and delicious. His hands sliding down her back drew her closer, slipped beneath the band of her panties, cupped the tender flesh. Releasing the nightgown, she drew both her arms around him and tested the fine sinew of his back, his shoulders, his neck. Her fingers nestled in his thick dark hair, and her lips drew him fully into her mouth.

She felt wild and free, insane with wanting. Her knees throbbed with a warm weakness, and she pressed herself against his body. The strength of his hunger crushed her tender pelvic bone. She caught her breath in awe and delight at the power of this man.

"Fiona," he murmured. He drew away slightly and lowered the nightgown that was draped over her bosom. At the sight of her breasts, full and beautiful, desire flooded through him. He cupped one globe and ran his thumb over the burgeoning nipple.

He knew better than to push her. She wasn't the kind of woman who would slip easily into bed with a man after a few drinks and some light flirtation. She was different. If he rushed, she might back away. She might run. He couldn't risk it. But oh, waiting wasn't going to be easy.

Her breasts, large and full for such a taut, honed woman, taunted him over the crumpled fabric of her gown. Fiona wore her sexiness unconsciously, like a she-leopard's sleek and sensual beauty. Her naiveté, coupled with the womanly curves and hollows of her mature body, made her all the more desirable.

"Rogan," she was whispering as his thumbs tested the petallike skin beneath her heavy breasts, "I feel very... very..."

Nothing adequate would come to complete the sentence, so she left it unfinished. She gazed in amazement at this body—her body, though it felt as though it must surely belong to someone else. It blossomed and throbbed with life. Trying her best to remain scientifically detached, she noted the myriad changes she was undergoing at the hands of this man. It was a marvel.

"Rogan," she said softly, "just look at what you've done to me. From a purely objective standpoint the changes are... remarkable. My breathing and heart rate have accelerated. I feel flushed. My normal circulation has altered. Blood seems to have pooled in my knees, and I can't think straight. It's as though my brain has been slightly deprived of oxygen."

Mirth danced in his eyes as he listened. "Is this a treatise on female sexuality, Fiona?"

"I *am* a scientist. My outlook is an integral part of me. Analysis comes naturally. I'm not the emotional, sentimental type of woman, you know."

"Hmm." He ran one finger down her bare skin and then circled a rosy crest. "You'd better add this to your data base. We'll do a controlled test, shall we? Note what happens when I stroke this breast. See how your nipple contracts and rises? It's almost seeking my touch. You'll notice a sharp tugging between your thighs.''

"Yes," she acknowledged, her eyelids drifting shut.

"The control breast, however, shows little response. It's still very soft and warm. But if I begin to caress it, you'll note that it immediately responds in a similar manner. A sweet, tightening ache begins throbbing down deep inside you, doesn't it? Now, if I were to lower my head and cover your nipple with my mouth, like this . . .''

She caught the back of the chair and held on.

"The warmth of my breath causes an even stronger biological and psychomotor response—scientifically speaking, that is. When I stroke my tongue around the circular edge of your nipple . . . like this . . .''

"Rogan . . . oh . . .''

"And when I lap your breasts with hot, wet strokes . . . you'll find that you begin to tremble and your body starts to ache for release.''

"Yes.''

"Perhaps I should investigate. For research purposes, of course.''

"Oh, yes. Perhaps so.''

As his hands moved over her bare flesh, he continued to speak. "My body, on the other hand, has undergone different but equally remarkable changes, Fiona. If you begin to stroke my chest, you'll notice that I'm very warm.''

He took her fingers and slipped them beneath the cotton fabric of his T-shirt. The crisp hair under the fabric felt hot and slightly damp to her touch. Each breath seemed labored, yet he continued to speak in that low monotone that held her transfixed.

"Now, accepting as fact that your skin is ultrasensitive along your neck and over your breasts, it would seem to follow that my skin might be equally sensitive. Why don't you experiment?''

Obeying as though she were indeed nothing more than a mute robot who could only follow orders and respond as bidden, she placed her lips on his neck. His hands began to follow the curve of her back and hips, sliding under her thin cotton panties and stroking the tops of her thighs. She touched his skin with her tongue and marveled at the heat emanating from it.

"Rogan," she murmured, "I don't feel very... scientific anymore. I can't keep my distance. I'm losing objectivity."

"Really?" he said with mock surprise. "Dr. Thornton, how astonishing."

She smiled. "In fact, I think I could just keep touching you for hours. I like the way your lips feel on my skin and the way your hands are so strong and rough. And I think if you would just kiss me again... mmm, yes... like that..."

"Now, here's what I want you to think about," he said into her ear, aware that at this moment he might win her— or lose her. "You're more than a scientist, Fiona Thornton. You're a woman. Beautiful. Sexy. Desirable. And here we are, way out in the middle of Africa with nothing but the moon and the stars and your body and mine. Not a thing to stop us from enjoying each other. You think about that, Fiona, would you?"

She was still nodding when he pulled her nightgown over her breasts, kissed her lips one last time and walked out of her tent.

"Memsahib," Nguyo called from outside. *"Memsahib,* wake up. Bwana McCullough is ready to go and see the elephants."

Fiona sat bolt-upright in her bed. *Rogan.* The image of his face washed over her in a trail of hot ripples.

"Nguyo, what time is it? Is... is breakfast ready?"

"It is almost seven o'clock. Breakfast was prepared long ago. Many pancakes have already been eaten by Bwana McCullough." He paused a moment. "And nearly all the syrup."

She couldn't believe she'd slept in. All night she'd tossed on the camp bed, trying to sort through and analyze the flood of changes Rogan had unleashed. She felt wild and free... embarrassed and shy. She wanted to spend the rest of her life in a sexual frenzy... and she never wanted to see another man as long as she lived. She could hardly wait to see Rogan... and she wished he'd never come into her life.

"Memsahib?"

"*Just* . . . just a moment, Nguyo. Tell the *bwana* I'll need to shower and eat before we can go."

"Yes, *memsahib*. He is repairing the Land Rover now. It will be ready by the time you have prepared for the day."

"The Land Rover?" Fiona stuck her head through the door flap.

Nguyo grinned as he jabbed a finger in the direction of the vehicle. "The *bwana* has told me the gears are not good. He is going to make them better for you."

"I didn't know Rogan was a mechanic."

"Oh, *memsahib,* that man can do many things."

"Yes," she acknowledged, "he certainly can."

"But he was not happy about the hole in the front fender. When I told him that the big elephant, Margaret, had pushed her tusk into your Land Rover, the *bwana* became angry."

"Oh, he just doesn't understand Margaret." Fiona studied Rogan from a distance. He was bent over the Land Rover, one elbow jutting into the air and his head buried in the vehicle's engine. "What's he wearing, Nguyo?"

The African beamed. "These are the clothes of Wilson, *memsahib*. Very clean, very well pressed. Even starched."

"*Our* Wilson—the night watchman? But he's a Maasai."

"These are his Nairobi clothes, bought from a *duka* in Narok. Shorts, socks, T-shirt. Very nice?"

Fiona stared at the baggy green shorts, something an old-time English colonist might have worn. The safari shirt that had accompanied Rogan's chic tourist outfit covered a faded blue T-shirt emblazoned with the slogan Only Elephants Should Wear Ivory. The bush shirt blew open in the breeze, its tail flapping loosely at his thighs. And on his feet the new suede boots were covered with red dust.

"Very nice indeed," Fiona muttered. "He's becoming a veritable Humphrey Bogart. Next he'll be wanting to set sail on the *African Queen*. Excuse me, Nguyo. I'll be ready for breakfast in a few minutes."

Whistling, the African set off down the path toward the thatched kitchen. From the Land Rover a matching tune

began. The notes intertwined, lifted through the sunlit sky
and were carried away by the breeze.

"There's James again," Fiona said, spotting the lone bull
as she traced her binoculars across the horizon. She and
Rogan had spent the morning rambling across trackless,
scorched plains in search of elephants. It was almost noon,
and the old male was the first they'd seen.

"He's by himself today," she went on. "I don't see any
sign of Margaret or her family around here. They're probably nearly to Mount Longonot by now."

Rogan leaned across the Land Rover roof and studied the
sloping mountain. "So Longonot's a volcano?"

"Yes, and so is Mount Suswa, to the southwest. See it
there?" She moved aside as Rogan's shoulders maneuvered
the turn inside the open hatch. "Suswa has caves that are
full of bats."

"Bats produce guano. It ought to be mined. The stuff
could be a great money-maker for the local population."

"Rogan, do you always think in terms of money and in-
come potential?"

"Usually. Is there something wrong with that?"

She considered a moment. "I can see it going either way,
actually. The sort of man you are...if you wanted to, you
could be driven, aggressive, combative, intimidating. I have
a feeling you might be able to manipulate people into anything you want."

"Whoa. Don't turn me into Hitler."

"It's a possibility."

"Look, I may be a leader—but I'm not evil. I just do
what I need to do to stay where I am in the world."

"But you could be so much more than you are." She
wondered why she was spilling the thoughts that had rolled
through her head all night. It shouldn't matter to Rogan
what she thought of him. And yet, she wanted him to see the
vision she'd had.

"What are you talking about?" he said, a gruff note of
irritation in his voice. "There can only be one person on
top—and I decided a long time ago that that person's going

to be me. I've worked damn hard to become the man I am today."

"Why? Why have you worked so hard?"

He flicked a blade of grass from the roof. "Well...I guess I have an inner drive to be the best."

"Why?"

"If you knew anything about my past, you'd know why. I had some things to prove. I had to show the world who I was and what I could do. A guy like me had to prove things to his father, you know."

"But your father died three months ago."

"So?"

"So, now who are you proving things to?"

He stared down at the scratched green paint on the Land Rover roof. The truth was, since his father had died, something had died inside him, too. He'd spent his whole life trying to show John McCullough that his son was somebody. Somebody worth noticing, worth paying attention to. But Fiona was right. His father was dead. Now what?

"What did you mean about my potential to be more than I am?" he asked, changing the subject. "Would you explain that?"

"If you opened yourself up," she said, softly, "rather than trying to dominate, you might learn empathy. Your leadership skills could be used in positive ways. You could inspire people. You could become a truly courageous man."

"What kind of courage are we talking about here, Fiona? I fly planes, I race cars, I'll tackle any kind of risky sport—skiing, speedboats, motocross, boxing. Mountain climbing. Caving. I love a challenge. Anything there is to conquer, I'll give it a try."

She studied him in silence for a moment. "True courage," she said, "is not the power to *conquer* the world, Rogan. It's the power to love it enough to save it."

"Now, wait a minute here. You're equating courage with love? Is that how you handled the charging elephant that rammed this Land Rover? Did you just sit there and *love* that elephant into submitting?"

"Of course I did. Margaret was very upset because I'd inadvertently driven between her and Mick, her youngest calf. It happened a few years ago, when Mick was just a new baby. The M family had been attacked by poachers not long before. They'd killed two of Margaret's sons. I understood how upset she was. So when she gored the Land Rover, I drove far enough away until she felt comfortable again. It was really my own fault. But we have an understanding now.''

"You trust her not to charge you again?''

"Oh, she regularly charges. It's usually just a bluff. She's a grumpy old thing. But we're on good terms.''

"I don't believe this, Fiona. You mean you'd just sit and let an elephant charge you?''

"Well, I wouldn't hold it against her. Look, here comes James. You can see he's in musth. That means he'll be a little irritable.''

"Fiona, I don't think you should let these elephants get so close to you,'' Rogan said, taking her arm and turning her to face him. "What if something happened? What if you got hurt—seriously wounded? One of them could easily rip you open with a tusk or crush you. These elephants weigh a *lot*.''

"Twelve thousand pounds for a full-grown male. The females are half that. But don't worry, I've never known an elephant to purposely hurt a human. In fact, they'll go out of their way to avoid it. They're gentle creatures. Very loving and kind. I've lived with them for years. I trust them, and that's that. Now, are you going to take notes or not?''

She felt oddly pleased that Rogan seemed concerned for her safety. Not that she'd ever been particularly worried about it herself. She knew the elephants too well to be afraid of them. Rogan was flipping through the notebook, frustration written in the downturn of his mouth.

"So what did you tell me about James?'' he asked.

"He's in musth right now. That means he's sexually active and in full rut. Musth is a stage bulls periodically go through—kind of like estrus in the females. I've started noticing that these two conditions seem to coincide. I'm fairly sure a bull in musth can put females into estrus and vice versa.''

Rogan was writing, but his thoughts weren't on bull elephants. They were on Fiona's soft words and clear eyes as she'd told him that she thought he had the courage and the power to make a difference in the world. The power to save the world, she'd said. It was a new thought, and he turned it over in his mind as he took down her words.

"James is smelling the air," she whispered. "He's probably looking for females. Notice the swollen temporal glands between each eye and ear? They're streaming with a thick liquid. During musth, the male has a sharp, pungent odor. Can you smell him?"

Rogan lifted his head. It shocked him to see that the bull had wandered to within yards of the Land Rover. Head high, the animal was testing the air with his trunk. He smelled rank.

"Keep writing," Fiona said. "James is showing characteristic male musth signs—head lifted, chin tucked in and ears waving. His aggression level seems higher than usual. He's constantly dribbling urine. His sheath is covered in a light green scum, and his legs are wet."

"Scum?"

"Yes, on the sheath covering his penis. Can you see that green coating? Early researchers thought the bulls had some sort of horrible disease. But it's just musth. Okay, steady. He's going to charge us."

At that moment James rumbled and flapped his ears. Shaking his head, he thundered toward the Land Rover.

"Hell, let's get out of here," Rogan shouted, hurling the notebook through the hatch and grabbing Fiona.

"Stop!" She wrestled free and put one hand on his arm. "Just watch. He's only bluffing."

Rogan held his breath as the enormous elephant plunged toward them. The ground shook. The air seemed to vibrate. White tusks flashed. Gray ears fanned the air. Rogan clenched the Land Rover roof. At the last moment the bull skidded to a halt, stared with angry eyes and then shook his head and backed away.

"See," Fiona said. "He's just irritable because he's in musth. Now he's wandering off again. Trying to find some females."

"This is ridiculous," Rogan exploded. "That elephant is a menace! You can't stay out here and subject yourself to this, Fiona. You shouldn't be wandering around in the middle of Africa bush without a gun. You shouldn't be out here, period. It's too dangerous."

"Really, Rogan. It was nothing. Just a sexually excited male. *You* ought to understand about that."

She winked and slid through the hatch onto her seat. "Coming down, Rogan?" she called, turning the key in the ignition. "I want to check on Rosamond and the R family."

Chapter 7

Sun slating low through the grass coated the individual blades with gold. Seeds the color of platinum and the shape of arrowheads clung to each shaft. Impalas and Thomson's gazelles wore saddles of gilt. Zebras' stripes glinted silver and ebony. A family of hyenas, their scraggly fur burnished with copper, slunk over a rocky crest. Weaver birds returned to gourd-shaped nests that hung shimmering from silhouetted acacia branches. A flock of vultures drifted, circling above a distant gorge like debris preparing to be sucked down a drain.

"We should look into that," Fiona said almost to herself as she drove the Land Rover across the dry earth.

"Look into what?" Rogan had been staring out the window, his eyes fixed on a herd of shaggy, bearded wildebeests.

"The vultures. Something over there—probably a lion—has made a kill. I usually try to examine the dead animal the vultures are waiting to clean. Assuming I can find it, that is."

Rogan studied the birds as, one by one, they floated to the ground in long, lazy spirals. He'd always thought of vultures as dirty scavengers in the ecological pecking order. The

low men on the totem pole. But Fiona had spoken of the
birds as waiting to "clean." It was as if she saw them not as
shifty-eyed beggars, but as upright citizens who performed
a useful job.

Once again he was struck by her holistic view of the
world. Animals were a part of the whole life cycle, blend-
ing with plant life in supreme accord—as long as humans
didn't get in the way and mess up the delicate balance. As
much as Fiona loved the elephants, she admitted that they,
too, had their place in the fragile web of nature. She had
spoken of her worries when elephants began eating acacia
shoots, of their voracious stripping of baobab tree bark, and
of the horrors of human garbage in an elephant's diet. Everything had to blend in order to work. And it was man who
so often threw the Creator's scales out of balance.

"I think they're landing just over that ridge," she was
saying. "We've taken care of the R family, and Nguyo will
keep dinner waiting, so I think we'll have just enough time
to check on that kill before dark."

The Land Rover bounced across a graded trail and then
swerved onto the grass again. It occurred to Rogan that
Fiona paid no attention whatsoever to the steady inroads
civilization had made in the Rift Valley. It was as though she
simply couldn't be bothered to travel on proper roads when
a more direct route led across uncharted savannah. She
never listened to the transistor radio unless Rogan mentioned wanting to catch up on news. She paid scant attention to Nguyo's carefully related messages that came in over
the radio transmitter, and she never returned anyone's calls
as far as Rogan had been able to determine. Nguyo or Sentero usually shopped for groceries and made her phone calls
at Naivasha. Piles of unread mail lay on a table in the
kitchen. Rogan had found the stack of American magazines she'd mentioned. They dated back to 1978.

"Now, do you think we should go around that pile of
rocks," Fiona was asking, "or cross through those trees on
the left?"

"The trees look a little more manageable."

"There's a stream hidden among them, but I suspect the drought has dried it enough that we can get across. Shall we give it a try? Oh, my goodness!"

She slammed on the brakes just in time to avoid a thundering herd of elephants. They tore out of the trees, their ears flapping and the whites of their eyes showing. Tightly bunched, they kept the calves in their midst. Mothers literally pushed the babies to keep them running at the frantic pace. Fiona threw the Land Rover into gear and stepped on the gas. Dust spewed out behind the vehicle as it swerved to follow the elephants.

"It's Margaret," Fiona said, coughing on the thick red powder that billowed through the floor and seeped around the window glass. "Did you see her, Rogan?"

"I couldn't tell." He didn't want to admit that all the elephants still looked pretty much the same to him.

"I saw Megan. And Moira was urging her calf. But I didn't see Madeline, did you?"

"No." He wished he could have been more help. He knew that to Fiona each elephant was individual, each was precious.

"Oh, I wonder what's happened," she called over the rattling metal. "I think they're heading for the south ravine about four miles from here. It's where Mindy died a few years ago. I've noticed the M group seems to feel safer there."

"Maybe you shouldn't follow them. Maybe the Land Rover is scaring them even more."

"They're not thinking about me. They're trying to get away from some danger. Did you hear an alarm call as we topped the ridge? I didn't hear anything. I wish Sentero were here. He would have heard it. He can hear them talking miles away."

"Talking?"

"Communicating. They rumble, bellow, grunt, groan, growl, moan, squeal, all sorts of sounds that we're only just beginning to understand." She shouted as she drove. "A lot of their communication takes place at infrasound frequencies. It's way too low for humans to hear. We can only feel it as a sort of throbbing in the air."

"Look, they're slowing now." Rogan watched as the elephants filed through a narrow opening and disappeared into a ravine. "Is that Mallory? That big one on the right?"

"Yes." Fiona nodded, giving him a quick smile. "She's helping Moira with her calf. And there's Madeline—and the baby."

She seemed to have relaxed a little. Taking out her notebook, she began to scribble what had transpired. She lifted her head and squinted at the disappearing animals, then bent to her work again.

"Where's Matilda?" she murmured. "Oh, there you are. And Mick. Yes, I see you...." She wrote for several minutes, then looked up. "Rogan, would you like for me to show you something? Or do you want to go back to camp and get your plane ready?"

He focused on the dark fear that was only now fading from her eyes. "I'd like to see whatever you want to show me, Fiona."

"We'll have to leave the Land Rover and go on foot. I should warn you, it's a dangerous time of day. Lions and cheetahs hunt at dusk."

"Let's go."

Without responding, she swung down from the vehicle. They followed the path of trampled grass toward the notch in the ravine wall. Slipping through a tangle of dried vines, they made their way along the sloping edge. Pebbles slipped beneath their feet. Almost nothing was visible through the dense thatch of trees and shrubbery. All at once Fiona held out her hand. Rogan took it.

"Look," she whispered, drawing him near. She pointed through an opening in the thick vegetation. "It's Margaret."

Rogan pushed aside a creeper and located the matriarch. She was walking along a dry streambed. Behind her followed the rest of her family, calm now, even though their silence held a definite undercurrent of tension.

"She's moving toward that small outcrop, do you see?"

Margaret stepped across the stream and began to stretch her trunk toward a collection of white objects.

"It's Mindy's skeleton," Fiona explained softly when Rogan gave her a quizzical look.

"Her sister?"

"Her daughter. Mindy was illegally speared by some Maasai warriors almost four years ago. The spear fell out, but the wound never had a chance to heal. An elephant's skin is so tough that it closes quickly and doesn't give the inner laceration time to drain. I watched Mindy fade, until she wandered into this ravine. And finally she died."

She said the words with such sorrow that Rogan slipped his arm around her shoulders and drew her against his chest. The elephants had moved among the white bones and were touching them gently with their trunks. Megan lifted one. Matilda and Mick turned others over with their front feet.

"Margaret always gives a lot of attention to Mindy's head and tusks," Fiona explained in a low voice. "See how she strokes her trunk tip along the jaw? She likes to feel in all the hollows and crevices of the skull. It's as though she recognizes Mindy. I think that, in a sense, she's caressing her daughter."

Rogan watched as the elephants performed the tender ritual. Even the newborn calves fondled and touched Mindy's bones. Mick lifted a rib and, after turning it for some time, tossed it in the air.

Margaret continued to brush her trunk over Mindy's skull. Finally she hooked the heavy bone and carefully moved it a few feet. She settled it in the grass near the other bones, then gave a deep rumble. The elephants slowly moved off, shuffling through the underbrush and disappearing into the darkness of the ravine.

Rogan held Fiona for a long time. Neither spoke. Purple twilight crept through the branches. A pair of delicate dik-diks, as small and fragile as rabbits—though their tiny horns and slender legs showed them to be antelopes—picked their way across the dry riverbed and vanished in the thicket on the opposite side. Somewhere nearby a baby cried.

When Rogan stiffened, Fiona smiled. "It's just a lesser galago," she whispered in his ear. "A bush baby. Can you see it in the tree there? I've been watching it for some time now."

Rogan finally focused on the small primate with its wide, childlike golden eyes, furry body and curled ears. The animal stared for a moment, then cried again.

"You'd think it was human," he said, a shiver sliding down his spine. "Sounds like a tiny abandoned baby crying for its mother."

Fiona let her gaze drift over Rogan's face. The furrow in his forehead had smoothed and softened. His mouth was relaxed, lips gentle and quiet. Blue eyes turning to her, he searched.

"Fiona," he began, but didn't know what he wanted to say. So he kissed her instead. A silent, tender kiss. And then he turned her in his arms, rested her head against his shoulder and stood, drinking in the twilight, the silence, the woman.

"Nguyo will be furious," Fiona said as she drove the Land Rover toward camp. "He understands if I'm a *little* late, but he hates it when the sun has set and I'm not home. He says I ruin his dinners, but really, I think he's worried about my safety."

"Isn't Sentero always with you on these long treks?"

"Oh, Sentero and I have only been working together for about nine months. He had trouble lining up his research grants after college in Texas. And now that he wants to begin his doctorate, he has to go to Nairobi a lot to arrange things from there. I hope he eventually decides to work with me on a permanent basis. He's great. We get along very well."

She was smiling as she drove. Rogan wondered how it could be possible that he had come to envy a man who had long, beaded earlobes and dressed in checkered cloths. But he did covet the smile that Fiona wore for those she treasured. He'd seen it at Moira's birthing and this evening in the ravine. He'd seen her special smile when Nguyo had presented his famous spice cake. And now she wore it for Sentero.

"What's he like, anyway, this Maasai who graduated from U.T.? I'm having trouble putting him together."

"I'd trust Sentero with my life," she said immediately. "He's a wonderful man. Generous, kind, honest, intelligent. He cares about his country. He's working for the future of Kenya."

"I don't know why, Fiona, but something about him doesn't feel right to me. Maybe it's just those strange eyes."

Fiona drove in silence, and Rogan wondered if she were angry with him now. He knew he shouldn't have made that last statement. But he'd learned to rely on his instincts. And they told him Sentero held some deep secrets.

Maybe it was just the thought of Fiona drifting around out here in the bush with hungry lions and charging elephants, and nothing but a man with a spear to protect her. Or maybe he was just miffed that she reserved that special smile for someone other than him.

She looked beautiful as she drove through the pale lilac light of dusk. Her eyes shone, and her magnificent hair tumbled around her shoulders. Rogan had the discomforting realization that if he weren't careful, when he left Fiona and returned to Nairobi, something inside him might remain out here in the wilderness. It also came to him that he ought to get away. Soon.

Things were beginning to feel uncomfortable. He had the strangest sensation that he wasn't himself. Not truly. Somewhere in the deep silences and the silver moonlight and the golden elephant grass, he had begun to get tangled. Things clung to him. The dry orange dust. The smell of heat and sunshine. Wood smoke. He felt he was being slowly and insidiously invaded.

And this red-haired woman...she was tangling him, too. The light in her camouflaged eyes told him that mysteries lay hidden in their depths. Mysteries he wanted to unlock. Her lips beckoned. Her hair tempted. Her smile lured.

"I'm going to skirt that gorge where the vultures were," she was saying, half to herself. "It might be just light enough to..."

Her voice trailed off. Rogan sat up as she slowed the Land Rover. Her eyes had focused on something in the distance. Brow narrowed and lips just parted, she stared.

"What's the matter, Fiona?" Rogan asked.

"Down there . . . in the river. Do you see it?"

He searched the dusk. "It's not light enough to see much of anything. Wait a minute...that little hump? Is that what you're talking about? That's not a hump, Fiona. That's a... I'll be damned, that's a baby elephant."

He grabbed her hand as it rested on the steering wheel. She didn't move. The tiny creature stood in a couple of inches of water, its ears flapping and its head lifted piteously to the sky. As Rogan watched, he began to make out other shapes—low, slinking shapes that circled the calf and edged toward it.

"Hyenas," Fiona whispered.

"Where's the mother? That's not one of *our* babies is it? Not Madeline's or Moira's?"

"I don't recognize it. Must be a newborn. It's been abandoned."

"I didn't know an elephant mother would do that." He felt angry, filled with irrational rage at the thought of anything being abandoned by its mother. "What's going to happen?"

"The hyenas will kill it. Soon, I suspect."

"Like hell they will!" Rogan flung open the Land Rover door and jumped to the ground. Shouting and waving his arms, he ran down the slope toward the river.

Frightened, Fiona drove after him, honking the horn. "Rogan!" she shouted. "Get in here! You can't do this. The hyenas will come after you."

"I'm not going to stand by and let them kill that elephant!" he yelled over his shoulder.

She slammed on the brake and the horn at the same time. "Get in! We'll try to chase them away."

He leapt into the still-moving vehicle. As she drove, he hung out the door shouting at the predators. "Get away! Scat! Damn it, Fiona—step on it. One of them's nipping at the baby's leg."

She wasn't sure why she suddenly became possessed, but Fiona drove straight into the group of hyenas. With a series of eerie yips and laughing barks they scattered, their hunched backs fading away in the dim light. The elephant calf screamed with alarm at the sight of the rumbling Land

1over bearing down. Smooth gray ears fanned the air as the elephant swung its trunk back and forth.

Rogan was preparing to jump out of the Land Rover a second time when Fiona lunged across the seat and grabbed his arm. "What are you doing?" she shouted. "You can't go out there, Rogan. Those hyenas will be back within minutes. They'll tear you to shreds."

"I'm not just going to sit around and wait for them to attack that baby. Are you?"

He pinned her with such a black scowl that she shrank away from him for a moment. Panting for breath, he looked like a madman. His hair swept over his head in disarray. The crisp new safari shirt must have gotten caught on the Land Rover's metal frame, for it had ripped across the back. One pocket dangled. His blue eyes flashed.

"Rogan," she said softly, touching his arm with her hand, "do you remember the vultures we saw over the ravine earlier? I think this calf's mother must have been killed. Margaret and the rest of the M family may have heard her rumbles of panic from several miles away. They were escaping when we nearly ran into them."

"How did the calf's mother die?" he demanded.

"I don't know. Poachers. A Maasai spear. The drought. It could be any number of things."

"But a mother elephant wouldn't just leave her baby alone, would she? The elephants I've seen today—they're not like that."

Fiona wondered at his insistence. "No," she whispered. "Never. Something has happened to the mother. I'm afraid this baby doesn't stand a chance for survival."

Rogan stared at the newborn. "You're going to let the hyenas kill it, aren't you?"

"You studied biology. You know there's a delicate balance in nature. And especially out here in the African bush. With the human population crowding into the wilderness, the drought and the huge numbers of pregnant elephants, not many of the new babies will have a chance to live. This baby is . . . it's the first casualty."

"You don't mean that. I can't believe you're just going to drive away and let it be butchered. You love these elephants, Fiona."

"I'm a scientist. There are things I'm forced to accept. There's nothing I can do—"

"The hell with that!" He grabbed her shoulders and shook them. "You're a human being, Fiona. You love and you care. You've cried over these elephants. And you're going to help me save this baby."

"Rogan, I don't have the facilities to tend—"

"What about the courage to love something enough to save it? What about that, Fiona?"

"Oh, Rogan."

"Have you got a rope?"

She didn't know exactly why, but at that moment she tossed every shred of her careful training, her ordered sense of detachment, out the Land Rover window. She leaned over the seat and unlatched the metal trunk bolted to the vehicle's floor, then drew out a long coil of hemp rope.

"Take this rifle," she said, pressing a compact .22 into Rogan's hands. "Don't shoot unless you have to. If poachers killed its mother, the sound will scare the calf into a panic."

She tied the rope into a noose. "Keep me covered with the rifle while I walk down to the stream. I'm going to tie one end to the Land Rover, because the baby may bolt when it feels the rope. I'll need your help if that happens."

"Fiona." He caught her arm as she pushed open the door and started to slide to the ground. "It's the right thing to do."

"It's a mistake," she said, her eyes suddenly filling with tears. "You don't understand, Rogan. It's a terrible mistake."

As she left him and made her way down the slope, she angrily brushed away the drops that clung to her lashes. It was all a mistake. Taking the helpless elephant calf away from its natural predators was interfering in the normal sequence of nature. And she'd made a rule never to interfere—only to observe. Even more troubling, trying to rescue the baby proved that the words Rogan had hurled back at her held a measure of truth. By saving the calf, she was stepping away from the detached scientist she had always been. She was allowing herself to feel.

It was all Rogan's fault. He'd disordered everything in her life. Once she had known who she was and what she wanted. Now she was unable to sleep at night. During the day, she spent time hoping for another of his drugging kisses; she found herself dissolved in inexplicable tears, and she was breaking the cardinal rule of the experienced scientist.

Approaching the stream, she saw that the baby had lifted its trunk to sniff the feared smell of human. Clearly a newborn, the calf wobbled and stumbled as it attempted to move away from her. In the last remnants of fading light, she discerned the pink on the backs of the calf's ears—and by this sign she was able to calculate that it was less than six weeks old.

She could hear Rogan moving down the slope behind her. She weighed calling him for help as the little elephant grew more and more distressed with each step she took. But when she set foot in the stream and stood in silence for several minutes, the calf began to calm. Its trunk tip lifted and began to explore the front of her shirt. It moved toward her. She held up a hand and allowed the baby to touch her skin.

"I'm going to walk to the camp," she said in a low voice.

"What about the rope?" Rogan asked behind her.

"No, I don't think I'll need it." She stroked the baby's fuzzy head and tried to imitate the low rumbles of comfort she had recorded mothers making to their newborns. She caressed the baby as it continued to explore her.

"Come on, now," she whispered. "Come with me, will you?"

Turning, she began to walk up the slope of the ravine. The calf flapped its ears and shook its head.

"Come, *toto*. Come now."

The baby took two wobbly steps in her direction.

"That's it. Follow me."

Moving at an elephantine pace, she set out across the grassland. The baby stumbled after her, and in a moment she felt its trunk settle along the back of her neck. Together they walked through the near-darkness. Rogan followed just behind in the Land Rover, its headlights shining on their path.

Nguyo set up such a howl of dismay at the sight of the elephant calf that the baby nearly bolted away into the darkness. It was all Fiona could do to calm and reassure both the animal and the human.

"Memsahib," Nguyo gasped, "lions will come in the night to eat this elephant. They will attack us!"

"We're just going to have to keep watch over him until we can decide what to do."

"I will not watch that elephant, *memsahib.* I am a cook. And you have missed the dinner I prepared—grilled chicken breast with a special sauce made of—"

"Excuse me, Nguyo," Fiona interrupted. "Rogan, I want you to radio Clive Willetts. We're going to need milk and other supplies. I need to contact the game wardens and the wildlife federation. We're going to have to find someone willing to take care of this calf. Maybe the Nairobi Game Park has a facility..."

Rogan was smiling as he approached from the Land Rover. The scene in the lamplit camp clearing lifted his spirits for some reason he couldn't quite understand. The baby, though tiny for an elephant, stood almost three feet at the shoulder. It kept bumping against Fiona and exploring her body with its long gray trunk. Barely holding her ground against the onslaught of elephantine nudges, she was carrying on an animated monologue—lists and lists of requirements and analytical data that no one was listening to. Nguyo, rattling out names of ingredients that had gone into the wasted dinner, kept up a nervous dance at the edge of the campfire. Every time the elephant moved toward him, he backed away.

"Rogan, did you hear what I said?" Fiona asked. "I'm trying to explain the difficulty this situation has put me in, and you're standing there with a silly grin on your face."

"This is wonderful," he said softly. "This is great."

"This is going to become a catastrophe if you don't start paying attention to me. Now, you've got to contact Clive Willetts—"

"I'll fly out tonight. I'll pick up the milk in Nairobi and have it back at the camp for you by midnight."

"It's dark."

"Don't worry. Tell me what to get."

She scribbled the name of the soy-based human infant formula that was the only type of milk able to sustain elephant life. "There'll be a supply of it at the wildlife federation offices. It's used for several species of orphaned and wounded animals the game wardens bring in. You'll have to contact Mr. Ngozi, the director. Here's his number. We can't wait. This baby is starving," she said as the calf butted her from behind and sent her stumbling into Rogan's arms.

Rogan held her tightly for a moment. "I'll be back in a couple of hours. When you hear my plane, train the Land Rover's headlights on the airstrip. Fiona, it's going to be all right."

He kissed her lips, stroking her hair as he gazed at her. And then he was fading into the darkness. In moments the airplane's propellers could be heard beyond the stream. They whirred to life, lifted the plane into the air and sent it roaring across the tops of the acacia trees toward Nairobi.

As sunrise slanted over the hump of Mount Longonot and filtered through the long dry grasses of the Great Rift Valley, Fiona sat alone near the dead campfire and stared at the baby elephant, who was wandering weakly across the bare, trampled earth.

Rogan had not returned.

It occurred to her to wonder why she had ever believed he would. He wasn't from her world. In the first place he hadn't understood why the calf should have been left to the hyenas. He'd interfered and forced himself on her in every way. He'd destroyed her serenity.

And yet, for some unknown reason, she'd come to trust him. When he held her and kissed her and told her she was beautiful, she believed him. When he'd insisted on saving the elephant, she'd gone along—never mind that everything in her training had taught her it wouldn't work.

Exhausted from trying to corral the calf all night, she stood and made her way toward the kitchen. Disappointment in Rogan—and in herself for being so foolish—was a palpable taste in her mouth. She would have to radio the game wardens. They would frown on her actions, of course. In the Rift Valley there was no facility and certainly no manpower to care for an orphaned elephant calf.

An animal orphanage just outside the Nairobi Game Park had room for some of the smaller species. But it closely resembled a zoo, and with the large number of schoolchildren visiting, there wouldn't be room for a growing elephant on the premises. A woman had given over her estate on the slopes of Mount Kenya to the rearing of giraffes. And there were people who took in orphaned monkeys or lion cubs and nursed them back to health. But an elephant calf?

She punched the requisite buttons on the transmitter, which began to buzz and crackle. Nguyo wandered in, bleary-eyed and resentful.

"The elephant is tearing out your tent stakes," was his greeting.

Fiona hovered between rescuing her home and continuing to scan the transmitter. "Bwana McCullough didn't come back last night," she said. "I have to call the game warden."

"Sukari is in your tent, *memsahib*. That elephant will frighten your cat."

"Nguyo, can't you see that I'm trying—" The makeshift kitchen walls trembled as a roar blasted over the camp. Bits of thatch drifted onto the clean pots and pans.

The African lifted his head. "Just as you wished, the *bwana* has returned in his airplane. Now everything will be much worse."

Fiona stared at him, half-angry at the rush of elation surging through her veins. "Rogan," she whispered.

"Go to him, *memsahib*."

"But you said everything will be much worse.... What do you mean?"

Nguyo shrugged. "Now you will keep the baby elephant in our camp. You will forget the importance of your true work."

"Don't be ridiculous. I'm only going to take care of the calf until I can find someone else to tend it. You'll see, Nguyo."

"Yes, *memsahib*. We will see."

She was tempted to slam the door on the knowing little man and his dire predictions, but instead she stomped across the clearing to rescue her tent. In the distance Rogan waved as he leapt over the stream.

"Fiona!" he shouted. "Everything's taken care of. I have the formula. It took a lot longer than I'd expected, but I've got three boxes full of the stuff. Where's the baby?"

"Tearing up my tent."

Rogan laughed. It was a deep, wonderful, rich sound. Fiona paused and stared at him. His hair rustled in the morning breeze, lifting and parting without the slightest hint of ever having been combed. A thick growth of rough, black whiskers shadowed his jaw. Bright blue eyes sparkled with life beneath his dark brows.

"This is amazing," he said, chuckling. "A baby elephant. How about that? Hey, come here, kiddo."

"The calf is a male."

"Come here, son." He deepened his voice on the final word, then winked at Fiona. "Would you look at that? He's coming! Here's a bottle for you, old buddy. Mr. Ngozi fixed it up before I flew out this morning. He wanted to show me the correct measurements."

Fiona watched as the little elephant abandoned the uprooted tent stakes and began to nudge Rogan's chest. The man reached out and gently stroked the calf's fuzzy forehead.

"Yes," he whispered, "I've brought some milk for you. Yummy, yummy milk."

Fiona stifled a laugh as Rogan attempted to catch the waving gray trunk and hold it to the bottle's nipple. "That's his nose, silly," she said. "He can't drink through his trunk."

"Dumbo did in the movies."

"This is real life, Rogan. Hold the bottle to his mouth."

Rogan dribbled a little milk onto the calf's lower lip. The baby tasted it and lunged for the nipple. Sucking contentedly, the elephant eyed Rogan with utter adoration. His trunk slipped around the man's neck and began to fondle an earlobe. Then the trunk tested the man's ear, found it comforting and warm and nuzzled peacefully.

Fiona had to turn away as Rogan gazed into the elephant's eyes, for there came across the man's face such an expression of bliss that for a moment her vision blurred with tears and she was unable to swallow the lump that rose in her throat.

Chapter 8

"I had decided you weren't coming back," Fiona said.

She was staring at Rogan over the breakfast table. He had cleaned his plate of three fried eggs, half a dozen fresh biscuits, an entire bowl of sliced papaya and what seemed like gallons of hot tea laced with milk and sugar. Totally absorbed, he sat in his torn safari shirt and dusty shorts, a crooked smile lighting his face every time he glanced at the elephant calf.

After downing almost two quarts of milk, the baby had hunkered down into a patch of cool grass and shut his eyes. The sound of soft snuffling snores drifted through the clearing.

"Not coming back?" Rogan asked, his brows lifting in surprise. "I told you I'd be back. Things just take a little longer to organize out here than they do in New York. You didn't think I'd just run off, did you?"

"Commitment doesn't really seem your style."

At her words, the smile died from his lips and he clamped his mouth shut. He knew he couldn't argue. Oh, he was committed to certain things—McCullough Enterprises and all that went into making it a success. But Fiona had been right in one respect. He didn't often choose to give himself to anything that required a personal devotion. About the closest he ever came to charity was once a year when, for tax purposes, he signed away millions of dollars to various nonprofit organizations.

Fiona had seen beneath the impetuous Rogan of the moment to the businessman who normally existed on a detached, unemotional plane. Commitment *wasn't* his style. And lately he'd been acting completely out of character.

He thought back over the previous evening's events—Ginger's shriek of shock when he'd appeared unannounced at the apartment, Clive Willetts's morose head-shaking over the elephant story, and, finally, the chastisement he'd received from officials at the wildlife federation. Mr. Ngozi had told Rogan that the Kenyan government would be very reluctant to allow a wild elephant to be held privately in captivity and that there was no safe place the federation knew of to keep such an animal.

Now that he actually had a quiet moment to think about it, Rogan wasn't sure why he'd been so determined to save the elephant in the first place. As Fiona had argued, she knew best about the balance of nature. But the thought of leaving that baby to be torn apart by hyenas...

"You'll have to feed the calf every three hours, day and night," she was saying when he finally focused his attention on her. "He should take approximately eight quarts of milk over a twenty-four-hour period. You'll want to keep a record and watch his consumption carefully."

"Me?" Rogan clunked a glass of mango juice on the table. "Hold on a second, now—"

"You'll have to make sure he stays in the shade. Baby elephants are always in their mothers' shadows. He mustn't get too hot, and he'll need plenty of playtime and exercise."

"Wait a minute, here."

"No, *you* wait a minute. You're the one who insisted we bring the elephant to my camp. You're going to have to care for him. Day and night. You'll have to make sure he has access to fresh elephant or rhino dung to establish the right balance of flora in his stomach. When he's older—maybe nine months—you can start adding greens to his diet. When he's two years old, you can wean him. Then, assuming you can integrate him into an established herd and socialize him properly, you can get back to your publishing."

"Two years old? Fiona, you're being ridiculous. I can't stay out here. I have a stack of messages a foot high in Nairobi right now. Clive has been complaining about my use of the airplane. Air-Tours double-booked groups of tourists, and he and the other pilot are going to need both planes. I told them I'd try to get back to Nairobi this afternoon."

"And when am I supposed to get back to *my* work? Or is your foot-high stack of messages that much more important than my years and years of research?"

She pushed herself back from the table and stood. Rogan sprang to his feet. "Now, Fiona, let's be reasonable."

"Reasonable! I suppose you think it's *reasonable* for me to just drop everything and take care of a baby elephant for two years? Never mind that I'm right in the middle of an important study of elephant family interrelationships. Never mind that Harvard just asked me to collect data on elephant communication. Never mind that *International Animal* has contracted me to write a series of articles on the effects of drought. Never mind that Sentero and I have begun a revolutionary study on the correlation between estrus and musth. A study that Sentero hopes to use as the basis for his doctoral dissertation. Never mind that—"

"Okay, okay. Calm down." Rogan raked a hand through his hair. "Just settle down."

"I had a well-ordered life before you invaded my privacy, Rogan McCullough. You've turned everything into havoc. My camp is a near wreck. Nguyo acts like he may quit any minute. Sentero's gone off to Nairobi, and nothing is being recorded. The Rift Valley is in the midst of a terrible drought. Babies are being born every day. And now you've saddled me with an orphan elephant to—"

The sound of a terrible roar drowned her words. The calf, eyes still shut in sleep, lay kicking and screaming with panic. Gray ears flapped, their delicate bones snapping and popping. The long trunk flailed helplessly through the air.

"What is it?" Fiona cried, grabbing Rogan. "What's the matter with him?"

Holding her tight, he ran across the clearing to the thrashing body. "It's . . . it's like a nightmare—"

"Or poison! Oh, Rogan. What if that milk was bad? What if we've poisoned him?"

Rogan bent to the little elephant and began to stroke his head. "Come on, boy. It's okay now."

Fiona knelt at the other side of the baby and rubbed his heaving sides. "There, *toto*. What's the matter now, sweet boy?"

"He's calming down. Okay now, little fella. You're okay."

At the sensation of touch, the brown eyes slid open, and the elephant struggled to his feet. Instantly he lunged into Rogan and wrapped his trunk around the man's neck. If it were possible to say that an elephant could snuggle, this one did. His two-hundred-fifty-pound body rubbed against Rogan, and his throaty rumbles subsided to almost a purr.

"He seems okay now, doesn't he?" Rogan whispered as he and Fiona touched the baby's skin.

She nodded. "I think you were right. It was a nightmare. I've heard elephants can have them. I read an article by a woman who was studying how animals adapt to zoos. She wrote about the terrible nightmares elephants experience—especially when they've witnessed something horrible in their past. Mourning can go on for months. Some elephants have been known to die of grief, no matter how much proper care and medication they're given."

"He was dreaming about his mother's death," Rogan said softly. "I think he was reliving it."

Fiona's mind made an involuntary leap to memories of her own mother's violent death...the horror and pain...the sorrow that nothing had been able to heal.

"I need to go out to the site of the kill," she murmured. "No animal predator can successfully bring down an adult female in good health."

"You think it was poachers, then?"

"Maybe."

"I wonder which elephant family the baby belongs to. Maybe there's a mother in the herd with milk to spare."

"Possibly, but I doubt it. Without an adequate supply of water and fresh vegetation, any mother's milk supply is going to be down. A lactating female will have enough trouble nourishing her own calf without taking on an orphan."

Rogan scratched the little elephant between the eyes. He had a rather thick growth of coarse black hair on his forehead and back. Together with his soft pink ears, that gave him an almost comic-book appearance. The calf explored Rogan's face with the soft two-fingered tip of his trunk.

"He seems to like your ears," Fiona whispered.

"Naturally," Rogan returned. "I have highly sensitive ears. Would you like to sample this one while the other's occupied?"

"I'll pass," she said with a smile. "It's a curious phenomenon, though. Your ears must somehow resemble his mother's teats."

"Great, Fiona. Thanks for the romantic interlude."

Chuckling, she stood and stretched. "Well, have a good day, Rogan. I'm off on my rounds."

"Now, hold on." As he rose, the calf let out a rumble of dismay and began to butt Rogan's legs. "You're not going to leave me here."

"I certainly am."

"Fiona." He caught her arm. "We *both* rescued this elephant. I saw your face when you thought he'd been poisoned. You can't abandon him any more than I can. We're in this together."

"I'm not together with anyone or anything. I work alone. I live alone. I'm completely self-sufficient. Just like you, Rogan. Perhaps that's why we don't get along. We're two of a kind, you and I."

"I gather you're not real big on commitment either, then."

"No, I'm not."

"All right, I guess that settles it."

"Settles what?"

"The elephant. Since neither of us has the time or energy to be bothered with him, and since neither of us is willing to make the long-term commitment, I guess we'll just herd him back to the stream and let the hyenas have him. What do you say, huh? Does that sound good?''

Fiona gazed at the little shaggy-haired calf. He had wandered away a few paces and had begun exploring his trunk. For a moment he swung it back and forth in a huge rubbery arc. Then he lifted his head and began to toss it up and down. Finally he sent it whirling around in a circle.

''Oh, Rogan.''

''Well, Fiona? You ready to turn him over to the hyenas? Want to let the vultures pick his bones?''

By this time the elephant had tired of swinging his trunk and had popped the tip into his mouth. He stood sucking it and eyeing the pair of humans with the look of a trusting child.

''Oh, Rogan,'' she sighed again.

''Look, Fiona...'' He touched her arm, turning her to face him. ''Why don't you go on out into the field this morning? Get some research taken care of. I'll stay here and feed the little guy. Then you come back at lunch and we'll talk. In the meantime I'll see if I can think of something. After all, solving problems and coming up with grand schemes is sort of my specialty.''

''All right,'' she whispered. She looked into his eyes. His blue, blue eyes. Soft dark hair. Unshaven chin. Sensual mouth. Tattered bush shirt.

If there had ever been a moment when she wanted to abandon all her scientific detachment and be wildly, emotionally female, this was it. She felt a huge, unbidden urge to throw her arms around Rogan's neck, kiss him passionately, gush about the elephants, giggle and caper around the campfire and then demand that the fairy tale never end. Demand that this stubborn man and his baby elephant and everything wonderful they had brought into her life would stay just as they were forever.

Instead, she swallowed the knot in her throat and walked away.

Fiona returned to the camp just as Clive Willetts's airplane bounced onto the landing strip. She pulled the Land

Rover under the shade of the acacia tree and sat for a moment, watching the scene in the clearing.

Rogan was crouched in the dust, one arm around the little elephant and the other holding the large milk bottle. The calf, trunk nestled along Rogan's neck and toying with his ear, gazed adoringly at the man. Soft gray ears fanned the air, lifting and scattering Rogan's hair. In the background Nguyo trudged back and forth with arms full of dishes. He was whistling—always a good sign. Occasionally he said something to Rogan, who responded. And they both laughed.

Fiona rested her forehead on the sun-warmed steering wheel. Though she had firmly denied the existence of any heavenly power since her mother's death so many years before, she suddenly found words forming on her lips.

Dear God, how had this happened? What could she do? Once there had been a man in a stiff wool suit who demanded she allow tourists in her camp. Now, as she lifted her head, she saw a man who fit in, whose skin was darkened by the sun, whose clothing matched the soft taupe grasses and whose boots were red with African dust. She saw a man who whispered into an elephant's ear. A man who stroked his fingers through a baby's dark hair. A man who belonged.

Oh, Lord. She had to send him away. If Rogan had changed, she had been transformed. For the first time since...well, she couldn't ever remember a time...she craved a human touch. She ached for the sight of this man's smile and his deep laughter. Worse, she longed to hear his voice, arguing, teasing, discussing—it hardly mattered. She wanted to talk. Human words. Human expressions. Human feelings. She needed them all. And she was scared to death by that need.

Trembling, she slid out of the Land Rover. She would send him away. Never mind about the elephant—she would take care of him somehow. But she knew she had to make Rogan leave if she were ever to get her old life back. And the most terrifying thought of all was the realization that she wasn't sure she wanted her old life back.

"Fiona!" Rogan lifted a hand as she approached. "Two quarts since you've been gone! How about that? He's getting real frisky, so watch out."

When the elephant calf caught her scent, he pulled away from the bottle and bolted across the ground. Wobbly legs flying, he greeted her with a loud rumble. Head raised, ears spread and flapping, he tucked in his chin. His trunk looped around her arm, then unlooped. At the same time he backed away, spun in three complete circles, then bumped into her legs with his bottom.

Trying not to laugh and frighten him, Fiona responded in kind. She caught the elastic trunk and wrapped it around her arm. She lifted her head up and down. Then she turned circles and backed into the baby.

"What the hell is she doing there, Mr. McCullough?" Clive's voice broke in among the human and elephantine rumblings.

"It's the greeting ceremony," Fiona explained. "All the elephants in a family do it when they've been apart. It's usually very intense and emotional."

"I'll be damned." The lanky pilot scratched his sparse mustache. "Well, anyway, here's your man, Mr. McCullough. He's a Kikuyu from up in the highlands. He tells me he was a *cyce* on a big coffee farm, and he thinks if he can take care of horses, he can take care of elephants."

Rogan and Fiona both stared at the compact African. Cleanly dressed in a neat pair of gray trousers, a navy sweater and a striped shirt, he looked as if he had just stepped out of an office in Nairobi.

"My name is Moses," he said, holding out a hand. "I will work for standard wages and one weekend off per month. You must provide my bus ticket home. I will sleep in the camp, and I will require my food. Now, this is the elephant?"

Obviously this *was* the elephant. Moses took the bottle from Rogan's hand and within a few minutes had the calf sucking contentedly. As he moved the baby into the shade, he called back over his shoulder, "You may return to Nairobi now, Bwana McCullough. All will be well."

Rogan looked at Fiona. "I, uh." He cleared his throat. "I took the liberty of radioing Clive and setting things up."

"But I don't have the funding to pay this man."

"It's okay. I'll take care of that. It's the least I can do."

"Yes," she said. "Well . . ."

"Well, everyone," Clive filled in the silence between them, "I guess it's time to leave. Do you two have things worked out now?"

Neither spoke for a moment. Fiona tried to moisten her lips, but her mouth was dry. So this was it. Rogan and his money had solved everything in one neat package. The elephant would be taken care of. Rogan would fly to Nairobi and then to New York. She would return to her research. And that was that.

"Yes," she said softly, "everything's been worked out."

"Will Air-Tours be flying in here, Mr. McCullough?" Clive asked.

"No," Rogan said. "That's not going to be possible."

The pilot nodded, as if to say he'd known all along the plan wouldn't work. "So, Dr. Thornton, where are the elephants these days? I have two groups in this week. I thought I'd fly them over the park and let them have a look at your friendly pachyderms."

He had pulled a map from his hip pocket and was spreading it wide. Fiona stared at the familiar lozenge shape of the Rift Valley Game Park nestled between the two volcanic mountains, Longonot and Suswa. With her help Clive had partitioned the map into the same grid she used for tracking elephants.

"The M family is in D-2 heading north toward Longonot," she said, pointing out the position. "The Js are in A-3. They're looking for water. You'll find the Os in D-7. They're near the Suswa bulls—Jesse James and his gang. You've been seeing the Cs a lot lately. They're in E-4 right now, but I wouldn't advise flying over them. They're very jumpy. Poachers killed Calliope yesterday."

"You don't say. That's too bad. Did they get her tusks?"

Fiona nodded, trying to block the memory of the bullet-riddled elephant whose face and trunk had been hacked away. "She was the calf's mother."

"Well, it's a good thing you saved the little chap and I found Moses to watch him. Now he'll have a chance to grow into a big tusker like his mum."

"If he's lucky," Fiona said.

"Well, thanks for the tips, Dr. Thornton. If you're ready, sir, we'll start back. Your secretary's nearly frantic with messages for you. I'll get your plane going."

"Yes, well . . ." Rogan murmured as the pilot set off. "Fiona, I'll set up an account for you to use for Moses' salary. And . . . I'll write to find out about the elephant."

"Of course."

"Is there anything you need from Nairobi? Anything I can do for you?"

"No."

"Well, then . . ."

"Goodbye, Rogan." She held out her hand.

"I've enjoyed my visit." He took her hand and held it. His thumb stroked her palm. "Fiona, I—"

"Rogan, you'd better go."

"Yes." His lips brushed her cheek, and then he was pulling away, heading across the stream and climbing into the nearer of the two Air-Tours planes.

"Nguyo," Fiona said as she passed the cook. "There will only be me for lunch. And you should know that Moses has joined our camp crew to look after the elephant."

"Yes, *memsahib*." Nguyo looked forlornly at his table, all set for a great company. "I prepared a wonderful egg salad."

"I'm sorry, Nguyo."

"Will the *bwana* return one day?"

"No. He's not coming back again."

Nguyo lifted his head as the planes flew over the camp. "Perhaps you are wrong, *memsahib*. Perhaps he will return."

"No."

"But he has forgotten to tell me *kwaheri*. And he failed to say goodbye to his elephant."

"Well at any rate, he told *me* goodbye."

"No, *memsahib*. If you will remember, it was you who told him goodbye."

With that Nguyo turned his back and began removing plates and silverware from the table.

As Rogan's plane flew over the camp, he searched for one last look at Fiona. He couldn't find her. It felt to him as though she had already become reintegrated with her world. Her red hair had melded with the rich soil, her bronzed skin with the shadows of the trees, her clothing with the shades of the grasses. She had rid herself of the alien invader and instantly adjusted to life without him.

Things weren't going to be so easy for Rogan. Remembering his father's comments to Clive about Africa, Rogan felt the first touch of affinity with his late parent. In Africa John McCullough had been able to relax, to rest. In Africa he'd felt like himself. Now Rogan knew what that meant. He began to glimpse an understanding of the mysterious, powerful father he'd hated and loved with an intensity that had driven him for more than thirty years. Maybe his father was not so different from himself.

Rogan flew low over a thicket of thorn trees lining a river, then lifted the plane so as not to frighten a herd of zebras grazing nearby. Sun beat on the top of the aircraft and seemed to melt through the metal roof onto his head. Clive's plane flew not far to one side, its silver wings as bright as mirrors.

A group of long-necked giraffes, their shadows tucked neatly beneath them, wandered in the direction of Mount Suswa. Rogan wondered where the Ms were today. Was Margaret searching for water? Was Mallory hovering close to Madeline's new baby, keeping watch? And what about Mick? Was he tossing dust over his back, or running with ears flapping toward a patch of not-so-dry grass?

Rogan flipped on the radio and contacted Clive. "See any elephants down there?" he asked.

"Not a chance. They're almost invisible from the air. That's why I ask Dr. Thornton to tell me where she's been tracking them."

"What's that? That shiny patch just to the southeast."

"A little water hole. The Maasai use it for cattle. It's just outside the park boundary. The King family built that old stone house down there. That and the water hole. The Kings were colonists, you know. But the house is empty now. Falling apart."

"Too bad... Hey, is that an elephant? At about two o'clock?"

"I'll be damned, sir—you have sharp eyes. Those are the Suswa bulls. Mean old devils. Swing down and take a look at the tusks on those chaps."

Rogan banked the plane and zoomed over the three bulls. They shook their heads and trumpeted at the sound of the engines. Their huge bodies looked small from this height, vulnerable somehow. There were so few of them. And their hold on this golden kingdom seemed so tenuous.

As soon as he got to Nairobi, Rogan decided, he would radio the camp. He would find out how the little calf was managing in the hands of Moses. He would ask Nguyo what he was planning for dinner. Was there any spice cake left? Maybe Nguyo would copy the recipe for Rogan's own cooks back in the States. And what about the rest of the camp? Were the vervet monkeys behaving themselves? Any sign of rain? Was Fiona planning tomorrow's outing?

Fiona.

An ache that tightened the muscles in his chest gripped him as he thought of her. She was still so close. And so far, out of reach, intangible. He could almost smell the lemon-flower scent of her hair. The memory of its red-gold waves tumbling down her back seemed so real. He felt he could almost touch her smooth skin. He could see her camouflaged eyes, mystical and enigmatic. He could taste her full lips, feel her fingertips stroking his back, hear the husky timbre of her voice as she spoke his name.

Damn, it was a good thing he was getting away. He couldn't allow himself this intensity of feeling. He didn't want the burden of responsibility that came with caring. Fiona was too much for him. She was too strong, too honest, too real. He preferred a surface sort of woman. One who didn't have too much to give, but didn't take too much, either. The sort of woman his father...

His father. John McCullough. A man who craved power and wealth. A man who couldn't commit, not even to his own wife and child. A man who skimmed the top, who refused to deal with anything strong, honest and real.

How Rogan had hated his father. He'd hated the man not because he was his father, but because he wasn't. He'd despised the man, he'd fought him, he'd struggled to prove himself to him...and, in the end, he'd become just like him.

Rogan let three days go by. He forced himself to concentrate on his work. Ginger reported that a man who had a hotel on the coast wanted to work a deal with Air-Tours. The CEO of his huge oil refinery operation had wired, asking for a meeting the minute Rogan could get back to the States. Megamedia had been calling every day, trying to finalize the buy-out of McCullough Enterprises. Rogan's personal manager had phoned to find out whether to open the Florida home for the traditional end-of-winter bash, or whether Rogan planned a ski trip to New Mexico. There were calls from several stores in New York with messages that Rogan's new spring suit and casual-wear selections were ready, calls from dealers with new airplanes or cars on the market, calls from his accountant, calls from six foundations inviting him to gala dinners.

Rogan sifted through the pile of messages. His leather-bound appointment book perched on Ginger's stocking-clad knees as she filled line after line with crisp black-ink notations. He met with the Mombasa hotel owner. It wasn't a particularly good deal—not the sort of thing he would normally go for. More like a losing proposition, if the truth were known. But it would give Air-Tours some business. And business would keep it alive.

"Now, about the museum benefit on the fifteenth," Ginger asked on his third morning back in Nairobi. "Shall I send a wire and tell them you'll attend? It's in Washington—and you've already set up a meeting in New York for the morning. But if you flew down—"

"Yeah, okay," Rogan growled, waving a hand as if shooing a fly. "Just put it down."

"And I've been on the phone with the airline. Shall I go ahead and make reservations for us to fly out tomorrow morning? You could talk to that fellow in Amsterdam who's interested in a partnership—"

"Tomorrow morning?" Rogan looked up. "Leave Nairobi tomorrow?"

"You do have a meeting with Megamedia in New York on Friday. It would give you a little time—"

"Ginger, where's the nearest radio?"

"There's a stereo by your bed, sir. I'm sure a radio comes with it."

"Not that sort of radio. A transmitter. The kind of thing you can call places with."

"Clive Willetts has one at the airport. That's where I called you from when you were out at that camp in the middle of—"

"Get my coat, Ginger."

"But, sir! I have all these messages to go over with you. And there's the—"

"My coat, Ginger."

"With all respect, Mr. McCullough, I don't think it would be wise for you to go out in public right now. You haven't shaved since the meeting with the hotel owner two days ago. And your clothes—"

"Where the hell is my coat?" He stalked across the room and rummaged through the closet. Jerking the mended bush jacket from its hanger, he tossed it over one shoulder. "Call down to the limo, Ginger. I want to go to the airport."

"Yes, sir. What about your conference call with Megamedia? It's scheduled in ten minutes."

"Tell them to call back later."

"*Later?* It'll be the middle of the night in New York, Mr. McCullough. Sir—"

The door closed before she could finish her sentence.

Striding into the Air-Tours hangar, Rogan saw at once that it was empty. Both planes had flown out with tour groups. Clive's would spend a week crossing three game parks, he remembered. The other, piloted by Oliver Kariuki, would fly around Mount Kilimanjaro and Mount Kenya.

Unlocking Clive's small office, Rogan spotted the large black radio transmitter. He sat behind the desk and fiddled with the buttons and switches. Unable to produce more than a spatter of static, he jerked at the desk drawers looking for a set of instructions. Locked. All of them.

That irked him. It was one thing to keep private, confidential materials locked up. But Air-Tours was just a simple charter company. Securing the company files was probably Clive's idea of maintaining an image as a businessman.

Pushing buttons again, Rogan finally managed to tune in on the channel wavelengths. And at last he heard Nguyo's voice through the buzzing transmitter.

"This is Rogan McCullough, Nguyo," Rogan shouted. "How are things at the camp?"

"Bwana McCullough, is that you?"

"Yes, Nguyo, it's me. How is everything?"

"I am preparing steak with black pepper. Very delicious, *bwana.*"

"Sounds good. How's the elephant?"

"Moses does not like our camp."

"I'm sorry to hear that. What about the elephant? Is the baby elephant still there, Nguyo?"

"Two elephants now, *bwana.*"

"*Two* elephants? Calves?"

"Sentero found another one in a ravine. Last night they knocked down your tent."

"How's . . . how's Fiona? Dr. Thornton . . . how is she?"

"Quiet."

"Quiet, did you say?"

"Not talking."

Rogan stared at the Air-Tours logo embossed on a stack of writing paper. He could see her silence. He could feel it. Her mouth closed. Her eyes hidden. Her face half in shadow.

"You would like this steak, *bwana,*" Nguyo said. "Lots of fresh black pepper. And mango chutney. I make it myself."

"How about spice cake?"

"Today I have baked my very special coconut pie. It's good. Perhaps you should taste it, *bwana*."

"Perhaps I should."

"I will select for you a very thick steak and a very delicious slice of my coconut pie. Goodbye, Bwana McCullough."

As the radio crackled, Rogan shouted through the empty hangar to the limousine driver, who was polishing a windshield. "Hey, out there! Hey, Duncan Gitau! Find out how I can rent an airplane, would you?"

"An airplane, Mr. McCullough?"

Rogan grinned. "I've got a dinner engagement."

Chapter 9

Fiona drove the Land Rover along the track toward her camp. Evening sun silhouetted the acacias and baobabs. Dust, pink-lit and fine as talcum, sifted through the cracks beneath the doors and settled on her boots. A stack of papers slid back and forth. An ink pen rolled and bounced around the floor like a skinny man at an amusement park.

"Shall we search for the J family tomorrow, Dr. Thornton?" Sentero asked. "We haven't recorded anything on them in a week. They were near Longonot last time. We could check up on the Ms, too."

Fiona nodded but said nothing. Sentero flipped through a few sheets of paper attached to a clipboard. His long earlobes dangled against his neck as he searched the file.

"In the J family you recorded four females in estrus two years ago," he said. "Janice, Jennifer, Jill and Jody. It would be a good idea to find out if there have been any births."

"Yes."

"What about the poaching? They've killed Calliope and Cindy. And we haven't seen the old bull, Custer, lately. Do you think the killing is stepping up? Should we alert the wardens?"

"They need to know."

"Dr. Thornton, I've been thinking about what we discussed earlier—about the new age-set being initiated. Perhaps I should speak to the Maasai elders."

Fiona sighed. "If you would, Sentero."

She didn't feel like talking. The day had been long and discouraging. That morning they'd found Cindy's carcass not far from Calliope's. She, too, had been shot and butchered for her tusks. The C family was jittery and hiding nearby in a thicket of trees. At the sound of the Land Rover, they bolted. In the same moment Fiona realized that Charlie, the young bull, had been wounded. Blood dripped from his mouth and trunk as he struggled to keep up with the others. His tusks were tiny. He wasn't even old enough to have marketable ivory, but the poachers had shot him anyway.

And then Sentero had mentioned the initiation of a new group of young Maasai men. Fiona knew from experience that every few years the Maasai clans circumcised all teenage males within a certain age-group. When they recovered from their ordeal, these youths would be called *Ilmoran*. Warriors. To prove their bravery, they would spend months searching for wild animals to kill—even though hunting was against the law in Kenya. Lions were the favorite, but elephants often fell prey to the spears of Maasai warriors.

With the poachers, the drought, the age-set initiation and the calves being born, the Rift Valley elephants could not hope to fare well. Fiona felt the ominous certainty that, from now on, every few days she would begin to find dead elephants. Matriarchs and old bulls slaughtered by poachers. Young females pierced by spears. Calves collapsed from starvation.

And there was nothing she could do. Oh, Sentero could talk to the elders. But they would never agree to call a halt on their warriors—even though they knew the *Ilmoran* could be prosecuted as poachers or shot on sight by game wardens.

She could speak to the wardens themselves. But how much could a few ill-equipped men do against efficient poachers armed with semiautomatic rifles? Especially when the killers were motivated by the fortune to be made from a world hungry for ivory trinkets, earrings and tiny carved boxes.

And the drought. Of course, only God knew when that would be over. Why? she questioned for the hundredth time. Why couldn't it rain? At least the babies would be spared. A new generation.

No, Fiona was under no illusions. She knew wobbly elephant babies could never take the place of the stately old matriarchs who carried with them the lore of generations, who knew where to dig for water during the dry seasons and where the best patches of grass could be found. But, given a chance, the babies would grow and learn and one day fulfill their own destinies on the golden plains.

"Airplane," Sentero said.

Startled, Fiona lifted her head and scanned the camp. She could see a small plane on the distant airstrip—it was something modern and red. Certainly not one of Air-Tours big Catalinas. Her heart sank.

Chastising herself for allowing the thought of Rogan McCullough to enter her mind, she worked to focus on other matters. Who might have flown to the camp? Another researcher? Someone from one of her supporting wildlife societies or universities? When should she drive to the park headquarters to speak to the wardens? What would Nguyo have prepared for dinner?

But, as the past three days had proven, nothing—not even drought and poachers—could erase Rogan from her thoughts. Again and again she had imagined him climbing the stairs to a huge jet, settling into his first-class seat and winging away to Europe and America. She had no doubt that it wouldn't be long before he forgot all about his brief interlude in Africa.

Fiona had been a mere annoyance to him, that was all. An irritation. He would probably sell Air-Tours, since it wasn't making enough money to suit him. And before long he would be settled back into his world—negotiating deals, flying planes, racing cars, buying houses, whatever it was multimillionaires did.

She, on the other hand, had been left in a silent world filled with his memory. When she rose in the morning, she thought of their breakfasts together by the campfire. When she settled into her Land Rover, she found herself almost wishing it was Rogan's heavily muscled body in the next seat and not the thin-framed Sentero. Even when she was studying the elephants, she seemed to hear his deep voice, low and murmuring, as he spoke his observations. His handwriting filled pages of her notebook. The T-shirt he'd worn hung drying on the line.

And alone in her tent at night, she faced long, quiet hours when thoughts of Rogan McCullough would sift through her mind. Snatches of conversation replayed. Memories of his smile. His laugh. His blue eyes gazing into hers. She would close her eyes and curl into a tight ball and try to will him away. But in the end, she would hear his voice again....

"Rogan McCullough," Sentero said. "He has returned, Dr. Thornton."

"What?" Fiona shifted her focus from the dusty road to the camp, bathed in shadow. A jolt ran down her spine as she recognized, standing beneath an acacia, the dark figure with broad shoulders and shaggy hair. "It *is* him," she breathed. "What's he doing here?"

"No doubt he wants to check the elephant calf."

"Oh, that must be it."

"Perhaps he has developed a new plan for bringing his tourists to the Rift Valley."

"Yes, maybe so."

"Of course, at this moment you will notice he is waiting for *you*."

"Well, I don't think—" Fiona unconsciously smoothed her hair as she pulled the Land Rover to a stop beneath the tree. She wished she'd worn something other than this faded yellow T-shirt and olive drab trousers. And if she'd just put on a hat, she wouldn't have such coral pink cheeks.

"Oh, hell," she muttered.

"Hello to you, too." Rogan lifted a hand as he approached the Land Rover.

"What are you doing here, Rogan? I thought we'd resolved everything about the tourists."

"Thought I'd drop in for dinner." He slipped an arm around her shoulders. "And I wanted to see you again, Fiona."

"Have a pleasant evening, Dr. Thornton," Sentero interrupted, speaking in Swahili. His face a mask, the Maasai strode into the fading dusk. As he rounded the kitchen, the tip of his spear glinted in the last rays of sunlight.

"That guy gives me the heebie-jeebies," Rogan said. "What did he say just now, anyway?"

"It's nothing. He was just wishing me a good evening."

"I don't see why he can't speak English and say what he has to say outright. If he went to college in Texas—"

"Rogan, please." She pulled out of his embrace. "Why did you come back? I thought you were going to the States... to your work. I thought we had settled everything."

He studied her hazel eyes, memorizing them lest he ever forget again. "Nothing's settled, Fiona. You know that."

"But the baby elephant is fine. Moses is looking after him. And the other one we brought in seems to be responding."

"Fiona."

"Sentero's come back, and he's going to talk to the Maasai elders about the initiation problem. You don't know about that, but it's a terrible situation. We've contacted the authorities about the drought. And we're gong to tell the wardens about the increase in poaching."

"Fiona..." he said again.

"Rogan, I explained to you, I won't allow tourists in the camp. I'm only just now getting back to my research. I thought we'd settled all that, because I can tell you right now, I'm not going to back down."

"Nothing's settled, Fiona. I missed you."

She looked away and bit her lower lip. It came to Rogan then that he'd never known a woman quite like this one. For some reason the desire he felt for her was no longer on a purely physical plane, where at first he'd hoped to keep it. He wanted to meld with her, not just sexually, but in some strange mystical sense, he wanted to take her inside him. He wanted to carry her wherever he went. Her copper hair, her incredible eyes, her shy smile.

"Did you miss me, Fiona?" he asked.

Her head turned, just a little. "I've been very busy, of course. There's the research and the poachers . . . and the drought . . . and two calves. . . ."

"While I was gone, did you think about the afternoon we spent sitting on the Land Rover roof watching elephants, Fiona?" He stroked her hair, cupping a mass of it in his big hand. "Did you remember the way we danced under the stars? At night in your tent, did you miss the feel of my arms around your body, holding you close and warm?"

"Oh, Rogan." What else could she say? The touch of his fingers in her hair felt like heaven. The warmth of his breath on her neck sent tendrils of fire shooting across her skin. She slipped her arms around him and allowed his jaw to graze her cheek. His mouth touched her ear. She shivered.

Lifting her head, she trailed her lips over his skin. And then their mouths met, hungry with wanting, bold with need. His tongue stroked hers, tangling and dancing in the moist depths. She caught his lower lip between her teeth, then ran her tongue along it. Groaning, he crushed her tight, enjoying the rapid rise and fall of her breasts against his shirt.

"Oh, Rogan," she said for the second time, because it was all she could manage. She wove her fingers through his thick hair and sighed with delight as his hands cupped her hips to hold her close.

She'd never needed anyone's strength before, not since Margaret had been taken away and she'd learned to live on her own. But now, oh now, she drank in this man's power like a sponge absorbing water. His firm muscles moved under her fingers. His beard scratched her skin like fine sandpaper that marked her with his brand.

"Fiona," he breathed into her ear, "I want you to come with me. Let me take you to Nairobi. We'll be together. We'll relax. I want to be with you . . . just us."

Her eyes lifted and traced his face. "Nairobi? But I can't leave. My research—"

"Let Sentero do it for a few days. You managed without him while he was in Nairobi. Let him take over for you now. Please, Fiona."

"But the elephants. We have two of them now, and they're so rowdy."

"Moses can watch them."

"Moses isn't working out very well, I'm afraid, Rogan. He keeps forgetting the feedings. And he's afraid out here in the bush. He won't admit it to me, but Nguyo says he's terrified at night."

Rogan studied the bright hazel eyes, so serious, so intense. What was he going to do about Fiona Thornton? He didn't want to just leave her out here again. There was something between them now. He could feel it in her kisses, in the depth of her response to him. He could feel it in himself. It intrigued him, and he wanted to find out what it meant.

But he couldn't force Fiona to go with him, either. She was tied to this place and these animals with stronger bonds than those that tied her to some visiting man she happened to enjoy kissing.

"Dinner's served," she said softly. "Will you stay, Rogan?"

He listened to the muted melody of the bamboo xylophone as it drifted across the evening. A pair of wild doves added their own laughing five-note call to the refrain. Crickets began a high-pitched, whining chirp. And somewhere in the streambed a frog set up his nightly croak.

"I'll stay for dinner," Rogan answered. "But, Fiona, I want you to think about what I've asked. You've turned me down on everything else. Come with me to Nairobi for a few days. You need a rest. And I'd like the chance to be with you a little longer. I'd like to get to know you better."

"The only place you can really know me is here, Rogan. In the bush. This is where I belong."

"Just think about it, will you?"

She nodded. He tucked her under his arm, and she rested her head against his shoulder as they walked toward the campfire. You don't know, Rogan, she was thinking. You have no idea how easy it seems to me now just to leave everything and do what you ask. For the pleasure of looking into your blue eyes and the tingle of your hands on my skin, I feel I could walk away from it all.

But—she realized even as she was thinking those thoughts—this is merely a physical attraction. It's only temporary. You have your life, Rogan. And I have mine. And a pair of blue eyes and warm lips can't change that.

After dinner they settled beside the campfire. The elephant calves were visiting Wilson, the watchman whose clothes Rogan had once borrowed. He had agreed to take over the night feedings in place of Moses, who was too much trouble to awaken anyway. Nguyo had placed a kettle of steaming tea, two china cups, cream, sugar cubes and a plate of buttery cookies on a small table between the two rickety chairs. After the ritual of deciding tomorrow's meals with Fiona, he had retired for the night.

"Fiona, would you—" Rogan began.

"I can't dance tonight, Rogan. Really, I'm just too tired." She also knew too well that if she allowed herself to dance with him, she would lose that fine edge of control she had draped over herself during dinner.

"That's all right," he said, watching her intently. "I'm tired, too."

"Let's just drink our tea, then."

"What I was going to ask was if you'd let me tell you the reasons why I'd like to take you to Nairobi."

"Oh." She reddened a little over having jumped to conclusions about his wanting to dance. "I just can't go to Nairobi, Rogan. I don't like the city, and there's so much to do out in the valley that I—"

"Fiona." He caught her hand and pulled her around so that she was forced to meet his eyes. "Just give me half a chance here, would you?"

"All right."

"Now, I'm supposed to be heading back to the States. I really ought to leave tomorrow. I've got meetings and all kinds of appointments set up with various people and organizations. But the only thing that really has to be taken care of is the company that wants to buy out my business."

"Someone is buying McCullough Enterprises? But what will happen to you?"

"The point here, Fiona, is that I have to meet with Megamedia. But they have a small branch office in Nairobi and a bigger one in London. I think I can handle a lot of this with conference calls."

"And? What does that have to do with me?"

"And then I'd be free for a few days in Nairobi."

She thought about the idea for a moment. He was proposing her little fantasy come to life—they would be together. But what good was that? If she spent any more time with Rogan, it wasn't going to be easy to stay casual. And she didn't want any deeper involvement. Did she? No, of course not.

"Rogan, the thing is, I just don't see the reasoning behind this," she explained carefully. "From a logical point of view—"

"The hell with logic, Fiona. Put away your scientist's brain for a minute and let yourself feel a woman's emotions. I saw your face this evening when you realized I'd come back. I felt the way you kissed me."

"I *am* a woman. But I don't intend to spend the rest of my life flitting around with my emotions on my sleeve. I intend to be a scientist. I've worked hard to control my feelings and keep myself detached. That's the way I *want* to be, Rogan. Please try to understand."

He heard her words, and he knew she meant them. But look at her! All he could see at this moment was Fiona the woman. Her smile, her glowing eyes, her long neck, her hair drifting in copper waves around her shoulders, her full breasts beneath her yellow T-shirt, her long legs, her small toes inside those big boots. But he knew he couldn't have just the woman and not the scientist. They went together.

"Okay," he said. "Okay, here's why you should come to Nairobi tomorrow morning. Logically speaking."

She leaned forward, almost willing him to come up with something.

"I've lined up a meeting with the national museum in Nairobi," he went on, putting it together as he spoke the words. "I'm planning to work a deal with the executive board to promote both the museum and Air-Tours in one package. You come to the meeting. I'll give you fifteen minutes to talk to them about your elephants.''

"Fifteen—"

"Half an hour. No interruptions, I promise. And..." He scanned his brain. "And there's this embassy thing I was invited to. A party. We'll go together. I'll introduce you to diplomats from everywhere."

"Burundi? Zimbabwe?"

"What about them?"

"They're two of the countries in Africa that haven't signed an agreement to allow Switzerland to monitor the trade in registered tusks. Most of the illegal ivory poached in Kenya goes through Burundi or Zimbabwe, Rogan."

"Hell, yes, we'll talk to their ambassadors. Sure thing. Why not?"

"And?" she asked. "Are there any more reasons why I should go to Nairobi?"

He smiled and shook his head, letting out a breath. "Well, let's see now. If you can't count eating out in the finest restaurants, shopping for new clothes, going to the theater, walking hand-in-hand and dancing and kissing and—"

"No. I can't, Rogan."

"How about if I got you a spot on Cable Television News? I know their correspondent in Nairobi. He worked for McCullough Enterprises years ago, when he was just starting out. He could interview you. CTN, Fiona. That's big time. Worldwide exposure."

She looked down at their entwined fingers. "I've never been on television."

"Just talk about the elephants. Talk about Margaret and the others. Talk about the babies."

"Rogan," she said, "you drive a hard bargain."

"Then you'll go?"

"I'll think about it." She stood, feeling soft and biddable—and frightened by her own vulnerability. "Good night. I'll see you in the morning."

"Fiona." He rose and caught her arm. "There's something I've been thinking about."

"Yes?"

Why had he stopped her when it was so obvious she wanted to leave? What did he want to tell her? He couldn't just say how good it had felt to see her smile when she first caught sight of him under the acacia tree. Or how much she'd been on his mind the whole time he was in Nairobi alone. Or the way nothing seemed so important anymore, so rushed, so imperative. His priorities had begun to shift around. They were all out of whack. And, despite Ginger's frantic pleas and the urgent messages from New York that he'd been choosing to ignore, each morning his heart felt full.

Could he just up and tell Fiona that since he'd met her, he'd found himself doing things that were completely out of character? Cancelling meetings. Wandering around by himself. Forgetting to shave. Stooping to examine the magenta, crimson, pink or gold bougainvillea shrubs that grew along Nairobi's streets.

"I bought a notebook," he said.

She studied his blue eyes and felt their intensity. "A notebook."

"With blank pages."

She nodded. "Oh . . . blank pages." What other kinds of notebooks were there? And why was he telling her this? And why did his fingers feel so strong on her arm? Each one pressed separately into her skin and sent messages that she couldn't read, that melted her, that made her want to touch his hair and stroke the side of his face.

"I've been writing in the notebook. Collecting things." He felt ridiculous now. Why was he even bothering? When he was a kid, no one had ever wanted to hear about his dumb collections. And it was clear she wanted to get away.

"What kind of things?" she was asking.

"Oh, just stuff. Never mind." He laughed, trying to make it all sound light and inconsequential.

"Rogan, what are you collecting? I'd like to know."

"Well . . ." He studied the moon, wondering how he could make what he was about to say sound manly and sexy and all the things he wanted her to think he was. "Well . . . flora."

"Flora? You mean, flowers? Leaves, plants, specimens, that sort of thing?"

He nodded. "I started with bougainvillea. I noticed that they don't really have petals—at least, not flowers of any consequence. The colored parts are bracts. So I broke some off and pressed them in the *Financial Strategy 2000* book I bought in the airport the other day. And then I got to looking at the Cape honeysuckle growing up the wall of my apartment. And I found some frangipani trees, but when I tried to save the specimens, they turned brown. That's when I bought the notebook and started writing down my observations. I began to see all these different varieties of hibiscus. I wandered into somebody's yard, and an old lady with hair like cotton came out of the house and took me all around her garden, showing me things. And, I don't know... hell, it was just something amazing."

He felt stupid, realizing how he'd run on and on about some old lady's garden and a bunch of flowers. He looked at the moon again, wondering how he was going to get out of this. He would have to use some sort of tactical maneuver to connect his ramblings with a point that would sound sensible.

"Will you come with me, Rogan?" Fiona was saying. She pulled her arm a little, and since he was still holding it, he followed her. "I want to show you something."

She took him into her tent and turned up the lamp that hung from a hook overhead. Swishing the cat off her cot, she motioned Rogan to sit. Then she set a big philodendron on one side of a black metal trunk and opened the lid. She rooted around placing things on the floor.

He let his eyes run down the curve her back made as it joined her hips. Small, round, tight hips. Her hair covered her shoulders and fell halfway down her back. The yellow T-shirt molded to her skin, gathering in the back where she'd tucked it into her jeans. The swell of her bottom pulled her pants' waist into a sloping V that pointed to the line formed by the seam between her buttocks.

Rogan imagined what it would feel like to sidle up behind her and cup his hands around her bottom. He would like to slide his hands down her thighs and over her knees.

And then, his chest hard against her back, he would like to take her breasts and lift them just a little. He would like to rub the yellow T-shirt over their tips until her nipples stood up underneath and begged for his touch.

He rubbed a hand over the back of his neck and tried to make himself concentrate on other things. Her slender arm, bronzed by the sun. Fine gold hair, almost invisible, swept down it. She was touching things the way he'd imagined her touching him. Stroking with her short nails, cradling gently, smoothing, lifting and stroking.

But it wasn't his body beneath her touch. Instead, she fondled a small photo album. A child's diary with a tiny brass key on a ribbon. A thick, hand-knitted wool sweater. Two teacups with red roses and green leaves on a pink background. And, finally, a large book.

"Here," she said, swinging around without standing, "my father gave me this years ago. You can borrow it, Rogan."

He took the book and gazed at the slick cover imprinted with brilliant red blossoms and bearing the black-lettered title *Plants of Kenya.*

"I used to read it all the time," she went on, moving to sit beside him. "See, inside I saved actual specimens of each of the species I found. It was sort of a dream of mine to collect every one."

With tapered brown fingers she flipped the pages one by one. The book's spine lay between his thighs, each side across his lap. As she moved her hand down the page, he could feel the pressure on his leg. Her shoulder leaned into his. Her hair settled against his arm. With her fingertips she stroked the paper-thin petals of the dried flowers.

"Floss-silk tree," she murmured. "Flame tree, red-hot poker tree, jacaranda, desert rose. Africans use the desert rose sap as an arrow poison, did you know? It's toxic. Here are some yesterday, today and tomorrow blossoms. Look—purple, cream, white. All from the same shrub. Candle bush, angel's trumpet, snow on the mountain, poinsettia, hibiscus, crown of thorns."

"Looks like you got them all."

"Not the baobab." She smiled. "You know those fat trees with bark the elephants love to eat?"

"*Adansonia digitata.*"

She laughed in surprised delight at his instant recital of the scientific name. "Baobabs hardly ever have leaves. And you almost never see them in flower. I tried and tried, but I couldn't get a specimen. And I've lived in Kenya all my life. Nearly, anyway."

"Nearly?"

"I was sent to boarding school in England once. That experiment didn't last long. And then, of course, I did some of my graduate-level university work through institutions in the States."

"Why didn't your boarding school experience last long?"

"Oh, England . . . well, you know."

"No."

She lifted her head. What did he expect her to do—blurt out all the pain she'd worked so hard to bury? Just come right out with everything as though it didn't matter? As though she could just casually shrug about her past and the things that had hurt so much?

"I suppose my experience was something like yours," she said finally. "All the things you don't like to talk about, you know. About your parents and the memories."

"I don't see how there could have been any similarity at all between your life and mine, Fiona. Did your parents get divorced, and did your father take you on ski trips with his mistresses? Did your mother marry five different men in a row and hate each of them within a month of the wedding?"

"My mother died?"

"How?"

"Well . . . they killed her."

"Who killed her?"

She gestured vaguely in the air. "They. Somebody. People."

"Somebody just killed your mom? Murdered her?"

"Rogan, really, I think you'd better go now." She brushed her hand across her forehead. "I have to compile some data from this morning. And I have a full day planned for tomorrow. If you don't mind . . ."

"Fiona." He took her shoulders, wanting to tell her that she could talk to him—talk about anything. He wanted to hear it. She could say the words that were so hard for her. She could cry if she wanted to; he wouldn't mind. She could be angry. He would take her anger and hold it for her.

But when had he ever shared *his* tears or anger? When had he ever spoken of those things that were so painful? He understood her. And inside himself he saw that there were reasons why she hadn't left his mind for one minute when he was in Nairobi. Reasons why her face lit up when she had seen him standing in her camp that evening. And the reasons had to do with the fact that the two of them were alike—both buried in work so they wouldn't have to feel, both hiding memories that hurt too much, both sidestepping anything that required emotional commitment.

"Fiona, thank you for the book," he said finally, because he couldn't make the words he wanted to say come out. "I'll read it tonight."

"You can take it with you, if you want. Just send it back to me when you're finished."

"Okay. Thanks."

"Well . . ." She stood, not wanting him to go, but not knowing how to make him stay.

"Breakfast tomorrow, then? And you'll let me know about Nairobi."

"All right."

He walked to the triangular patch of night that showed through her tent door. "Fiona—"

"Rogan—"

He turned and retraced the steps he had just taken. She came into his arms, her own sliding around his back. Her face tilted to his, and their mouths met. Hungry, exploring, needing. His lips moved over her cheek, her ear.

"Fiona," he whispered.

"I'm glad you came back."

"I thought about you all the time."

"I thought about you, too."

His big hands curved over her shoulder blades, and then his fingers laced around the back of her neck. He ran his thumbs into her hair as his mouth sought out every damp velvety curve of hers. He'd kissed women before, but never one who took his breath right out of his chest and sent his heart into double-time so fast. He'd never felt himself respond so quickly, with such urgent demand.

Her body felt good, soft and hard at the same time. He cupped her hips the way he'd imagined and pulled her against himself. Her breasts pressed against his chest, and she turned them just slightly as if she wanted to be stimulated by him. The motion sent fire surging through him.

Taking the yellow cotton knit between his fingers, he tugged it from the waist of her jeans. She shivered visibly. Her nose was tucked between his collar and his neck, her lips hot on his skin. He drew his hands upward, inside her shirt, and touched the warm flesh beneath the fold of her breasts.

With a sigh she lifted her arms and spread her fingers through his hair. He trailed circles around her bare breasts, tightening each orbit toward the center. Her breath came in tiny gasps.

He didn't know how much longer he could stand upright, his body was in such turmoil. He wanted to lay her down on that cot and touch her until she was sobbing with need. His fingertips slipped around the crest of one breast. She sucked in her breath and stiffened as he began to stroke her nipple. Over and over, squeezing lightly, tipping it up and then down, heightening her pleasure. He moved his hand to the other breast and drew his fingers to the hardened tip.

Her hips began to move against him, pressing and searching. He used one hand on her bottom to press their bodies together, pelvic bones jarring with the shock of meeting. Her legs slid closer, one on either side of his. He lifted his thigh and pushed it against the soft mound beneath her jeans.

"Oh, Rogan." She felt as if she were coming apart in a thousand pieces. Her breasts throbbed and tingled, sent sweet aching trails to the pit of her stomach. Her legs had gone weak. She was melting inside, liquid with wanting.

"I could touch you all night," he murmured, his breath hot in her ear.

"I could let you."

"Will you let me, Fiona? Will you let me make love to you? It's what I want more than anything right now."

She lifted her eyes and let her gaze linger on his face. His brown-gold hair. His shadowed jaw. She heard her own breath hard in her chest. She felt his heartbeat, strong against her fingertips. To let this man part her body as no other man had done... to let him touch her in places she'd never been touched... to give him permission to enter her and take her and sow seeds of passion and pain...

"I need time," she whispered. "I have to think."

"Don't think, Fiona. Feel. Feel your body. Feel what you want. What you need. Let yourself go."

She touched his lower lip, loving the curve it made. "Give me time, Rogan. Please."

He stepped back, his breath ragged. He looked over her face, her swollen lips, the bright stain his rough beard had left on her cheek. He let his eyes wander down her body, the wrinkled yellow T-shirt, her full breasts with nipples teased into arousal, her jeans tight around her thighs.

"I don't want to," he said.

"Please," she whispered.

"Come to Nairobi with me, then?"

She swallowed. "All right."

"You will?"

"For CTN and the museum and the embassy party. For the elephants."

He nodded, backing toward the door. He felt like a kid again, a teenager dizzy with elation. "Okay. Okay, that's fine. For the elephants."

She watched him leave, his face bright with a smile she'd never seen before.

Chapter 10

When Rogan emerged from his tent by the stream, Fiona was deep in conversation with her staff. The two baby elephants trotted around the dead campfire, running with floppy ears. Due to the elephants' orphan status, Fiona had given them names that would not tie them to any particular family. She hoped they would form their own bond group— a goal that now seemed achievable. When Johnny tripped on something and fell, Fiona stopped speaking and moved to help. But instantly the older orphan—a female, christened Olivia—rushed to Johnny's aid. She nudged his gray backside, pushing with her trunk and front foot until the little calf was standing again.

Smiling, Fiona lifted her eyes and watched Rogan make his way across the clearing. He wandered toward the shower, his head high, his focus on the branches of the acacias and the monkeys cavorting there. He wore a soft expression, completely readable. He looked nothing like the man who had first come to her camp in a wool business suit, with carefully parted hair. He looked happy.

Before stepping into the shower he raised one hand. She waved in answer. Then, feeling the dark eyes of four men on her flushed cheeks, she returned to the conversation.

Her leaving, she realized, was not something they had anticipated. Nguyo wanted to know what to do with all the fresh fruit he'd just bought in Naivasha. And should he send the coconut pie with them on the airplane? Wilson wondered when she would be back and whether he was supposed to keep up the night feedings during her absence. Moses complained, restating for the third time that morning that he'd been hired to watch only one elephant and asking whether she intended to employ another man to look after Olivia. Sentero studied her in silence, his dark eyes shifting from the woman to the shower to the woman again.

"I'll be away two or three days at the most," she assured them. "Just to speak to some people in Nairobi about the elephants."

Nguyo shook his head, dark eyes forlorn. Moses looked at the pair of baby elephants resting in the shade. Wilson tapped his flashlight against one leg. And Sentero stared at her, his face revealing nothing.

In time breakfast was eaten and all the arrangements made. Rogan, clean shaven and dressed in tan trousers and a blue shirt with a button-down collar, insisted on carrying Fiona's half-empty canvas knapsack to the plane. She had on her least faded pair of khaki slacks and a white blouse sent as a Christmas present from her father years ago. She had never worn it.

Now, feeling silly in long puffed sleeves and a stand-up collar buttoned to her throat, she leaned through the airplane door and called last-minute instructions to the men.

"Be sure the babies don't get too hot," she shouted to Moses over the drum of the propellers. "And keep an eye on the M family for me, Sentero. Check Rosamond's wound again, will you? I'm afraid it's festering. And Charlie, too. He can't last much longer. Wilson, if you see anyone suspicious around the camp at night, radio the game wardens. And, Nguyo—"

Rogan's hand closed over hers. She turned to find him smiling patiently. "Everything will be all right, Fiona."

She nodded, her heart beating too fast. "And, Nguyo, if you have some extra time, there's mending in a basket by my cot. Just slacks with the knees gone."

"Yes, *memsahib*."

"And keep an eye on Sukari for me."

"Yes, *memsahib*."

"I don't want him to feel neglected. And check that he has fresh water."

"Fiona." Rogan drew her gently inside the plane and reached over her to shut the door. "Relax now. They'll manage."

Relax? How could she possibly relax? She wedged her hands between her knees as Rogan taxied the small plane down the airstrip. What if something happened to one of the elephant calves? What if Moses quit while she was away? What if Sukari panicked and ran off? And then there was the matter of this tiny plane—she'd always hated flying. It seemed so uncertain. And Rogan. What about him? How could she possibly be doing something so impulsive as abandoning her staff, her research, the elephants, just to go cavorting off to Nairobi with this man she hardly knew?

She sucked in her stomach as the plane lifted into the air. Oh, she'd thought about Rogan. Thought about him nearly all night. Thought about the wonder of him. And the magic. Of course, that was all he was. Illusory magic. These amazing feelings wouldn't last. They couldn't. Yet here she was in her poufed blouse zooming over her camp and heading for the city.

She disliked Nairobi. Such a big place. So many people. Dangerous things could happen in cities. Dangerous things *did* happen. She couldn't be expected to simply walk down the street without any fear. Not after what had happened to her mother.

Yet Rogan would expect that of her. He would expect her to be normal. To follow him to his embassy party and to astonish the museum directors with her wisdom about the elephants. He would expect her to blend into his world. And what else would he expect?

She glanced at him. His strong profile was lit by the rising sun, outlined in gold. The light danced through his eyes, skipping on the white flecks and darkening the navy circle around each iris. He was smiling that little smile from the night before. One corner of his mouth turned just enough to make a crease in his cheek. His skin glowed from the razor; his ears were clean and scrubbed; his hair clung to his neck, still damp.

Fiona thought about the conclusions she'd come to in the night. She had forced her mind away from the magic touch of Rogan's hands on her body. She'd made herself think about practical things. About her work. About the elephants. And finally her thoughts had come around in a circle, back to Rogan.

Why not? she had decided. Scientifically speaking, the human body was made for sexual intercourse. Female breasts were formed with both nourishment and pleasure in mind. She was certainly old enough to have this new experience. And with Rogan she'd felt for the first time what animals must know during the rutting season—the mating instinct.

That was all it was, after all. Just a natural animal drive. Why shouldn't she accommodate it? Look at Margaret and the other female elephants. They went through their lives without weighing consequences. They felt the mating urge; they went into consort with a bull in musth; they mated several times and then they went on their way. Very simple. Uncomplicated.

Of course, twenty-two months later tiny elephant calves were born from those unions. But Fiona had considered that angle, too. What would be so awful about having a baby? She could incorporate that change into her life. In a way it might be good for her. She'd begun to realize that she enjoyed the human touch. She liked having someone to talk to and share things with. If she had a child, she would welcome the difference. And, like the elephants, she would carry on with her life in the same way she always had.

She glanced at Rogan again. He was studying the clouds just overhead. His hands, strong and tanned, skillfully guided the small plane. He read dials and pushed buttons. And every now and then he leaned over and looked out the window.

Rogan was intelligent, Fiona had concluded. A man with good genes. A handsome face. A healthy build. Just the sort of male she *should* seek out for mating. It made sense. She unwedged her hands and tried to relax against the seat.

"There's the edge of the park," he was saying, giving her that slow smile. "Ever seen it from the air?"

She shook her head, wishing her stomach wasn't lurching. It was just the plane ride, she told herself. It had nothing to do with her train of thought or the way Rogan was watching her with those blue, blue eyes.

"Look down," he urged. "See that old empty stone house and the water hole? Clive tells me they're right on the park's borderline. And can you make out Mount Suswa just to your right? It's kind of far away."

"Oh, yes, I see it."

"Won't be long before we fly over the escarpment and into the highlands. Did you bring a sweater? Nairobi can be chilly at night."

"Yes. A sweater. I brought one."

"Great. Okay, Nairobi, here we come."

A long white limousine met them at the airport. Fiona climbed onto the lushly padded leather seat and wedged herself into a corner. Rogan took her hand, holding it lightly as they drove through the city. She shut her eyes, willing away the honks and growls of traffic, the sway of the car as it swung around corners, the ding-ding of bicycle bells.

In no time the limousine had pulled into the shadow of a high marble arch. The door opened, and Fiona stepped out onto hard pavement. Rogan cupped her waist, his fingers trailing along her arm as he thanked the driver and described plans she couldn't bring herself to listen to.

And then they were climbing cool marble steps. Walking through a door held wide by a smiling, red-coated African. Standing in a carpeted elevator that swished up and up with stomach-sinking swiftness.

"Here we are," Rogan said, a note of pride in his voice. "I rented this place for my stay in Kenya. Great location. Lots of space."

She tried to smile as he fitted a key in the brass lock. The doors were huge and antique, carved and studded with brass. Brought up from the coast, she imagined, where they had once graced an Arab house. Rogan gave her a small nudge to move her into the front room.

Instantly a tall skinny woman with hair that stuck straight up from her head in little blond spikes leapt to her feet and hurried around a huge carved desk.

"Mr. McCullough—you're back! Oh, thank God." Seeing Fiona, she stopped suddenly, her ankles nearly giving way atop her high heels. "You've . . . you've brought someone."

"Ginger Smeade, this is Dr. Fiona Thornton," he said.

"The elephant researcher. Oh, pleased to meet you, Dr. Thornton."

Fiona shook the proffered hand, amazed at the length of the fuchsia nails extending from the secretary's fingers. How did she ever type?

"Mr. McCullough, I have a stack of messages for you, sir," Ginger went on, breathless. "Megamedia has been on the phone for hours with me, and I just don't know what to tell them. They've been sending telegrams, too. And Mr. Barnett called from New York. He's very concerned, sir. And then there's the man in Frankfurt—"

"Ginger, would you be so good as to show Dr. Thornton to the guest suite? And see if you can round up something for us to drink. I'm parched."

"Yes, sir. But about the messages—"

"Go ahead, Ginger. Show Dr. Thornton around. I'll take care of things."

As she walked through a second set of carved doors, Fiona looked behind her at the man who now stood at the desk. A telephone receiver was wedged in the crook of his shoulder and neck; his fingers flipping through a stack of papers; his eyes scanning the desktop.

"Yes," he was saying, the softness gone from his voice. "I need New York, please. . . . Yes, get me New York. . . ."

Fiona followed the secretary's swaying hips through a massive living room and down a long hall. The bedroom door opened onto an immense room, one side lined with closets and the other revealing a smaller boudoir area with a love seat and plants. There was a grand bathroom with rows of lights over the double sink, a big pink-marble tub, fluffy white towels.

"When your suitcases are brought up," Ginger was saying as she opened one of the closet doors, "you can hang your clothes in here."

"Oh, this is all I've brought." Fiona lifted the knapsack that hung by a frayed loop from her index finger. "I'm not staying long. I'm just here to... to talk to people about the elephants."

"Of course." Ginger smiled, fuchsia lips spreading over white-capped teeth. "Is there anything you need, Dr. Thornton?"

Yes, Fiona wanted to say. I need fresh air and green trees and dust on my feet. I need my elephants, and I need Sentero's dark eyes watching the landscape, and I need my white cat curling onto my lap.

"No, thank you," she managed. "Everything's fine."

"Well, then. I'll just go get those drinks and see what else Mr. McCullough needs." The secretary stared at Fiona, up and down. Then she smoothed the peplum on her purple linen suit and hurried out of the room.

Fiona sat on the end of the bed. She stared at her safari boots, worn and creased and reddened with dirt. She stared at her hands, knotted around the wrinkled knapsack. Then she stared at the immense room, the gold-and-crystal chandelier, the mauve silk bedspread, the heavy curtains muffling sound from the street below. Blinking back a tear, she fiddled with a string on the hem of her blouse and tried to figure out what to do with herself.

"Ready to go?" Rogan burst through the half-open door to find Fiona slumped on the edge of the bed staring at her feet. "Fiona? What's wrong?"

She raised her eyes. "I shouldn't have come. I need to get back, Rogan."

"Hey, now." He strode to the bed and lifted her. "I just had a few things to take care of. I'm free for the rest of the afternoon. Let's go out. I'll buy you something to wear to that embassy thing tonight. What do you say?"

She met his eyes, wondering if the man who pressed hibuscus flowers was still in there somewhere. "I don't accept charity, Rogan. Besides, these clothes are fine, and I don't want a dress. I'd never wear it again."

"So what if you never wear it again? We'll wave my magic credit card. How about that, Princess Sunrise?"

She pondered the proposition and didn't like it. Though she knew Rogan probably had no ulterior motive behind his offer, she remained a little suspicious of him, all the same.

"What's wrong, Fiona?" he was asking. "Tell me."

"I'll admit I've thought about buying myself some new clothes. I just haven't gotten around to it. But I don't need your money—"

"Fiona, you haven't allowed me to contribute to your project in any way so far. Let this be my donation to the cause. Look on it as an investment with good returns at the embassy party tonight."

"Well...as a donation... Still, I just don't feel comfortable in cities, Rogan."

"I'll be with you every minute. Come with me now. We'll have a good time."

She walked beside Rogan out of the bedroom and down the long hall. He stopped at the end of the corridor before a full-length gilt-framed mirror. He turned her around, letting her take a long look at herself—at the red-gold hair, the girlish white blouse tucked into worn trousers, the dusty boots.

"Remember this," he whispered in her ear. Then he led her out into the front room, where Ginger was sorting through a file. The secretary looked up.

"Going now, Mr. McCullough?"

"We'll be back by six." He started for the door, then stopped and swung Fiona toward the secretary again. "Ginger, what colors would look good on Dr. Thornton?"

"Colors?" Ginger stood and cocked her head. "Colors, oh, let's see. Red, maybe? Orange. And pink. Any shade of pink."

"And fabrics?"

She stuck the end of a fuchsia spike into her mouth and sucked. "Velvet. Brocade. And knits."

"Thanks, Ginger." Rogan winked. "Catch you later."

He wheeled Fiona out into the hall and strode toward the elevator. Chuckling, he slipped his arm around her waist. She stepped through the steel doors feeling even more queasy than she had before.

"Red?" she said as the elevator sucked them down. "And pink? And Rogan, brocade and velvet. Please, I—"

"Oh, think of this kind of like you do Nguyo and meal planning. Whatever Ginger suggested, we'll do just the opposite. Personally I'm picturing you in green silk."

Hand in hand Rogan and Fiona walked the streets of Nairobi. They lunched at The Thorn Tree, a sidewalk cafe under the spreading branches of a three-stories-tall acacia that had been planted in the city's center. They wandered in and out of galleries and boutiques, examining necklaces of amber, malachite, amethyst and tiger's eye...fingering dyed batik dresses in shades of purple and yellow...touching fine olive-wood carvings...studying oils and watercolors of Africa and her animals.

At first Fiona clung to Rogan's arm with a grip that almost cut off the circulation. She kept glancing behind her. She jumped when a car backfired. But as the afternoon wore on, she began to relax. The press of people held mostly friendly faces. When someone bumped her arm, there came an instant apology. Rogan kept her attention focused on the wonders of the shops, the aromas of curry and cinnamon and freshly baked bread in the little stalls, the array of bananas, papayas, mangos and tomatoes being hawked by street vendors.

"This is it," he announced as Fiona emerged from the fitting room of a dress-filled boutique. "This is the one."

She pivoted in front of a three-sided mirror, staring at herself with flushed cheeks. The gown, a rich blue-green silk, curved over her bodice to reveal smooth creamy shoulders, a swelling bosom, a narrow waist and—beneath the hem of the full skirt—a pair of long, shapely legs. Pale silk stockings, at Rogan's insistence, were added to a stack of lacy lingerie. Matching blue-green pumps covered in sequins went into a sack, along with a cashmere shawl in a complementary shade of midnight blue.

Later in the afternoon another boutique provided a simple matching jacket and skirt in bright yellow linen. The short skirt, split on the side to reveal a stretch of thigh, was accented with a pair of brilliant canary high heels. As she left the store, Fiona clutched the bags against her chest, unable to believe she was the owner of such up-to-date, expensive, well-matched and fitted clothing.

"Now your hair," he said, turning her into a beauty salon.

"Rogan, I like my hair just the way—"

But in moments she was seated in a reclining chair, enjoying the feel of practiced hands massaging her scalp with thick lather. Her hair was treated to the luxury of rich conditioner, fluffed with a modern electric blow-dryer and finally curled and styled high on her head. When the stylist turned the chair to the mirror, Fiona gasped so loudly that everyone in the salon turned to look.

Her hair, swept and piled on her head, gleamed with copper lights. Tendrils almost too wispy to see softened her face at the ears and nape. The lifted hair revealed things about herself Fiona had never known. She had high cheekbones that gave her eyes an exotic almond shape. And her neck. How long it was. Long, thin, meeting her shoulders with swanlike grace. She turned, admiring her own ears for the first time in her life. She smiled and realized she had a lovely mouth. She blinked and saw long dark lashes flutter.

Next she was handed over to a woman who showed her how to apply makeup. Soft foundations and translucent powders made her skin glow. Gentle liners, shadows and mascaras brought her sparkling eyes to life. Contours blushed her cheeks. A stray brow hair was plucked here and there. And finally a glossy lipstick showed just how full and pouty her lips really were.

When Rogan walked into the salon after her three-hour ritual, Fiona stood, turned and walked to him feeling like the newest, prettiest, sexiest woman alive. And his eyes agreed.

* * *

"Fiona," he said in a low voice as they stood together at the embassy party. "It's almost midnight. Are you ready to leave, princess?"

"Will my dress turn into a T-shirt and jeans at the stroke of twelve?"

"No, but I might change into an ogre if I'm forced to keep staring at your shoulders without getting a chance to touch."

She laughed and took a last sip of champagne. Everything felt swirly. Ladies in gorgeous gowns tittered with men strutting in black-tie tuxedos. Faces from Asia, Africa, Europe and South America mingled and swam. Languages, accents, laughter and music floated through the high-ceilinged ballroom. Scents of rich perfume blended with the aromas of exotic food—curries, tropical fruits, old wines.

Rogan had introduced Fiona to a diplomat from Zimbabwe. The man had listened to her animated words about the plight of the elephants. Then he'd smiled, commented, "How very interesting," and sidled off to find himself another drink. But Rogan had blotted out her disappointment by whirling her onto the dance floor. His arms came around her, his eyes memorized her face and she drifted away in pools of deep blue.

Oh, she'd had too much to drink. She was well aware of that, considering that tea and mango juice were her primary beverages in the bush. The day had toppled her off balance—from the morning's plane ride away from her camp to the afternoon of shopping to the utter physical transformation of Dr. Fiona Thornton. She felt frightened and light and so, so vulnerable. The champagne had blunted that fear a little. She had let herself laugh and meet people. She'd graced Rogan's arm, chatting inanities that she imagined were proper and polite.

And all the while she tried to keep in mind that this was simply part of the human mating dance. The fluff and brilliance and perfume decorated the strutting peacocks of the world of people. Rogan was her suitor, trying to win her with touches and compliments, with his handsome suit and his gifts—just like a weaver bird won a mate by building the perfect nest, or a bull elephant won by dominating the other males.

And Rogan dominated. How he dominated. His smile sent the women into flutters. His handshake held a power that transfixed men. He stood tall and handsome, the white shirt matching his smile, the black bow tie accenting his bronzed skin.

"All right, I'm ready," she said when his hand slipped up the back of her bare neck. And she *was* ready. She'd made up her mind to experience this. Rogan was the mate she'd selected. The time was at hand.

He escorted her through the ballroom and into the limousine. He drew her close in the darkness of the leather padding and kissed her lips.

"Fiona," he murmured, "you're beautiful."

"Yes," she concurred, "beautiful." She allowed her eyes to drift shut, savoring the feather-light touch of his fingers on the soft skin above her bodice. Yes, she thought. I am beautiful. I'm a beautiful, beautiful woman. And this is my chosen mate. The male who selected me, whose touch sends my body into arousal, at whose hands I will experience a natural human function. It's simple and natural, she told herself, swirling again…natural…mating…intercourse…a basic drive . . . an instinct . . . no big deal. . . .

She was snoring softly when Rogan drew her against his chest and carried her to the elevator. As the lift rose, he studied her face, knowing that this woman did things to him no other woman had ever done. Knowing that she was special. She was different. Knowing she was worth waiting for, no matter how long it took. Knowing—somewhere deep inside himself—that when they finally joined together, it would be stars and diamonds and ribbons of silk. It would be magic.

Fiona woke with a gasp and sat straight up in bed. Where was she? A mauve spread lay rumpled over an expanse of bed bigger than her entire tent. Sunlight spilled between pleated curtains. Hot tea, plates covered by silver warmers and a red rosebud crowded a bamboo tray beside her bed. The aroma of eggs and bacon drifted through the room.

Grabbing her throat, she glanced down at herself. White nightgown. Her old one, from home. Buttoned to her neck. The blue-green silk dress draped over the love seat in the boudoir. Sparkly pumps perched together on the Persian carpet.

"Oh, dear Lord." Once again she caught herself in prayer. She shut her eyes, tenderly touching her breasts. They felt just like they always had. She lifted her gown, spread her knees and peered between her legs. The same silk panties she'd put on for the embassy party peeped between her thighs.

Flopping back on the bed, she flung an arm over her eyes. Oh, what had she done? What *hadn't* she done? Why hadn't she done it? Who had taken off her dress? Where were Sukari and her philodendron and the chime of Nguyo's xylophone?

"Good morning, Princess Sunrise."

She bolted upright again as Rogan walked into the room and sat beside her. "Planning to eat any of this, or are you going to laze around all day?"

"Oh, Rogan." She touched his arm. "Last night, I—"

"You fell asleep in the limo. I guess I wore you out with all that shopping and beauty parlor business."

"My head . . . I don't know what happened. I just drifted around, and everything felt so different."

"Champagne and dancing. They'll do a person in every time. Especially when her normal bedtime is eight-thirty."

"Rogan, I'm sorry. I know you wanted—"

"I got everything I wanted, Fiona. I wanted time with you. I wanted to hold you in my arms, to dance with you, to take you places and show you the world I live in."

She looked down at her hands, smoothing the mauve bedspread. This wasn't the behavior of a spurned male in the heat of mating season. This was kindness, understanding, tenderness.

"Our museum meeting's at ten," he was saying. "After that I'll take you to lunch at the Norfolk Hotel. And then we'll meet Fred from CTN at two."

"All right."

"Wear the yellow suit."

"Rogan..."

"You're beautiful, Fiona. Beautiful in the morning. Beautiful at night. Even beautiful when you're snoring."

"I snore?"

"Very quietly."

She brushed a hand over her eyes. His lips stroked across her cheek. "See you in an hour."

Fiona couldn't imagine taking an hour to shower and get dressed. But the water was steamy, the soap filled with cream and lather and sweet perfume. Thirsty towels drank beads of water from her skin. She rubbed lotion over her legs and arms. She practiced with the makeup. And she brushed out her hair so that it tumbled in thick burnished waves over her breasts.

Finally, with only minutes to spare, she dressed in the yellow suit and emerged into the living room. Ginger glanced up, and her mouth fell open, revealing her set of capped teeth and a wad of spearmint gum. Rogan stopped dictating.

"Fiona," he breathed.

Color crept up her neck and settled in hot points on her cheeks. A vague memory slipped forward—a little girl in a lacy pink Easter dress standing on a porch. White-gloved hands clasped a shiny white purse, and hips swayed shyly back and forth.

"Why, Fiona...how adorable!" a young voice said. "Look, John, isn't she beautiful?"

And then another, deeper voice. "I should say so. Takes after you, Mavis, darling. My, my, my."

The memory faded, and with its leaving came the sharp sting of tears. Fiona tried to remember her mother's face...the red-gold hair...the smiling eyes...but she, too, had faded.

"Fiona?" Rogan was at her side.

She swallowed and forced a smile on to her lips. "Shall we go? I'd hate to keep the curators waiting."

Ginger swept up a file from the desk. "Here, Mr. McCullough. The file for your meeting with Megamedia." She placed it in his hands, but her eyes were on Fiona. "You look great, Dr. Thornton," she said. "I mean, it's a regular miracle."

"A temporary miracle," Fiona answered, recovering. "I'll be leaving tomorrow morning, Miss Smeade. Would you please find out whether Clive Willetts will be free to fly me back to my camp? I'd like to leave as early as possible."

"Sure. Of course, Dr. Thornton."

And then Fiona and Rogan were on their way. The museum meeting rushed by. Fiona's presentation drew a rumble of approval from the board. Several questions were asked, and pledges of support given. There was talk of setting up a special fund for the Rift Valley Elephant Project.

At lunch Fiona imagined herself completely contained—the museum meeting had gone better than she'd expected; she was fully prepared to face the cameras of CTN. She felt confident, efficient.

But then Rogan took her hand and offered her a basket of bread.

"Would you like a roll, Fiona?" he asked.

As she reached for the basket, she suddenly heard the whispered voices again.... "Bread, Fiona, darling? Mummy baked it just for you. And marmalade? Oh, sweetheart, do have a bit of butter."

And the deeper voice. "You bake the best homemade bread in eleventy-seven counties, Mavis. I swear it. I'd lay money on you any time."

"Darling!" And then a high, tinkling laugh that tumbled down into Fiona's heart.

"Fiona?" Rogan touched her cheek. "Fiona, what's the matter? Is something on your mind?"

She focused on his blue eyes. "Oh...oh, it's nothing. I was just remembering something. Something I'd forgotten."

He watched her, wondering.

But she was stunning before the cameras. The interview went beautifully. Fiona startled everyone with her impassioned speech. Fred asked if CTN might come to her camp and film a segment on the elephants of the Rift Valley. She said she'd consider the possibility and let him know.

And then Rogan slipped his arm around her and they walked together to the limousine. In the car he held her hand, toying with her fingertips. He said nothing, and she couldn't bring herself to speak.

They rode the elevator to the apartment, and Rogan gave Ginger the rest of the day off. "Relax here, Fiona," he said, opening her bedroom door. "I'll be at my meeting with Megamedia until around six. Then we'll have supper together."

She nodded.

"And, Fiona. If you want to stay another day, I'd like that." He touched her arm, pulled her to him, kissed her lips. "I'm not crazy about the idea of sending you off tomorrow."

As he shut the door behind her, she sank onto the bed. The voices slipped over her again: "John, darling. I just can't send her off. She's too little. Let her stay here another year."

The deeper voice. "What about school? You don't want her to grow up ignorant, Mavis."

"Better ignorant than lonely. She's obviously intelligent—that'll work in her favor. But she's so shy, so small and fragile. She's just a child, John. I'm afraid she'd be easily hurt."

"All right, Mavis. Keep her with you. Fill her with all that extra love you seem to think she needs. And when the time comes, we'll figure out a way to educate her."

Fiona squeezed her eyes shut, seeing the faces. Oh, her mother. Her father. How long ago it had been. And how very warm and secure.

With the heel of her palm she ground tears into her cheek and shook her head. Why now? Why was she suddenly swamped with memories of what she had lost so long ago? Why did she feel like that little girl again, wanting warmth, wanting comfort, wanting security...wanting—no, aching—for love?

Chapter 11

When Rogan returned from his meeting in downtown Nairobi, he found Fiona seated alone, staring out the window, one fingertip trailing down the ivory tusks on the telephone table. Bare feet emerged from the ragged hems of her jeans. An old navy T-shirt clung to the curve of her back.

"Fiona?" Rogan walked toward her, uncertainty in every step. Though her physical appearance had slipped into the old norm, emotionally she seemed drained, evaporated and so silent.

She turned and gazed at him, her eyes deep. "How was your meeting?"

"Looks like I can have the deal wrapped up in a few weeks. If I decide to make the final move."

Her mouth curved into a faint smile, then she returned to tracing imaginary lines down the tusks.

"So, what have you been up to while I was gone?" Rogan asked, setting his briefcase on the floor and loosening his tie. "Been busy?"

"I answered the telephone for a while. But then I gave up and let it ring. I didn't know what to tell everyone. They all wanted you."

"Aw, don't worry about the phone. It's the bane of my existence. I leave it off the hook half the time anyway.... So, what else have you been doing?"

"Are these yours?" she asked, tapping the tusks.

"The apartment came furnished. They were in here with all the other stuff."

She returned to tracing.

He decided maybe a change of scenery would do her good. "Would you like to eat out, Fiona? Chinese, maybe? Or Indian?"

"I had cheese and crackers at sunset. I'm full, thanks."

He studied the back of her head, copper hair tumbling over her shoulders. She was despondent. He never should have brought her to the city. She didn't fit. She was right; this wasn't her world—it frightened her. The best thing he could do was put her on a plane and send her back to that isolated camp where she could drive across the trackless plains and study the elephants.

She'd been right, too, when she'd said they had nothing in common. Their worlds were poles apart. Rogan wandered into his bedroom, unbuttoning his shirtsleeves and rolling them to his elbows. Fiona might have performed superbly for two days in his sphere, but he had to recognize her behavior as just that—a performance.

What had he expected, anyway? Had he hoped to show her life in the fast lane, the pleasures of money, the importance of knowing all the right people? Had he hoped to impress her with things he was beginning to doubt himself? Did he really expect her to respond to a man who had lost his drive to reach the pinnacles of power?

He'd tried to force her out of her world and into his. And look what it had brought her.

"Is it those tusks?" he asked, coming out of the bedroom in his bare feet. "Is that what's bothering you, Fiona?"

She turned, her eyes revealing a trace of surprise at his tone. "They bother me, of course. I...I keep thinking about the elephant they belonged to once. Maybe she was a matriarch, with lots of sons and daughters and a mind full of

wisdom about where to find the best patches of grass and
how to search out water during the dry season, and..."

She fell silent, knowing she'd told him the truth, but also
knowing there was much, much more. Could she tell him
how things had been flooding through her for the past few
hours? Things she hadn't thought of for years? She felt as
though this man...his human touch...his tender
words...had opened her inside. Doors had swung wide and
windows had lifted. She was tasting her own feelings. She
was reliving things she hadn't even known she remembered.

"Rogan, I—" she began, standing. But he was already
behind her, reaching around to grab the heavy tusks.

"Here, I'll just put these things where they belong." He
strode across the living room and hurled the curved tusks
into the huge stone fireplace. Their weight shattered a half-
burned log. "I'll set them on fire tomorrow. Isn't that what
the Kenyan government said to do with ivory? Just burn the
stuff? Will that make it go away, Fiona? Will that erase
some of the pain?"

"Rogan—"

"Damn it, Fiona! What would make a difference? I'm
just one man. I can't round up all the poachers and stand
them in a firing line. Believe me, if I could, I would. It's not
going to be taken care of that easily. Look, I'm sorry if it
hasn't worked out. I thought you might have fun in the city.
You know, shopping, eating out, stuff that would relax you
and take your mind off things. And I wanted to be with you.
But I guess it was a mistake. You're miserable, and I'm—"

"Rogan, will you please stop talking?"

His mouth shut, and he watched her walk across the
room, her bare feet silent on the thick Persian carpet. She
looked like the sunrise coming to him, her hair glowing, her
slim body covered in shades of indigo. He wanted to hold
her and take away everything that hurt her. It angered him
to realize that for all his big-time money and connections,
he didn't have the power to make her smile. He couldn't heal
her.

"Rogan," she said, forcing herself to look into his eyes,
"there are other things."

She crossed her arms under her breasts and stared at the sooty tusks. When you hadn't spoken your deepest thoughts in twenty years, how could you just start all at once? Words didn't form on your lips so easily. Inner feelings were reluctant to be dredged out of hiding.

But she knew Rogan was confused and hurt by her demeanor. He deserved an explanation. More than that, perhaps—she sensed that she wanted to talk. And she knew that after this night, she would never see him again. She would be safe. He would be like a priest—hearing her inner wounds, touching them with a healing hand and then vanishing to let her live her life as she chose.

"Other things?" he asked. "More than the elephants?"

She smiled. "The elephants are my work, Rogan. And I guess I am a little obsessed with them. But I'm not just a scientist. There have been other things in my life."

"Other things." He repeated the two words.

She let out a breath and lowered herself to the stone edge of the raised hearth. "Since I met you..." she began, searching for ways to say what she wanted him to know. "Since I met you, I've been remembering things. Things about my life. I guess I'd shut them away a long time ago. But the way you've talked to me and...and treated me in the past few days, I've slipped back into touch with those other sides of myself. It's been a little strange for me. Difficult."

She felt him settle beside her on the hearth, his long thigh parallel with hers. She could see the end of his knee straining against his slacks—the flat cap of bone and next to it the hard ridge of muscle that ran from groin to joint. Elbows resting on his thighs, he linked his fingers loosely and kept his eyes from her face. She was thankful.

"A long time ago," she said, her voice just above a whisper, "when I was young . . . five years old . . . we went to the States to visit my father's family for Christmas. Boston."

When she stopped speaking, he tensed. He wanted more than anything to reach over and take her hand. Or cradle her in his arms. But he was afraid she would slip away from him.

"Boston," he said. "Big city."

"Yes." She sat in silence. He heard her swallow twice. "We went Christmas shopping one evening. Snow was falling. I remember walking through mounds of it, white on my black boots. They were very shiny boots."

"New ones, I guess."

She nodded. "And we were walking around a corner. I had a big white package under my arm. A new pipe for my father. A very special paintbrush my mother had been wanting...it had some sort of bristles that made it absorb the paint better. She was an artist, you know. And I was holding her hand, our gloved fingers all tangled up. Daddy was...my father was walking just in front of us with my grandfather. They were laughing about things they remembered. My mother was singing me a silly song she'd made up about snow...sweetheart, watch it blow...and which way will it go...it settles on my nose and seeps between my toes...it sparkles oh, so white like sugar in the night...and then I heard a...sound...very loud..."

She let out another breath and it came in trembles. Rogan took her hand and wove their fingers together.

"It was a car. Boys laughing and hanging out the windows. Shouting. Waving bottles. And a loud sound...a boom...or a bang...and a bright light. My mother fell into the snow, and I tumbled on top of her because our fingers were all tangled together. And then I heard screaming and shouting. Sirens. My father was running down the street and then running back to my mother. Someone picked me up. I wiggled and cried, because I wanted to be with my mother—her hand had felt so warm on mine. But then I saw, spreading across the snow all around her head, a stain like a red halo. And I don't remember anything after that."

Rogan stared at their hands. He couldn't make himself breathe deeply enough to fill his lungs. "Your mother..."

"She died. The police never found out who the boys in the car were. Just a random shooting, they told us. They killed my mother...just for kicks."

She rubbed the end of her nose. How could she ever convey the sense of emptiness she'd felt after that? The things that died inside her when her mother died?

"We went back to Africa, and my father kept teaching anthropology at the University of Nairobi," she said finally. "Margaret came to take care of me. Margaret Ochoa. She had big brown eyes and skin like ebony and a soft smile. She sang made-up songs the way my mother had. And she rocked me and told me stories."

"Like the one about Matalai Shamsi."

"And lots of others. My father seemed to sort of go away. He didn't talk or laugh anymore. He put my mother's paintings in a room and locked the door. He worked all the time, and he got angry if anyone bothered him. He shouted if I touched the yellow-tagged bones on his desk. He wouldn't let people come to our house. He had no friends. Then . . . when I was eight, he decided I should go to England to boarding school."

She gave a laugh that sounded more like a sigh and shook her head. "That was awful. They had to practically pry me from Margaret. I screamed and cried and dug my fingers into her skin. She kept saying, 'Okay, *toto* . . . okay, *toto*.' But it wasn't okay. I didn't last in England very long before they expelled me."

"Expelled you? What the hell for? You were just a little kid—what harm could you have done?"

"I ran away from school. Six times in the first two months. They couldn't find me for days at a time. I hid in wonderful places. Beneath a bridge. In somebody's barn. And finally they just gave up and sent me back to Africa. My father had me tutored. And that was that. I grew up. I met a woman studying lions, and she helped me with my graduate work and research grants. And from then on, I've lived with the elephants."

"What about Margaret?"

"I don't know. I never saw her after the day they took me away. She went to work for someone else, I suppose."

"So you were all by yourself all those years? Just you and your angry father?"

"It didn't matter to me, Rogan. I didn't like people any more than my father did. I was young, but I wasn't stupid. I figured out people had killed my mother for no reason. For fun. How could I trust anyone after that? People had torn me away from Margaret. People had beaten me with a cane for running away from school. People had laughed at me when I cried and hid under my bed. I didn't need anybody or want anybody. I was happy alone.''

''And you still are.''

She lifted her head. ''That's the strange part. Yes, I'm happy, and I'm content with my work and my life. But for some reason lately, things have begun feeling very...odd. I've started remembering my mother. My father and mother. Our family. I can remember laughing and singing songs. I can remember hugging and tumbling down a grassy green hill in my father's arms. For the first time in ages I've started wanting...'' She stood suddenly and walked across the room. ''Oh, I don't know....''

''Tell me, Fiona. What is it you've been wanting?''

She stood, her back to him and her arms tightly crossed, hugging herself. ''It's like I went to sleep years and years ago. And now I feel as though I'm awake. I want...I want to be...touched.''

He knew those words had taken great courage. He knew she could give nothing more. Slowly he went to her. His hands slipped up her chilled bare arms, and his fingers tangled between hers.

''Fiona,'' he whispered, ''I'm...I'm sorry. I'm sorry you've been hurt so badly. Not everyone is going to hurt you.'' He turned her around in his arms.

''People lie,'' she said. ''You might be lying.''

''I'm not lying. It's true that nobody's perfectly good. And it's true that there are people—a lot of them—who don't give a damn about anyone but themselves. But it's also true that there are people who care. People who try to do the right things. People who heal and save and fight for justice.''

''And which kind of person are you, Rogan?''

He studied her camouflaged eyes, and he knew the answer. ''I'm one of those who's been walking around in the middle. I don't murder or steal or poach elephants. But I've spent a lot of years focused on one thing—Rogan McCullough. I haven't really cared who I stepped on to get where I wanted to be. And I've had to do a lot of thinking about what you told me the other day."

"What was that?"

"You said I could use my assets to save the world instead of dominate it."

She studied his lower lip and the downturned line at its corner. "And?" she asked.

"And I don't know how to do that, Fiona."

"Well, I don't know how to let people into my life. I don't know how to let them touch me."

That wasn't going to be hard to teach, he decided. He cupped the side of her face and tilted her head. "Fiona, letting someone touch you is the easiest thing in the world. Remember the day you kept telling me all the scientific names for the different parts of your body? Well, sure, the human body was created with specialized functions... but we were also created for pleasure."

"I don't know... it just makes me feel very vulnerable when you start..."

"When I kiss you?" He touched her lips with his. Her mouth felt dry, as though she'd used everything up in telling him her past. He dampened her lips with his tongue and gently tasted her sweet breath.

"Yes, that."

"When I stroke the skin on your neck with my hands?"

"That, too." She shivered as his fingertips made tiny hot trails beneath her hair.

"Vulnerability is good sometimes, Fiona. Once in a while it's okay to let somebody else be in control. It's easy to let go of the reins you hold on to so tightly. It feels good just to relax with someone you can trust."

"Can I trust you?"

"Always."

At his vow, she tried to make herself remember her carefully constructed argument about the selection of mates and how Rogan was the one she'd picked for her consort. She tried to remember that it wouldn't matter when, like a bull elephant, he went his way and she went hers.

"Now is all I care about, Rogan. Can I trust you for now?"

"Now. And always."

He gathered her hair in his hands, wanting her to know she was cherished. Not for anything in the world would he hurt her—or allow anyone else to hurt her. She'd borne enough for one lifetime.

Drawing her into his arms, he rubbed the taut tendons in her back. His fingers kneaded away the knots of tension her words had brought. For a long time she waited in silence, absorbing his touch. And then her arms went around him, holding him, drinking in the warmth of his body.

"Fiona," he murmured, his breath stirring tingles through the hair over her ear, "Fiona, there are things about you that make a man wonder what the hell he's been doing all his life. You have such honesty, such immediacy. There's no pretense in you. Your inner spirit seems to radiate outward . . . through your shining hair and your smile. Did you know you have a certain smile that you save just for the things you love?"

"I do?"

"For the elephants. For Nguyo's spice cake."

"Spice cake!" She laughed. Then she grew solemn, afraid that he might see that special smile when she looked at him.

His blue eyes caressed her face. She took in his dark lashes, the tinge of sunburn still clinging to the bridge of his nose, the golden touches in his hair. Lifting a hand, she smoothed the hair above his ears, then let her fingers drift down his short sideburns and onto his cheek. His skin, shaved that morning, now wore a fine dark shadow of beard. She let her fingers play over the stubble, enjoying the mixture of rough and smooth, hard and soft, that made up this man.

"I suppose you've been told hundreds of times how handsome you are," she said.

"Not by you."

"I think you're very . . . very beautiful."

"Beautiful?"

"Yes. Blue eyes. Strong features. And you have such a wonderful mouth. When I first saw you, I thought I could just dismiss you from my mind. But I couldn't stop thinking about your mouth. Your lips."

Watching her mouth form the words, he felt his blood grow hot and thick. It flowed heavily, throbbing through his chest. It shortened his breath. It tightened his loins.

"Fiona."

She felt him struggling with his own thoughts. His hands were hard on her shoulders, gripping her flesh. She could sense him against her stomach and thighs, tensed and barely leashed.

"Fiona, I want your trust. I want that more than anything. I want you to know that I'd never do anything to make you lose faith in me. Not after all you've been through at the hands of uncaring people. Do you understand that?"

"Yes."

"The thing is, Fiona, I've never had much practice at being particularly noble and restrained. And when I hold you and kiss you... and when you look at me with those unbelievable eyes... hell, I just have a hard time holding back."

"Why are you, then?"

"I don't want to hurt you, Fiona. I don't want to be someone who passes through your life and uses you and then just goes on."

She let out her breath, ragged and moist. "Rogan, I expect you to go on. I want you to go on. But now... tonight... I want you to touch me."

It was the knife that sliced through the leash of his restraint. With a rush of breath, he caught her hard against him. His mouth sought hers in a kiss that grew from more than their words, more than their caresses. Inside him something ached for her. Something demanded her.

Her hands caught at his back, gripping the muscles beneath his shirt. She arched into his kiss, her lips and mouth moving against his as though she was compelled to taste every part of him. She felt him pull her shirt up, felt his fingers slide over the skin of her waist, felt her breasts tighten with anticipation.

Touch me, she wanted to cry out. Touch my breasts, my nipples. Make them hot and throbbing the way you did before. At just the imagined feeling of his hands on her, she felt herself move into him, her breasts cresting against the front of his shirt. Deep within her stomach a pulsing began. It curled and slipped down her thighs and then settled in her toes.

"Fiona," he murmured, "you don't know how hard it was for me last night. I carried you up to your bed. I laid you across the spread. You were so relaxed. So beautiful. Your hair tumbled out of that knot and spilled over the sheets. And then I unzipped the side of your dress and lowered that shiny blue-green silk...."

"I wish I'd been awake."

"You don't know...it was all I could do to keep my hands off you. To put you into that chaste gown and button up all those damn tiny buttons. It was like opening a birthday present and not being allowed to touch. And then having to wrap it back up."

"Touch me now," she pleaded.

He lifted her T-shirt and drew it over her head. With her arms raised, her breasts were tilted toward him, their tips beaded rosebuds. He bent and touched the full skin, his tongue moving from one faint freckle to the next. She shivered. When his mouth closed over her nipple, she sighed and ran her fingers through his hair. His tongue licked and teased her until sparks of fire ran up her neck, beneath her arms, down her thighs. Her whole being felt centered wherever his mouth moved.

"Rogan." How could she ask him to hurry? How could she explain that she couldn't hold herself together much longer? Things were sliding away. Her head drifted backward. Her breath rose and fell in faint sighs. She hadn't imagined ever feeling this loss of control—or enjoying it so very much.

When he lifted his head and returned to kissing her mouth, she began to unbutton his shirt. It didn't take long, and then she was able to sate herself a little by rubbing her breasts against the crisp dark hair on his chest. No...she wasn't sated...she only felt worse. Hungrier.

"Rogan," she begged again.

But he wouldn't hurry. He was enjoying her too much. Her breasts, large and round, touched his skin. Their taut pink nipples nestled in his hair and then surfaced when his thumbs tipped them, then sank into him again. Tiny purrs of satisfaction came from somewhere deep inside her. Purrs mingled with mews of need.

He cupped her breasts, thinking he could never get enough of them. But then she was calling his name again, as if pleading with him. He worked apart the zipper on her jeans, lowering the fabric over the soft mound of her flesh. She followed suit, tugging at his trousers with impatient fingers.

And then, knowing he wanted to make this last—and sensing she was already almost beyond the point of control—he lifted her in his arms. Sliding away her jeans and stepping out of his slacks, he carried her into his bedroom. She tumbled onto the bed and pulled him down with her. Her mouth searched for his; finding it, she drank and suckled.

As his mouth sought out her breasts again, she felt a wave crest over her head. She cried out loud and caught him tightly, clenching her teeth as the wave washed between her legs, throbbing at a point deep inside her and then rippling down to the tips of her toes.

"Oh, Rogan..." She fought for air. What had happened? She heard his slow laugh of wonder and delight. And then he was kissing her again.

"You're amazing, Fiona Thornton," he whispered. "Amazing."

But she didn't have time to ponder. Now his hands slipped over her belly. His flat palm smoothed her skin. She could feel him pressed against her, his body hardened on her thigh. Reaching, she began to stroke his flesh. He shuddered and pulled back.

"Hold on, darling. You're going to take me there before I'm ready."

She didn't know where she was going to take him. But she knew she liked the feel of him, hot beneath her hands. But when she reached for him again, he slid his fingers through the tuft of red-brown curls and deep into her moist, waiting body.

"Rogan," she gasped.

Licking her ear, he stroked her. He feathered each fold of delicate tissue. He tenderly lifted and ringed the essence of her womanhood. She held her breath. Her body began to sway with the rhythm of his touch. Her hands caught him and began to stroke.

"Fiona," he warned. He'd never known it could be like this. She was driven. It was as though her body had been denied too long. He felt her explode against him a second time, her thighs gripping and arching on his fingers. She cried out his name again and again.

But as soon as she sagged with the spent wave, he began to touch her again. She caught his shoulders as her need began to mount. More slowly this time. Her breasts rose and fell. Her head was tilted back, breath barely escaping through parted lips.

"Rogan, please. Oh, please."

She instinctively spread her thighs as he rose above her. He slipped through the damp curls and let his shaft continue to caress her. She reached and caught the flesh of his buttocks, digging her fingers into the hard muscle. He slipped through and over her, readying her. And then, when she lifted herself toward him, he allowed himself to seek her depths.

His body thrust into her. Tight. So tight. And then he reached a barrier.

"Fiona—" Her name was torn from his mouth.

She held her breath, her eyes begging as he searched her face. "Please, Rogan."

He gripped her, drawn by the utter need in her eyes. His shaft tore through her tender flesh. She squeezed her eyelids tight, fighting the pain. He paused, absorbing her. And then, aware of her so hot and taut around him, he began to stroke. Rising and falling gently within her, he built her pain into pleasure. His mouth wet her nipples again. His hands squeezed her hair.

She drew her legs around him, seeking to pull him deeper. Their mouths met, deeply hungry. And then, as her need lifted again, she moved into him. With all the strength in her body, she met him stroke for stroke.

When she thought she could bear no more, she felt him pause. His fingers sank into her shoulders. His body tensed. And then, in an elemental release, he shuddered with her.

The pulse and flow sent her over the edge. Catching him, she felt her body grip his in wave after wave of intense pleasure.

"Fiona..." He murmured her name as their passion buffeted them. "Fiona... woman..."

"Oh, Rogan, you were right," she whispered, rubbing her hands over his damp skin as though she would never get enough of him. "You were right. Letting someone touch you is the easiest thing in the world."

Chapter 12

Fiona curled against Rogan after their lovemaking, enjoying the warmth of his bare chest and the damp male scent of his skin. Her cheek pressed into his dark hair. The tip of her tongue reached to nuzzle his flat nipple.

"Fiona," he breathed at her touch.

Loving the sound of her name spoken in his deep voice, she smiled and buried her nose against his flesh. As always when she was experiencing something new, the inclination to analyze slipped in and out of her mind. It was something in her training, she supposed. Her brain ticked off the human sensations that drifted through her: detachment, lightness, a floating feeling and such drowsiness.

And yet she felt aware, too. There was pain. Physical pain that throbbed between her legs where she'd been torn, like a cocoon must tear for a butterfly to escape to freedom. There was pleasure, her body alive with a tingling glow that radiated over her breasts, down her hips and onto her thighs. And over all of it, there was the sense of Rogan.

Rogan. How wonderful he'd made her feel. She'd never known such passion. In all her years of watching elephants, of studying biological reactions, of carefully recording the mating act, it had never occurred to her to translate the experience to herself. She'd never thought about what it could mean to give over complete control of her body to a man. She'd never imagined herself capable of such intensity.

The memory of her response sent a shiver down her back. Rogan instantly drew her closer.

"What is it, Fiona?" he murmured.

"All these years, I've worked to suppress myself," she said, a smile touching her lips. "After my mother died, lots of feelings shut down of their own accord. And I struggled to hide away the rest. Later I didn't want to feel the pain of letting Margaret go. And I didn't want to be hurt over my father's withdrawal. Eventually—out in the bush—I just wanted to be as much like the Africans as I could. Like Sentero, you know."

"Sentero?" He drew away and looked into her eyes.

"Sentero is enigmatic. I like that about him. I never know what he's thinking or feeling. He's always right on track with our research. Nothing gets in the way of his observations. He's so emotionally level that his other senses have had the opportunity to heighten. He smells and sees and hears much better than I do. I wanted so badly to be like that. But now... in one strange night... all my hard work has... vanished."

"What do you mean, vanished?"

"Everything—all the feelings I'd locked away or buried—suddenly broke loose inside me. It's as if I went wild."

"I noticed that."

She laughed. "I feel free, Rogan. I feel emotional. I feel like all the dams inside me burst and everything rushed out."

"That's good, isn't it?"

She thought for a moment. "I don't know yet. I'm sort of in shock right now."

"You aren't the only one."

Lifting her head from his chest, she slipped up along him until they were eye to eye. She read the solemnity in his expression. And she began to realize that though she might have opened and been freed, Rogan had now shut himself away.

"Tell me what you mean, Rogan," she said softly.

He took a breath. "Fiona...I had no idea you were a virgin. I mean, I just thought...hell, I don't know what I was thinking. Probably I *wasn't* thinking. But I sure didn't expect to find you..."

His voice trailed off, mirroring the sense of confusion inside him. She stirred, and one hand came up to trace a line down his neck. For a long time neither spoke.

"I'm sorry it was a surprise," she said finally. "It didn't occur to me to tell you. I mean, I assumed you'd know."

"How would I know that, Fiona?" He caught her shoulders. "In my world, everybody's fairly well experienced. There's nothing new, no surprises. Sex has always just been something that eventually happened between two people. Part of the normal course of things. A good time."

"Didn't you have a good time?"

"Damn." He let out a breath. "Of course I did. I mean, it was...it was unbelievable. Fiona, what you just gave me was something very special. You've let go of a part of yourself. And you let me be the one to touch you in that way."

She shut her eyes, alarmed by the strength of his reaction. What did it mean to him, this lovemaking? What had it done to him to know she'd given him her virginity? She was afraid to find out.

"I'm thirty-one years old, Rogan," she said, trying to make herself sound as casual as the other women who had moved in and out of his life. "I decided it was time."

"But haven't you ever had a boyfriend, Fiona? In all those years, am I the first man who's known you so intimately?"

"Of course you are. How could I have had boyfriends? I was tutored by an old lady all through my teen years. I lived at home. We didn't go anywhere."

"But in college. Your doctoral work—"

"I told you, Rogan. I wanted nothing to do with people. I didn't trust them."

"But you trusted me. You trusted me with this."

"You told me I could."

"Fiona..." He gathered her closer, rocked to the core by the depth of her faith in him. No one had ever trusted him in such a way—trusted him to tread gently, to take care, to hold a precious gift in tender fingers. He was Rogan McCullough, the man who'd been accused of stepping on people on his way up. He was the guy women wanted, never loved. And he knew why they didn't love him. He couldn't commit to that sort of nonsense. He'd cultivated his image so that everyone would know it—women and men alike. You couldn't expect a lifetime of devotion out of Rogan McCullough. He didn't have it to give.

And now here was this woman, this woman who was so beautiful inside and out, who'd trusted him to touch her in a way she had let no other human being touch her. Ever. She had given him more than her body. She had let him breach the walls that had been her fortress nearly all her life. She'd given him herself.

"Rogan," she whispered, "since I'll be leaving in the morning, I was wondering if you might feel like . . . like engaging in sex again."

"Engaging in s—? Fiona, what we did here tonight isn't some scientific experiment."

"No, of course not. I never thought that. But I've just been lying here thinking about how it felt. And I thought I'd like to feel it again once more before we go our separate ways."

"I don't know, Fiona. I'm pretty blown away—"

Her lips covered his mouth. Her fingers touched his shaft. "Please," she whispered.

Clenching his jaw, he trembled, fighting for control. No, a man couldn't just use a woman the way Fiona expected him to. He couldn't love her and leave her like a honky-tonk cowboy in some worn-out country ballad. With other women there had been a sort of mutual understanding about sex. They'd silently agreed there would be no depth to it, no commitment, no real giving.

But with Fiona . . . He gazed at the top of her head, the spun-gold hair lit with an inner fire. With Fiona . . . He heard himself groan as her hands began to work magic on his body. . . . With Fiona everything was different.

Well, damn it, if she could give him such a gift . . . he could give in return.

Taking her in his arms, he gathered her to his chest. His mouth caressed the tender pink curve of her ear. His hands, seeming large on her slender body, curved down the lines of her back and molded to the swell of her buttocks. His thigh rose between her parted legs until it reached the damp apex.

As their tongues mingled, explored, danced, his hands found her breasts again. He pleased her, taunting her nipples, first with his fingertips, then with his mouth. Her body swayed against his thigh, an involuntary rhythm that pulsed to the beat of his touch.

"Oh, Rogan, you know a thousand ways to please me," she whispered. "I don't know anything."

His breath exploded from his chest. "Fiona...if only you were aware of what you do to me. You're natural in every reaction. Everything you do is so honest. So real. I can't believe the feeling. You're pure and beautiful and very, very sexy."

"Am I?" It was a new thought. A pleasing one. She shivered with delight at this shimmering facet of herself. Sexy. Yes, perhaps.

And with new found confidence, she slipped Rogan onto his back and sheathed him deeply inside herself. As she rose and fell, red hair atumble over her shoulders and cascading onto his chest, she lost all memory of biology and elephants and dark-eyed *ayahs*. She gave herself over to feeling.

Rogan's hands moved up her body, and his palms cupped the globes of her breasts. Her hips danced on his loins as she gave herself to him. She forgot that she was a female and he her chosen mate. She forgot that tomorrow she would be flying away from him.

And he, too, forgot. He lost all memory of the women who'd sifted in and out of his life like so much sand in an hourglass. He even forgot that Fiona was precious and new and had given him a miracle gift. Each knew only the other, only the height of cataclysmic release . . . and only the peace of sleeping twined with someone who could be trusted.

"Mr. McCullough, I—" Ginger stopped in the bedroom doorway. Her ankles caved inward. "Oh, God. I'm sorry.

You're usually up at six, and it's already nearly nine, and I just thought...and, well, Clive Willetts is here because he's ready to fly Dr. Thornton and...oh, excuse me. Please."

She fled.

Coming awake, Rogan peered at the empty doorway through sleep-blurred eyes. Against him, Fiona stirred. Her hands slid down his length, and her lips nuzzled his neck. She was beautiful in the morning. Drowsy, purring like a kitten and so damn beautiful.

"Rogan," she murmured, "I feel lovely inside."

"You are. Inside and out."

"Mmm. Is it morning?"

"Morning, and the rest of the world is bustling. What do you say I shut the door and we'll spend the rest of the day right here?"

She smiled, nestling a little more. "I'd like that...would you?"

"It'll be the best day of my life." He smoothed the skin on her shoulder, admiring the faint freckles and thinking that he would never get tired of looking at them. "I'll send up for some breakfast."

"Breakfast? Oh, Nguyo will..." Her head lifted out of the nest of sheets and blankets. "Rogan?"

"Good morning, Fiona."

"Oh, my heavens!" She sat up. "What time is it? I'm supposed to leave this morning. What about Clive? What about my flight?"

"Calm down." He pulled her against him. "Stay with me today, Fiona. Here in Nairobi. I'll tell Clive to spend the day at the airport tinkering with his airplanes. And then you and I can do some of our own tinkering."

"Rogan." She felt a chill wash over her. She looked at the growth of beard on his chin. She felt the pain between her legs.

"Fiona?" His hand sifted through her hair.

"I need to get back to my camp, Rogan," she whispered. "The men will be wondering what's happened to me. And the elephant calves...and the research...I should go."

He watched her as she slid across the bed and clambered to the floor. Without looking back, she hurried into the bathroom and turned on the shower full force.

His gaze drifted to the tousled sheets, still warm from their bodies. He picked up a strand of long wavy golden-red hair from her pillow. It caught a shaft of sunlight that streamed between heavy curtains. He twisted it around one finger, studying the way the slender filament pressed into his skin.

As he ran a hand over the place where she had lain, his fingers touched a patch of dampness. He drew aside the sheet. Across the white fabric, her red blood spread in a faint pattern. He lifted the sheet higher and saw traces of her blood on his thighs.

Dear God. He couldn't let her go. Not like this. He moved to leave the bed, but she stepped into the room. Her wet hair had been pulled into a ponytail. Beads of water had soaked from her hastily dried skin through her faded green T-shirt. Khaki slacks covered her long legs. She was breathing heavily.

Her eyes looked huge in her face. Luminous. Close to tears. "I had a lovely time in Nairobi, Rogan. Thank you so much. For the clothes. And dinner. And everything."

"Fiona—" He came out of the bed, sheet around his waist and dragging across the floor. "Now, listen here, Fiona. I've asked you to stay another day. I think that would be a good idea, considering last night and the things we haven't talked about."

"I feel I said much more than I probably should have, Rogan. I ought to go."

He wadded a corner of the sheet and shoved it into his waist. "Fiona, I know we've had some disagreements in the past, but last night we...well, we shared something. And I'm not ready to just send you off into the boondocks like this."

"Rogan, please." She bit her lip for a moment, hearing herself preparing to express carefully formulated thoughts that had begun to sound like lies. "Last night we did what we both wanted. Neither of us is prepared to make anything more of it. We agreed we're not people who are good at committing. And we both know how different our lives are. We don't fit together. We don't belong—''

"That's bull! Pure baloney, Fiona. And you know it. You talked about yourself last night. You told me things—things I already knew about, in a way, because I'd felt them myself. Then later you gave me...you gave me yourself. Is that something you're just going to shrug off so you can get back to your elephants?''

"What am I supposed to do? Do you want me to turn this into something difficult? It was a simple act, Rogan. Just a simple act of human mating, wasn't it?''

"Was it?''

She stared at him, hands clenched on her ragged knapsack. No, she ached to say. No, it was wonderful and miraculous. I'm a new woman inside. I feel alive for the first time in my life. Truly alive. And it's all because of you, Rogan. You and only you. No other man.

She swallowed and studied the beam of sunlight filtering between the curtains and onto the wood floor. She couldn't speak.

"Your blood is on my skin, Fiona," he said.

She fought tears. Let me go, Rogan, she pleaded silently. Let it be the way I'd planned it. Let it be simple and animal and nothing more. Please, Rogan.

"I can taste you in my mouth, Fiona. Your body scents my fingers.''

"Rogan, please.''

"What about this, Fiona? What about our lovemaking? You weren't protected, were you? And I was a fool, trying to pretend you were just like other women. You...you could be carrying my child right now. What about that?''

"It won't make any difference. If it's true, I can have a baby and go on with my work. Elephants do it all the—''

"Elephants! Is that how you think of yourself, Fiona? That you're an elephant matriarch? Marching through life without human emotion, human need, human love?''

"I have to go, Rogan.''

She turned in the doorway, but his hand shot out and caught her arm. "Fiona, stay. Give us a day to sort this all out. Will you do that?''

She held her breath, knowing that everything inside her was weeping. How she loved this man's blue eyes. How she longed for his voice. How she wanted his wisdom, his strength, his warm arms. How she needed . . .

No, she didn't need him. She didn't need anyone. And if she stayed, she would only want him more. It would only be that much harder to leave.

"Rogan," she said, trying to swallow the lump in her throat and failing. "Rogan, goodbye."

On the airplane to Frankfurt, Germany, Rogan switched on the overhead light and stared through the darkness at an airline magazine. Ginger sprawled beside him, asleep. A thin wool airline blanket covered her legs and bare feet. Her high heels stuck out of the seat pocket. Her blond spiky hair was mashed down flat on one side of her head.

Rogan smiled for the first time in twelve hours. Ginger was the sort of woman a man needed to have around. She was reliable. She did her job. She didn't complain or talk about herself or expect anything out of him.

As opposed to a woman like Fiona. Obviously her type was trouble from the word go. She was stubborn, independent to a fault and self-centered. She couldn't focus on a damn thing except those elephants.

Rogan tugged at his collar and flipped a page in the magazine. His eyes scanned something about Dutch cheeses. Windmills. Tulips. Delftware. Maybe he would go to Holland. Spend a couple of weeks there just for fun.

Fun. Rogan flipped another page. He tried to think of things that would be light and enjoyable. Bike racing, maybe. Holland was so flat there wouldn't be much challenge in it. Maybe he should go to Switzerland. Climb a mountain. Or Monaco. Have one of his cars shipped over and race it.

He flipped another page. Oh, great reading material here. An article on grief. Just what a guy needed to be thinking about thirty-five thousand feet in the air. Death, dying, grief. He scanned the sidebar that listed the stages of mourning people went through. Denial, anger, bargaining, acceptance.

Well, it was obvious he'd never felt an iota of grief about his father's death. He wasn't in denial. He wasn't angry. He wasn't bargaining to get the old man back. Hell, no. The only thing Rogan was angry about was Fiona Thornton.

He skipped a couple of pages of in-flight entertainment listings and found the map at the end of the magazine. Red arcs zipped from city to city around the world, showing where the airline flew. His eyes traced the line he was on from Nairobi to Frankfurt.

Well, it was a damn good thing he was getting out of Africa. The place had never held much to attract him in the first place. He would sell Air-Tours and be done with the whole mess. And as for Fiona, she'd been just another passing fancy. Another woman, in and out of his life. No big deal.

His gaze traveled to the tiny spot on the map where the Rift Valley Game Park nestled beside the highlands. What would she be doing now? Probably settling onto her cot, turning out her lamp, rubbing her cat. Her hair would spill out over the pillowcase. She would tuck her feet inside that white nightgown. She would shut those camouflage eyes.

Damn it all. He deserved a little more from her than just a quick goodbye and fare-thee-well. He'd offered her half a million dollars for her elephants. He'd flown her to Nairobi and gotten her in to talk to some bigwigs. He'd even bought her a bunch of new clothes. Not that she owed him anything for all that, of course. But the least she could have done was...

Was what? What had he wanted from Fiona? He slid the slick pages of the magazine back until he found the grief article again. He studied the first two stages: denial, anger. Was it true she'd meant nothing to him? Was it true he was angry with her? Or was he mourning the loss of her red-gold hair and soft voice and gentleness?

No. A man only mourned something he'd loved and lost.

Leaning his head against the seat, he stared at the tiny light bulb. The last thing on the list of stages was acceptance. Acceptance. He couldn't imagine a time when he would ever accept the fact that Fiona was gone. That he'd lost her.

All right, he would give himself two weeks. Two weeks of vacation. He would send Ginger back to New York. He would postpone Megamedia and cancel all his appointments. Fun. He would just have fun zipping around Europe doing things he enjoyed. In two weeks, he had no doubt, he would be over this little episode.

Bargaining? What was that supposed to mean? Rogan studied the tattered airline magazine as he sat on the edge of his bed in a Swiss chalet. Après-ski boots barely warming his icy feet, he knew he should be heading for the Jacuzzi.

He lifted a gold pen from the hotel letter set and began marking through the list of mourning's stages. All right, he was over his denial. Two weeks without Fiona had taught him that. He couldn't negate the fact that she had come into his life. She'd touched him in a way no one else ever had. He'd cared about her. He'd wanted her—more than just physically. He'd wanted to know her and be a part of her life. And he'd lost her. She'd chosen to go off into the bush without him. He couldn't deny that, either.

Anger. Well, he wasn't mad anymore. After all, she'd been right. They really had nothing in common. She wouldn't last a week in New York with all the hustle and bustle, the traffic and people and parties and meetings that made up his world. And, of course, how could he exist in her isolated world? No, he wasn't angry.

His pen tapped at the edge of the third word—*bargaining.* He had no intention of trying to get her back by bargaining her into it. There was nothing to bargain with. The facts were all too clear. They'd met. They'd spent time together. They'd talked. They'd touched. They'd made love. They'd gone their separate ways.

He stared down at his boots. He'd always enjoyed late-winter skiing. The slopes weren't as crowded. The snow was heavy. But a week of sliding down mountains hadn't held its usual allure, for some reason. He was bored. He tossed the magazine into the wastebasket.

What would Fiona be doing right now? Certainly not sitting around in ski boots. It was late evening in Kenya. She would probably be sitting by the fire with a cup of hot tea.

Nguyo would be going over his menu with her. Maybe Sentero would be slithering around in the background, looking things over with his small black eyes. And the elephant calves? They were probably chowing down on their night feeding. Or settling into a patch of grass, their soft ears flapping with contentment.

He kicked off a boot. It had been two weeks since he'd seen Fiona. Maybe he should try to reach her. At least to find out if she was pregnant.

He wondered if she would be like the women his father had taken on ski vacations or cruises to Bermuda. If Fiona were carrying his baby, would she demand huge sums of money? File a palimony suit? Try to strip him of everything?

He ought to at least know if she could be pregnant. He really needed to find out for sure where he stood in this. Just from a logistical point of view. He reached for the telephone.

"I'd like to place a telegram, please," he said to the operator. He waited a moment while she connected him. "Yes, I want to send this to Kenya. East Africa. Send it to Dr. Fiona Thornton, director of the Rift Valley Elephant Project. Cable it to the safari lodge at Lake Naivasha. They'll get it to her."

"What will the message be, sir?"

Rogan studied his feet. There were a thousand things he would have liked to say. Things he wanted and needed to tell her. But Fiona had been brief with him. He would respond in kind.

"This is from Rogan McCullough," he said finally and gave the woman the address of the hotel.

"And what will the message be, sir?" she asked again.

"Just...uh...just put down one word. *Baby*. And a question mark."

"Baby?"

"That's right. Just *'Baby?'* Send it like that."

As he hung up, Rogan pulled the airline magazine out of the trash can.

* * *

Fiona was unloading a shipment of soy-based milk formula from Clive Willetts's plane when Sentero drove the Land Rover into camp. Fiona's hair, tied in a loose braid, whipped around in the wind that had sprung up suddenly from the west. She rubbed a hand over her forehead, brushing at the sweat that trickled down her temple.

"Is that it, Clive?" she called over the rush of wind.

His head emerged from the cargo compartment. "That's all they sent. Will you be needing more soon?"

"Of course. This is barely going to last us a fortnight." She gave a small kick to one of the blue-and-white cartons stacked beside the plane. "Look, Clive, I want you to get a message to the wildlife federation. Tell Mr. Ngozi I'm going to need antibiotics, as well as regular large shipments of formula. And I'll need him to send a vet out here the next time you come."

"Dr. Thornton, I can't fly into your camp on a weekly basis. Or even every other week. I have my regular work. And we've had rumors of a shutdown."

"A shutdown of Air-Tours?"

"I got a wire from Switzerland a few days ago. Mr. McCullough wants a detailed inventory of the assets. He said he's thinking of selling off. That means I've got to haul tourists about, write up this blasted inventory *and* plan for my own future. I've been bringing in these formula shipments as a favor."

"A favor to whom?"

"To you." He stared at her, pale hair whipping around his head. "Well, I'll admit, Mr. McCullough *did* instruct me to keep you in supplies. But that was before he started talking about selling Air-Tours."

"You still work for Rogan McCullough, Clive. And you're still bound by his wishes. Until you're told otherwise, I expect you to fly the formula to my camp."

"Yes, Dr. Thornton." A bitter line, unconcealed by the wispy mustache, formed around his mouth. "But I'd think you might consider the welfare of others once in a while."

Fiona grabbed a box of formula and wedged it against her stomach. "Stack another on this one, please, Clive," she snapped.

"Get Sentero to do it," he spat back. "I've a group of tourists waiting at the lodge for the plane."

He slammed the cargo door. Fiona felt fire flush her cheeks and heat her blood. She marched toward the pilot.

"For your information, Mr. Willetts," she fairly shouted, "I spend ninety-nine percent of my time considering the welfare of others. I have three elephant calves to care for now. *Three!* Babies are being born and orphaned in the park almost every day, and I could take in twenty if I had the room. But I have three here—and three is almost more than I can manage. Moses, the man hired to tend them, fled a week ago. My research has gone straight to hell. The camp is in chaos. There's almost nothing in the park for the adult elephants to eat, and they're starving. Maasai warriors speared James to death two days ago. Rosamond has a septic wound, and I'm out of antibiotics. I've been so busy considering the welfare of others, Clive, that I've let my own camp run out of food. Thank goodness Sentero had the presence of mind to drive to the lodge this morning and buy a few supplies or *we'd* be starving, as well—"

"Dr. Thornton."

"I'm not finished, Clive. You can tell your employer the next time you talk to him that he left me in one fine mess out here. He ought to just come and see what a wreck everything is—except that the minute I saw him, I'd run him off with my rifle for fear that he'd—"

"Dr. Thornton."

"What is it, Clive?"

"Sentero has something for you."

Fiona turned as the thin African stepped forward bearing a small slip of yellow paper. "A telegram," he said. "It was waiting at the lodge when I went this morning. It's from Bwana McCullough."

She snatched the envelope from his fingers. Squelching the mixture of anticipation, fear, desire and joy that flooded through her, she tore open the paper. Only one word stared at her.

Baby?

"Oh, good heavens," she said finally, slapping the envelope back into Sentero's palm. "If that's all he's interested in, fine. I can answer him easily enough."

She pulled a slim notebook from her back pocket and a pen from behind her ear. "Clive, send this telegram to your employer the minute you get to Nairobi."

She scrawled out her one-word response to Rogan's query. Then she folded the paper and handed it to Clive. Pushing the aching memories of Rogan out of her mind and into the wind where they could be swept away forever, she firmed her shoulders and bent to the cartons.

"Come on, Sentero," she snapped. "Load me up. We've got things to do."

Rogan was sitting on the balcony of his chalet sipping white wine and trying to pay attention to the Frenchwoman he'd met on the slopes that afternoon. A petite brunette with pale blue eyes and a wide smile, she had been chattering for hours about things that didn't interest him in the least.

Her après-ski outfit in vivid turquoise trimmed with mink should have kept him awake. She had left the front zipper undone almost to her navel, and the edges of her firm white breasts peeked coyly out from between the fur. But for some reason Rogan's eyelids drooped and it was all he could do to feign interest.

"So what brings you to the slopes, Rogan?" she asked, rolling the *R* in his name.

"Huh? Oh...elephants." He realized belatedly that he'd said the first thing that came to his mind. And it was the wrong thing.

"Elephants?"

He sat up and took in a breath of crisp evening air in hopes it would waken him. "Elephants. Yes, well, I was in Africa looking into one of my smaller business interests. I met a woman there who was studying elephants."

"Oh, you're recovering from a broken heart!"

"No, of course not. I'm . . . I was just—"

"But you have no idea how thrilled I am! I am the mistress of curing broken hearts." She wriggled coyly and squeezed her white breasts together with her arms as a giggle emerged from her painted lips.

"Really, Babette, I—"

"Oh, Rogan." She rolled the *R* again. "Don't deny me this pleasure. I've found there's nothing so exciting as a wounded man. Come inside with me. You'll see!"

Weary, Rogan stood, wondering how he was going to detach himself from this turquoise vixen with a fetish for broken hearts. He studied the snowy slopes, transfixed by the red-gold glow of sunset. Fiona's hair was that color. And nearly as shiny. He could almost touch it. Almost smell it.

Hell, he should probably go along with Babette. Maybe she *could* cure him. But the thought of lying with her the way he had lain with Fiona . . . the thought of touching anyone but Fiona . . . the thought of ever again kissing anyone but Fiona . . .

"Rogan!" Babette was hurrying through the doors and back onto the balcony. She grabbed his wrist. "Someone is knocking at your door, *mon cher*. You must come."

Vaguely aware that while he'd been staring at the snow she'd managed to disrobe, he glanced at her naked body, then looked away. As he walked to the bedroom door he realized that he felt not a shred of desire. Not one shred.

"Yes?" he asked, opening the door.

The portly chalet caretaker stood in the hall, a flat silver tray balanced on his palm. "A telegram for you, sir. From Nairobi."

"Nairobi?" Rogan began unfolding the pink slip of paper. For some reason he was suddenly wide awake. "Thank you, Herr Schönmaker."

As the door shut, nude Babette and the opulent chalet and the last vestige of exhaustion faded away. He uncreased the telegram and read the one-word response.

"Three."

For a moment he could do nothing but stare transfixed in utter shock. Then his head shot up, his mouth dropped open and his voice emerged like that of a frog in its death throes.

"Three," he said to the ceiling. "*Three* babies. Fiona is pregnant. I'm going to be the father of triplets."

Chapter 13

Fiona bent over her desk, Sentero at her side, a detailed grid map of the Rift Valley Game Park spread before them. As he read aloud the list of sites where elephants had been poached, she marked them with dots of red ink. In the past two weeks the park had lost eleven elephants to poachers. Eight males. Three females, one of them a nursing calf who had taken a bullet meant for her mother.

"There *is* a pattern here, Sentero," Fiona announced as she placed the final red dot along the eastern escarpment. "I have no doubt about it. It's almost like the poachers know each elephant family intimately. It's like they can predict and track the family's every move."

The African studied the diagram but said nothing.

"Can't you see what I mean?" she insisted. "Look, here are the Js heading south toward Mount Suswa. James is shot on a Wednesday, just over the road to Narok. Two days later Jack is killed at the foot of Suswa. But on that *same* Friday, the Ps are hiding in the bush near Nairagie Engare and someone shoots Paul. Now, how could the poachers have known where the P family was if they were busy tracking the Js?"

"Perhaps there are two groups of poachers."

Fiona slapped a hand on the map in frustration. "Maybe so, Sentero, but you know poachers never work this efficiently. They're never this fast. They never accomplish so much in such a short time."

He nodded. "Perhaps they are learning better skills. And the drought is certainly slowing the elephants."

He was right, of course. The elephants were so hungry they were risking exposure in order to search out the last remaining grass. And with continued exposure, more and more of them became victims.

"Still . . . look up here in the north," she argued, aware that her emotions were running high. "See how the pattern of poacher kills follows the pattern of elephant movements? I could understand if it were just one family being tracked, or even two. But members of five families are being slaughtered at the same time in different places. It's uncanny."

When Sentero said nothing, Fiona thought she was going to explode. She stormed up from her chair, toppling it backward onto the canvas tent floor. She strode to the door opening and gripped the central tent pole as she struggled for control.

Ever since Rogan McCullough had invaded her life, nothing had been the same, she realized. Her emotions had come raging up like molten lava. She cried at the drop of a hat. She shouted at the occasional warthog who happened to run in front of the Land Rover. She mourned the loss of each dead elephant with such intensity that it almost consumed her.

This couldn't go on much longer, she thought. She was a wreck. Her carefully regimented world was tumbling down around her—and she was crumbling right in the middle of it.

Oh, how she missed Rogan! Every single day that passed seemed to cut into her, carving one more notch in her heart. His smile haunted her. The blue of his eyes followed her in the huge cloudless sky. Even the dry grass seemed to mirror the soft golden lights of his brown hair.

"Dear God," she whispered. Prayer had become a regular habit as she begged for release from pain during the long weeks since he had flown away from her forever. Often she found herself with her head bowed and eyelids shut to the slow death of the elephants, to the barrenness of the landscape, to the unbearable ache inside her.

She knew she had never needed anyone in order to be a complete person. That still held true. For the first time in her life, however, she had come awake to her deep need for communion. She wanted someone to talk to. Someone to laugh with. Someone to love and to be loved by.

It seemed odd to her that in the midst of death and destruction—a perfect opportunity to rail against forces beyond her control—she had discovered that missing sense of communion within her own dormant spirit. She began to connect. Her prayers seemed to travel toward a divine ear. And though she received no quick answers, she knew she was heard.

There was no blinding light, no miraculous healing, no mystic transformation. The drought didn't end. The poachers didn't stop their killing. But in her life Fiona sensed a caring presence. She felt it in the breath of wind that brushed her face each night. She saw it in Nguyo's smile as he presented his latest dish. She heard it in the roar of lions on the savannah. She marveled at it with the soft nudgings of the baby elephants' trunks.

"Dr. Thornton." Sentero's voice rippled through her thoughts. His brown hand rested on her arm. "Dr. Thornton, Clive Willetts's plane has returned. Perhaps this time he has brought the vet."

She nodded, unable to speak.

"Dr. Thornton," he said again.

"What is it, Sentero?"

"You know the vet cannot heal all the wounded elephants."

"I know."

"You know also that God has given Africa one great gift."

She glanced up, trying to read the message in his small black eyes. "No, Sentero. I'm not sure about the gift God has given Africa."

"This gift we Maasai call *im-booti,* the seasons. Now we're in the midst of *alamei,* the dry season, when the sun scorches, the grass withers and the earth cracks. This is the time when cattle trails are dusty and rocks are bare. The people and the animals face despair, death, destruction. But one day God will spin the cycle and we'll have *alari,* the rainy season. Then a green blanket will cover the earth, streams will overflow their banks, crickets and frogs will sing, nights will be cold and the Maasai huts will begin to leak. During *alari,* we'll feast and sing and rebuild as we prepare for the return of *alamei. Alamei* will come and go, Dr. Thornton, just as surely as *alari* will come and go. *Im-booti* are God's great gift—and also His great curse."

Fiona studied the somber face, knowing from a lifetime in Africa that Sentero's words were true. Yet she was also aware that Kenya's rains had been known to fail for several years in a row—until there was such severe drought that other nations sent financial aid, doctors, nurses and shipments of food for famine relief.

And this was the worst drought Fiona could ever remember. Not only were the people growing hungry; the animals were starving to death. With the need for quick and easy money, poachers were slaughtering elephants at a faster rate than the creatures could ever hope to overcome through their normal reproductive cycles. Orphaned baby elephants seemed to litter the landscape, weak and hungry and dying.

And with the drying death of Fiona's world, she too felt dry and dead.

"Sentero, if the vet has come, please go and talk to him," she said softly from her place beside the tent pole. "Show him the three calves and ask him to examine them. In the morning we'll drive out and try to find the wounded elephants. Maybe there's something he can do."

Without answering, Sentero took up his spear and brushed past her through the tent opening. Fiona sagged onto the end of her cot and covered her face with her hands. She didn't want to escape, to run away. She wanted to fight—and win. But how? The odds were overwhelmingly against her.

Sukari crawled into her lap and began to groom himself, first with one damp paw and then with the other. Fiona rubbed the warm spot between his ears and heard him begin to purr. A smile crept over her lips as she stroked the cat's silky white fur. His tail wrapped around her arm, much the way the baby elephants' trunks twined around her in greeting.

Pondering the three small gray calves with their floppy ears and rubbery trunks, her heart warmed. The rest of Africa might be dying, but at least three elephants would survive. God willing.

But if the babies were to survive, they would need her care. Standing, determined not to give up, she had just pushed back the tent flap when a tall figure blocked the evening light.

"Fiona. Hello."

The voice rocketed into the marrow of her bones. She drew back, rigid with disbelief. Yet there he was. Rogan. Broad shoulders, khaki jacket and shorts, tan socks, dusty suede safari boots. It was as if he had never gone away but had only faded for a moment and was now in full view again. His blue eyes traveled over her face, down her body and back to her face again. His mouth was slightly parted, as if he wanted to speak but wasn't quite sure what should be said.

"Rogan." It was all she could manage.

"I came back."

She brushed a hand over her eyes. "Why?"

Life infused him suddenly. "Why? Your pregnancy, of course. Fiona, you didn't think I'd abandon you during something like this, did you? I wouldn't let you bear my children all alone out here in the bush."

"Your children?"

"I took the first flight out. It's all I could think about the whole way. My children. Our children, Fiona." He took her shoulders and gripped them as he spoke. "I want you to tell me everything. When did you find out for sure? Where did you have the sonogram? I want you to have the best prenatal care money can buy. And names, have you thought about names?"

She stared at him. "You've gone mad."

"I have not gone mad." He frowned, his eyes red-rimmed and tired from the long flight. "I'm serious as hell. You'll be examined by the best physicians. You'll be monitored carefully. I know you won't want to leave your work for nine months, but—"

"Rogan!" This time she was the one to grab his arms. "What in the world are you talking about?"

"Your pregnancy, damn it. You wired me that you're expecting my babies. Triplets."

"What!" A laugh of disbelief rippled from her chest. It was her first laugh in weeks, and it felt so good she did it again. "I'm not pregnant. In fact, my menstruation started two days ago."

"Your what?"

"My monthly period. Which may partly explain why I feel so grouchy and irritable—"

"Wait a minute here. You sent me a telegram saying you were pregnant with triplets."

"I did not. The telegram I got from you asked how many elephant babies were in camp. And I wired back the answer. Three."

Silence fell over the tent.

"Elephant babies." Rogan said the words in a monotone. "I wasn't asking how many baby elephants there were. I was asking if you were pregnant . . . if you were having a baby."

"You were?" The smallest tickle of a giggle welled up inside Fiona. She fought to squelch it.

"Yes. I was."

They looked at each other.

"You thought I was pregnant . . . with triplets?" Fiona asked, mirth infusing the words.

"You're not? You're not pregnant at all?"

She shook her head. "Not even the tiniest bit."

Rogan cleared his throat, crossed his arms and fought the urge to smirk. "So, there are three baby elephants in the camp now, huh? How about that?"

"Yes, three babies. Elephants."

"Well, what do you know."

Fiona bit her upper lip and stared at the tent wall. Images of herself pregnant with triplets mingled with pictures of the two silly telegrams and the three elephant calves and Rogan flying half the length of East Africa trying to think up rhyming names for his three expected babies.

"Well, it's nice to see you again, anyway," she said finally.

A deep chuckle rumbled from the depths of his chest. "Sheesh, Fiona. I thought...baby elephants...well, how do you like that?"

This time she couldn't stop the laugh. Her shoulders shook, and her head tilted back with mirth. Rogan watched her for a moment, enjoying the sight of her joyous mouth and sparkling eyes. Then he joined in the laughter, his own belly-deep guffaws mingling with her giggles.

"Triplets!" she snickered.

"I thought I was going to have to haul you away from here kicking and screaming to get you to a doctor."

"And you came all the way back to my camp...just to...just to..." She sobered suddenly.

"Just to find you," he said, the smile draining from his face. "I came back to take care of you. I came to be with you, Fiona."

"Oh, Rogan." Wiping a tear of laughter from the corner of her eye, she allowed him to draw her close. The warm scent of his skin flooded through her like an awakening. She shut her eyes and rested her head against his cheek. His strong arms slipped tighter, as if they would never be willing to release her.

"Fiona, I can't just walk away again," he murmured. "And I can't let you walk away from me, either."

Her fingers squeezed the fabric of his jacket. She ached to believe those words. Ached to know Rogan could fill her and she could fill him—and they could make it all work.

"I don't see how," she began. But his mouth covered hers with a kiss that burned away the pain of the past lonely weeks. His lips crushed hers in a bruising sign of desire and possession. His hands enfolded the back of her neck, cupped her head, tangled through her hair. His body sought her swollen curves and deep hollows.

"Fiona," he breathed. "I've been in hell."

She clenched her teeth, fighting tears, battling away the overpowering surge of emotion that rolled over her. Dear God! He was back. He was holding her again. His words held sweet promises. His body beckoned.

"Since you left, everything's fallen apart," she whispered.

"Tell me." His blue eyes searched hers.

"The drought . . . three calves . . . Moses ran away . . . and the poachers . . . and . . . and, oh, Rogan, I can't believe how much I've missed you."

She was crying. Genuinely crying. Rogan stood in awe, watching the tears stream down Fiona's cheeks. No one had ever cried over him. No one had ever cared enough. Something inside his heart came loose. He coveted her tears, he realized. He wanted the pain she had felt for him. For once in his life, he had been needed. Missed. Longed for. He—and not his business or his money or his influence—had been needed.

This was a rare thing, this woman's tears. Rare and precious. And he suddenly knew he would do anything to keep her feeling such emotion toward him. He would protect and nurture her emotions with his life.

"Fiona." He didn't brush the tears from her cheeks. Nor did he kiss them away. Instead, he watched them, hungrily memorizing their shine on the coral of her skin. "Fiona, tell me everything. I want to know about the elephants. Tell me about the drought and the poachers and how you wound up with three calves. Tell me everything."

She sniffled. How many years had it been since she'd let loose with such a flood of weeping? She wanted to feel foolish. But the tenderness written in Rogan's eyes erased anything but warmth.

"Let's go sit by the fire," she said softly. "Nguyo will be ringing for supper soon."

Nguyo's smile had never been so broad as that evening when he served his specially prepared dinner of roast chicken basted in garlic butter, fluffy brown rice with groundnuts, spinach salad and crisp white wine.

"I almost feel guilty, feasting like this when I know people and animals are starving out there," Rogan commented as he toyed with a curl of spinach.

"Don't feel guilty," Fiona said in a quiet voice. "Eat what you've been blessed with and be thankful for it. And then do what you can to help others."

"Save the world, you mean?"

She looked up, appreciating the tilt of his lips and the slight quirk of one dark eyebrow. "I told you that you could, Rogan. I still believe it. You have a gift."

He shook his head. "If I have a gift, it's for railroading people and amassing money."

"That's a worthy gift. Not many people can do it."

"It doesn't save the world, Fiona."

"It might."

She cut a bite of chicken and chewed it slowly, waiting for him to mull over their conversation. When he said nothing, she began to speak again, telling him about the situation in the Rift Valley. He listened, asking occasional questions as she explained the severity of the drought, the Maasai ritual spearings, the uncannily patterned paths of the poachers and the numerous births of baby elephants.

His gaze wandered behind her to the three little pachyderms cuddled together in the soft grass beneath an acacia tree. The smallest lay on his side, one gray ear flapping. The other two had hunkered down face-to-face. Johnny explored Olivia's face, touching her long sparse eyelashes and damp temporal glands with the tip of his trunk. Elephantine rumbles of contentment slipped through the clearing to mingle with the calls of night birds, the laugh of a hyena on the plains and the cry of a bush baby.

"I'll stay up and feed the babies tonight," Rogan said, interrupting Fiona's discourse on the wildlife federation and the need for a consistent supply of formula.

"It's all right," she protested. "I've been feeding them every three hours day and night for almost two weeks. I'm used to it."

"But I want to do it."

She pondered the idea of letting Rogan back into her world. Feeding the elephant calves would allow him to touch what she had been touching, feel what she had been feeling. It would bring them close once again. She wasn't sure she could handle it—because she knew that one day Rogan would have to fly away. And this time it would be forever.

"Rogan," she began, "it might be a good idea for us to talk tonight. I feel strange about all of this. I mean, you came back to the camp expecting to find me pregnant. I don't know exactly where you've been, but Clive Willetts told me you've been away from your work for almost three weeks. Things haven't been...normal...for either of us. My research is in a shambles. I just think we should talk over this situation."

His blue eyes traced the features of her face. Finally he spoke. "We both know what's going on between us, Fiona. We just don't know what to do about it."

She swallowed and turned to watch the elephants. His hand covered hers, large and warm. She shut her eyes, soaking in the human touch.

"Fiona, I want to take care of the babies tonight," he said, his voice deep. "I want you to get some sleep. We'll talk tomorrow."

"How long will you stay in Kenya this time?" She blurted the question before she had given herself time to think. Feeling foolish—like a lovesick school girl—she stood. "I'm sorry. That's none of my business.... Good night, Rogan."

She walked quickly to her tent. But he was behind her, taking her shoulders before she had time to step through the door flap. "Fiona, I'm here now. That's all that matters to me. I've lived three miserable weeks thinking about you and missing you and wondering how in hell I had been so stupid as to let you get away from me. I tried everything possible to make myself just get on with things. I decided I'd start my work again, so I cancelled the sale of McCullough Enterprises to Megamedia. I put Air-Tours on the international market. A fellow in Bonn has made me an offer. I spent time in Europe trying to have fun and make myself forget. I wanted it all to be over between us so I could just get back to my old life."

"It sounds like you succeeded."

"Like hell." He stared into her eyes. "I wanted you so badly I could taste it."

"Taste me now, Rogan." Lifting her face, she met his lips with all the pent-up hunger of those weeks apart. As they drifted into the tent, their hands groped for the satisfaction of holding flesh swollen with need. Their tongues danced. Primal sounds of need welled in their throats.

Rogan's fingers tugged the worn green T-shirt from the waist of her slacks. Tracing upward along her slender waist, he lifted the knit fabric over her bare breasts. They tumbled into his palms, ripe and ready for his touch. She sighed as his thumbs nudged their tips to life.

"I thought if I never felt this way again, I would die," she whispered against his ear.

Her hands worked the hard muscle along his back, absorbing the heat that radiated through his bush jacket. She nuzzled her nose in his hair and trailed her wet lips down his ear and onto his neck. With each caress of his fingers on her breasts, her hips ground into his, swaying with need. He clamped one hand over her bottom and pulled her close, so she could feel the effect she had on him.

Imagining their bodies together, the stroke of his fingers on her silken places and the hard thrust of his shaft between her legs, she trembled. Swift as a spark during drought, she had burst into an almost uncontrollable flame. Heady with need, she worked apart the buttons on his jacket and buried her hands in the swath of hair on his chest.

"Fiona," he groaned, "I can't think."

"Neither can I."

"I need you."

"I need you, too."

He lifted her in his arms and set her down on her narrow cot. Night birds and crickets went unheard. All he knew was her lithe body against his and her warm, damp mouth pushing toward his kisses. How he had wanted her! He couldn't imagine that he'd actually allowed three weeks of his life to go by without her. Insanity.

In the moonlight he could see her distended nipples and soft stomach. She had thrown back her head, red-gold hair trailing almost to the bed. Her long neck seemed to call to him. With eyes shut, she breathed deeply in and out, a husky sound emerging from her throat.

He bent toward the tent opening, reaching for the zipper, but at that moment she went rigid and caught her breath.

"Wait, Rogan!"

He paused.

"Rogan, I just remembered, I can't do this."

"Don't worry about it. Your monthly cycle is a natural part of you. It won't bother us."

"No," she said, shaking her head and pulling down her T-shirt, trying to catch her breath. "No," she repeated, "it's not that, Rogan. It's... it's me. I realized I can't do this. I can't make love with you again."

"Why not?"

"Because... because I'm not an elephant."

"Fiona—"

"Hear me out, Rogan." She tilted her chin so that she could meet his eyes and force him to know that she meant what she said. "When we were together in Nairobi, I thought I could just have a casual encounter with you and it wouldn't mean anything to me. I thought I could walk away from it as easily as a female animal who's mated with her chosen male."

"But?"

"But... I found out I was wrong. I'm not that sort of animal. I'm a human being. When you and I made love, we became somehow united. It felt mystic and magical to me. You became a part of me, and I became a part of you. I sensed a spiritual bonding with you. And later, when I had time to think about it, I saw that I had been wrong. Totally wrong. A person can't just have a sexual relationship with someone and expect it to mean nothing. At least, I can't."

His mouth had gentled into the softest of smiles. "Okay," he said.

"I'm not sure you understand," she went on. "I really mean this. As much as I've wanted you and longed for your touch on my skin and ached for the feel of your mouth on mine..." She tried to force herself back to the point. "As much as I've wanted a sexual experience, I can't allow it again. Not if I want to go on with my life. It hurts too much, Rogan.''

"All right."

"All right? You don't mind?"

"I mind. It's not going to be easy to leave you tonight. But you're right—you're not an animal. Neither am I. And I've been behaving like one for too damn many years." He touched her chin and lightly kissed her lips.

Then she watched him walk away, his broad back silvered by moonlight and his brown hair ruffling in the night breeze.

In the morning Rogan was gone. His plane had flown long before sunup. Nguyo was dismayed, of course, having prepared a huge breakfast of pancakes, sausages, omelets and fruit salad. Fiona stared at the empty airstrip, her mind and heart a blank, but it was only a moment before Nguyo hurried out of the kitchen with a note printed in large block letters.

"For you, *memsahib,*" he announced. "Perhaps Bwana McCullough wrote it."

Fiona took the note. "Did some thinking last night," it read in heavy black ink. "Back by sunset. Gone to save the world. Rogan."

"Is it from the *bwana?*" Nguyo asked, straining over her shoulder.

"He says he'll be coming back tonight."

The African nodded as he walked away. "Oh, yes. Of course he will return. Perhaps I shall bake a spice cake."

Rogan's plane flew into camp just as the sun flickered out over the horizon. Sentero had arrived in the Land Rover only minutes before. He and Fiona rotated the duty of feeding the three little calves with trying to continue their elephant research. Standing beside her, Sentero watched the plane taxi across the bumpy ground and come to a halt.

"A good pilot," he commented.

She smiled, watching Rogan climb out of the plane, long legs descending first, followed by his chest and head. "A good man," she stated.

Sentero said nothing but watched with her while Rogan sauntered over the almost dry stream and across the clearing beneath the acacias. He lifted a hand, a grin brightening his face in spite of the gathering dusk.

"Well, I took care of a few things," he announced, clapping Sentero on the back. "Got us a place to keep the three elephant calves. And more, if we find them."

"A place," Fiona breathed. "Where?"

He jabbed a thumb toward Mount Suswa, at this time of day just a small purple hump in the distance. "The old King house over by the edge of the park. The house itself is crumbling, but there's a water hole, plenty of trees, some stone cattle corrals and lots of acreage."

Fiona stared at him. His blue eyes looked downright merry as he gestured back and forth, describing his day. "Flew into Nairobi," he was saying while she tried to concentrate on his words and at the same time figure out how to tell him that his dream was an utter impossibility. "Took this fellow, Masika, out to the house in the plane about noon...place could use some work, but I'm a fair hand with a hammer and paintbrush...back into Nairobi...paid cash, but it wasn't much of a problem, thanks to the bank...got the papers right here...planning to work it all out with the wardens tomorrow—"

"Rogan!" Fiona finally interrupted him before she lost her temper. "Rogan, please. Listen to me, it may *sound* like a good plan to you, but—"

"It's a great plan. We'll borrow a truck and haul the little fellows over there. We'll straighten things up—"

"Rogan, stop. You can't be serious about this. I couldn't possibly find the time or the money to keep something like that going. Besides, I've lived here in this camp for almost thirteen years. I just can't see this."

"That's because *I'm* the one with the vision." Smiling, he flung an arm around her shoulders. "Come on, Sentero. Let's go sit by the fire. You two hardheads hear me out, and then we'll make a decision."

"But you've already bought the house!" Fiona protested as he urged her across the clearing.

"Damn right. Cost big bucks, too. But I figure it'll be worth it in the long run. Once I get the orphanage set up."

"Orphanage?" A slightly hysterical shriek emanated from somewhere in her throat.

"Sit down, Dr. Thornton. Now just listen."

Fiona watched him settle into a sagging camp chair. She formed a mental image of him seated behind a huge, polished mahogany conference table in New York as he prepared to propose some outlandish move to his stockholders. He positively beamed.

"What I've got in mind here is an elephant orphanage," he said, hardly able to keep his smile under control. "A place for baby elephants—orphaned by poachers or the drought or anything else—to find a haven. You or the game wardens can bring them in when you find them. We'll staff the place and keep it supplied with everything the little tykes need. Then, when they're old enough, we'll head them back into the bush and find a family that will accept them. That shouldn't be too hard if they're not still nursing."

Fiona shook her head. "Oh, Rogan, I can't see..."

"Now just listen, okay? We'll fund this thing by letting tourists come and see the operation. They'll love it. Baby elephants. It's perfect, Fiona. People will come out to the orphanage in tourist buses. They'll pay a fee to get in. We'll sell T-shirts and hand out packets of information on the need to save the elephants, and then we'll take any donations they happen to want to give. We'll plow everything back into elephant work. I can just see it—better equipment and more vehicles for the wardens to use in stopping poaching, plenty of formula for the calves, vaccines, even funding for your research. Can you envision what I'm saying here?"

Fiona glanced at Sentero. His face, as usual, was unreadable. She cleared her throat. "It's interesting."

"It'll work, Fiona. I'm telling you. I know how it can be done."

"So you just went and bought the house?"

"Sure. I didn't want to wait around on this thing. No telling how many of the little fellows are standing around right this minute with hyenas nipping at their feet.

"Well..." She looked at Sentero again. "Well, it does *sound* like a good idea. But I don't have time to manage such an operation, Rogan. And who's going to man the place? These elephant calves have to be fed and tended constantly. You know that."

"Like I said, I'm planning to talk to the wardens tomorrow. It can only be to their benefit to go along with me. The park will make money, the poachers will be deterred more effectively, and the elephants will have a greater chance of survival."

"So this is how you've decided to save the world?"

"Yes, ma'am. This is it."

Fiona looked at Sentero. He studied her in silence. After a long silent moment he placed his *rungu* stick on the ground in the Maasai sign that he had made up his mind to speak.

"Bwana McCullough," he began, "in Kenya we have a saying—a holed calabash cannot be filled. It means, the will of the gods cannot be changed. This has always been our belief. When something is set in motion, it cannot be stopped. The seasons run in endless cycles. Birth, life and death must come to all men. And I fear that you are proposing to fight a battle that cannot be won—even with money from tourists. Tomorrow go out and see the elephants. Then you will understand."

Taking up his *rungu* and spear, Sentero walked away from the fire without another word. Rogan studied the tiny orange flames that licked brown logs atop a pile of white ashes. A dry breeze lifted a strand of hair and sifted it across his forehead. In his jaw a tiny muscle flickered.

"Well, I guess we know what *he* thinks," he said finally.

"He's discouraged, Rogan. The situation is so terrible...." She struggled to keep images of the dying elephants from her mind. "But Sentero has forgotten that the Africans have another saying. One they believe in with equal strength."

"What's that?"

"Dawa ya moto ni moto," she said. "The remedy for fire is fire."

"And?"

"And I'm ready to fight, Rogan. I'm ready to fight with you to save the elephants."

Chapter 14

When the sun slipped above the escarpment of the Great Rift Valley and sent a golden light filtering among the silver grasses, Rogan and Fiona set out across the plain. The Land Rover jumped over rutted tracks and ground up hills, its riders bouncing with each bruising jolt. Behind the front seats the old wicker hamper Nguyo had packed slid back and forth, glasses and wine bottles clinking, hard-boiled eggs rolling, potato chips crumbling and fresh mangos absorbing each shock into their orange flesh.

"Where shall we go?" Rogan asked, glad to feel the wheel beneath his palms. It pleased him that Fiona had entrusted him with the Land Rover, put her faith in his driving ability on the rugged plains, acknowledging his growing intimacy with the park.

"Let's find the M family," she said. "I haven't seen them for almost a week. Sentero recorded them in D-4 three days ago. They were heading west."

"D-4. Let's see..." But before Fiona could clue him in, he pictured the grid map in his mind and located the spot. "Just north of the road to Narok."

He didn't see the smile that crept onto her lips as she relaxed into the gray vinyl seat. She shut her eyes, enjoying the play of sunlight across her eyelids and the warmth of the early rays on her arm where it rested on the open window. The scent of dried herbal grasses being crushed beneath the tires mingled with the ever-present red dust to drift through seams in the floor.

It occurred to Fiona that—contrary to what she might have expected—the return of Rogan had brought peace into her life. She'd slept well, knowing the elephant babies were in his capable hands all night. Their breakfast had been more pleasant than any she could remember. Nguyo's grin had been radiant as Rogan wolfed down seven pancakes, a matched pair of poached eggs and three slabs of ham. The aroma of hot black coffee and wood smoke, the sounds of doves cooing and the stream trickling, the antics of elephants frolicking with joy over their milk—all had combined to imbue the camp with a blessed aura of wholeness.

"Strange, isn't it?" she asked softly, speaking almost to herself in the familiar way she did when recording her observations.

He glanced at her and his face softened, but he said nothing.

"You were so annoying in the beginning," she went on. "I thought I'd never met anyone as bullheaded and politely obnoxious in my life."

"Politely obnoxious?"

"You were a gentleman about everything. But your ideas ... concrete water holes, a camp full of tourists, electric generators ... they were impossible."

She laughed a little. He reached across the stick shift and took her hand. Her eyes opened as he twined his fingers through hers.

"They may have seemed impossible to you," he said, "but I'm making them happen. Just not at your camp."

She thought of the old stone house she'd occasionally driven past at the park border. With its huge green acacias, fresh stream and water hole, the place had always held potential. But the once-manicured croquet lawn was now a tangle of weeds, the rock garden had all but died from lack of water and the house seemed to be crumbling.

Nevertheless, the image of it held a faint charm...a sense of peace. She could almost imagine lace curtains in the windows, a white wicker table and chairs on the lawn, gables freshly painted a deep green, bougainvillea draping over the verandah, bird-of-paradise blossoms clustering against the steps, a white cat purring in the sunshine....

"Like to drive over to the house this afternoon?" Rogan asked.

Fiona jerked.

"The place I bought," he clarified. "I think you'll like it. And it could sure use a woman's touch."

She ran a finger over the chrome door handle, absently dusting it. "I'm sure there's not much hope for that house. It must be nearly a hundred years old. The few times I've driven by, it's been on the verge of falling apart. You'll want to put your tourists in tents, I'm sure. For safety."

"Oh, the tourists aren't going to hang around there except to watch the baby elephants. The house will be a residence."

Her eyes darted to his.

"You should see the floors," he went on, leaving his comment without elaboration. "Old wood parquet. Beautiful stuff. It's been allowed to dry out, and some of the pieces have started to come up. But it's nothing that some gluing, sanding and waxing won't take care of. Apparently the roof leaks. I've hired that job out. Should be done in a week or so. The rooms will need new paint, too."

"White," she said quickly.

He looked at her and smiled. "White, huh?"

"It's...it's a good color in Africa," she finished, aware that she'd exposed herself. "It brightens things."

"Sort of stark, though."

"Not with pictures on the walls and furniture upholstered in deep shades. Houses in Africa tend to be invaded by the landscape. You open a window and it comes drifting in—scents, dust, sunlight."

"Even a monkey or two."

She laughed. "It's possible. White walls keep everything blended and pristine...even with the occasional invasion of a monkey or a stream of safari ants or geckos, who love to hide behind the pictures.''

''Okay, white walls. I can go for that. But what about the furniture? You mentioned something about upholstery in dark shades.''

''A soft, pale background, I'd think. Littered with huge cabbage roses in maroons and emerald greens. Wicker pieces in the garden. Those should be white. And a white table-cloth in the dining room. Deep curtains...something to block the sunlight. It creeps in so persistently. And book-shelves in the library. Does the house have a library?''

''Sure does.''

''I thought so. All the old colonial homes had them. You can put potted palms in there, and ficus grows well indoors.''

''What about that philodendron in your tent?''

She opened her eyes again. ''You can't have my philo-dendron, Rogan.''

But she had read the message behind his words. It fright-ened her to realize how she'd run on and on about his house, as though it was somehow partly hers just by osmosis.

It *wasn't* her house. She lived in a ragged green tent and was very happy there, thank you.

''Hey, is that Margaret?'' Rogan's voice held a note of excitement as he stepped on the brake.

Fiona sat up and scanned the barren horizon. Lumber-ing over a ridge as if they had all the time in the world came ten red-gray elephants. In the lead Margaret lifted her trunk to test the air. Her tattered ears flapped, and she shook her head.

''It is Margaret,'' Fiona confirmed. ''She's annoyed that we've found them.''

''They sure don't look too good this morning, do they?''

''They're starving.''

She said it so matter-of-factly that he turned to her, a knot of irritation in his chest. ''Well, what's going to happen here? Are they just going to drop dead with nobody even trying to prevent it?''

''What can we do, Rogan? We can't make it rain. It's al-ready almost April, and there's not a cloud in the sky.''

"What about bringing in food for them?"

"In my recent issue of *Zoology,* Dr. Hodges—he's an acquaintance of mine—reported the yearly diet of one zoo elephant at one hundred thousand pounds of hay, twelve thousand pounds of dried alfalfa, fifteen hundred gallons of grain, two thousand potatoes, sixteen hundred loaves of bread—"

"Okay, okay. I get the picture."

He sat slumped against the Land Rover door, watching the elephants file down the hill and begin to graze among a spindly stand of acacias. Megan and Moira tore at the young tree shoots, eating tender leaves and new buds. Margaret set to work on a giant gray baobab. Piercing the bark with her tusks, she tore sheets of it away to reach the spongy central core.

"That can't be good for the tree," Rogan said.

"It will kill it eventually. But Margaret's not thinking about the future. She's thinking about now. She knows she has to stay alive, because she's the only one in the family who can get them through this drought. She's lived through other dry seasons, and she can lead the others to hidden patches of grass and acacia stands. She even knows where water is buried beneath dried riverbeds. When there's no more water in the ponds or streams, she'll take Megan, Moira, Matilda and the others to the beds and teach them how to dig with their tusks for water."

Rogan absorbed her words as he studied the old matriarch stripping away the baobab bark. Beside her, Madeline's calf knelt to nibble at fallen scraps of the core, the wobbly gray trunk unable to perform such a delicate maneuver as picking them up. Mick, who'd always been Rogan's favorite in the family, stood alone, all his antics vanished and his head lowered.

"Mick looks depressed," Rogan said.

This time it was Fiona who reached across the open space and took his hand. She could see his throat working as he fought the emotion welling up inside him.

"You know," he said finally, "when I was a kid, I used to feel totally powerless. I hated it." He paused for almost a minute, struggling with words that didn't want to come. "I feel powerless now."

Fiona held his hand tightly, sensing his turmoil and knowing it was mirrored deep inside her own heart. "You're not powerless, Rogan. You've done something. You saved the calves, and you bought the house for them."

"Hell, that's nothing. Three babies, damn it—that's not enough. It doesn't help this situation."

"Yes, it does."

His expletive negated her words of support. He detached his hand from hers and crossed his arms over the top of the steering wheel. Staring at the floor between his parted thighs, he muttered inaudible curses.

"I hate this," he repeated. "When I was a kid, there wasn't one damn thing I could do about my situation. And I promised myself I'd never let that happen to me again. But here I am, ticked off and not able to do one blasted—"

"Rogan, you're not that little boy anymore."

"But I *was,*" he snapped, lifting his head. "I *was* that helpless kid. My father—John McCullough, real estate mogul—decided to sleep around with a show girl from Atlanta. Someone from the press took a picture of them together and the scandal was out. My mother screamed and cried and threatened him. He stalked around the house in stony silence. And there wasn't one damn thing I could do to fix it."

"You were only a child."

"I wanted to save her...protect her...."

"Your mother."

He nodded. "But I was pretty much lost in the grand shuffle. They shipped me away to boarding school. My father dropped me off at the gate and drove on to some appointment he had. I walked into the school office by myself, carrying my suitcases, one in each hand, and introduced myself to the principal. 'I'm Rogan McCullough,' I said. The man looked at me and smirked. From that moment on I decided that *I* was going to be the one at the top. *I* was going to have the power. I'd never let myself be helpless again."

"And you succeeded."

"Of course not. Not then. My mother whipped through six marriages—each one a bigger disaster than the one before. Gossip rags carried every juicy detail. My father got tired of the Atlanta show girl and found a model from L.A. Then it was a Dallas stewardess. I lost track after a while. They hauled me on a few of their vacations. My mother occasionally seemed to remember I was alive and sent me a new suit of clothes—usually too small. Once, nobody remembered to pick me up for Thanksgiving, so I spent the holiday with the dormitory cook. And let me tell you something, Fiona—I didn't want any pity like the crap I see in your eyes right now. I felt mad. Mad and strong and determined not to live the rest of my life being manipulated and controlled by other people. The minute I was old enough to take charge of my own life, I never looked back. I moved forward and upward. I became the one in charge. Anyone tried to push me into a mold, I fought them—because I didn't want to be powerless. Not ever again."

"But you think you are now," she said softly.

"Hell, what am I going to do about a bunch of elephants? I can't boss them around. I can't control the weather. I can't force everything to be okay out here."

"And you're angry."

"Damn right."

"Good." She smiled. "Now, how about lunch?"

She was reaching over the seat when he caught her arm and drew her toward him. "Fiona, what in God's name—"

"I wouldn't invoke the Almighty on this one, Rogan. I've realized He deserves a lot more credence than I've been giving Him."

"Fiona." The threatening clouds in his eyes sent a shiver down her spine.

"All right, I'm glad you're angry," she explained before he exploded. "Your anger means you care, Rogan. And . . . like I've told you . . . when *you* care about something, you can change—"

"Change the world. Save the world. Fiona, I can't do that."

"Yes, you can."

She kissed his cheek and leaned over the seat again. He stomped out of the Land Rover, slamming the door behind him. She glanced up from the trunk, which held blankets, ropes and tools. He was standing stock-still, arms crossed over his chest, staring at the elephants as they began to wander away from the acacias. His brown hair lifted from his neck. He wiped a hand across the bridge of his nose, then rubbed it on his trousers.

Holding a worn blue blanket against her stomach, Fiona slid out of the Land Rover. She sensed that Rogan needed to be alone at this moment, so she busied herself spreading the blanket in the Land Rover's shade and unloading the picnic basket. A flock of superb starlings swooped to the grass nearby and began to feed, their metallic green-blue backs and chestnut bellies shimmering in the sunlight. In the distance a pair of secretary birds minced through the scrubby growth with apparent distaste in every step. They studied Rogan now and again, their red-rimmed eyes staring and their wispy feather head-crests raised.

He didn't move while all the elephants slowly vanished into the brush. Even after they were gone, he stood rigid, unfazed by the approach of a small herd of zebras.

Fiona settled on the blanket, her feet tucked under her. She ached to go to Rogan and take him in her arms. But he might interpret the gesture as pity. Worse, she wasn't sure she could allow herself to touch him again. For all the desire she felt inside, she knew that to touch more than just his hand could be fatal. She would want more...she would want everything.

He raked a hand through his hair and turned finally, walking across the withered grass toward her. His face was emotionless, grim.

"Rogan—"

"Looks like the eggs got smashed," he said, his voice dead.

"Rogan, please. Let's talk about this."

"There's nothing to say." He sat beside her and picked up a squashed egg. He wondered whether there would ever be a time in his life when he could just let go of all the pain inside him. He wondered if he would always feel as fragmented as the egg in his hand.

How could he look into this woman's eyes and tell her everything he was feeling? Could he ever explain the pain in his past, the healing that her presence brought into his life, the anger and frustration he felt when he realized that, after all, he could do so little to make a difference? Where once he had held himself together with such rigidity, he now felt as though he were coming apart.

He didn't want the life he'd worked so hard to build for himself. It was empty. But he also knew he was impotent to matter *here*—to Fiona and to her work. He wanted to reach out and grab on to something, but there was only empty air within his grasp.

"Hell," he said.

"It doesn't matter."

"Yes, it does."

"Not really," she went on. "You just loosen the cracked part and it peels right off. See?"

She took the egg from his hand and deftly slipped the crushed peeling from the white. Dabbing the egg in a bit of salt, she presented it to him.

Her smile was as bright as the sunshine. The trace of a grin softened his mouth as he took the egg. Turning the creamy white globe in his hand, he gave a little laugh.

"You're beautiful, you know that?" he said.

"Did I ever tell you that when I was a little girl I had freckles everywhere? Zillions of them. My face looked just like an ostrich egg—milky pale, but scattered with tiny speckles. And my hair was positively orange. Margaret, my *ayah,* used to tease me and say that I was part Maasai. You know how the warriors ochre their hair until it's a gleaming orange-red? Well, that was just how I looked."

She was grinning as she sliced a sandwich in half. Rogan imagined her as a child, all freckly and cute. Long, gangly legs. Bright hair in a pair of thick braids. He wished he'd known her then. They would have had great fun exploring the brush, building forts, collecting feathers and snakeskins and strange stones.

"I thought I'd never look like my mother," she was saying, her voice wistful. "But somewhere during the years after elementary school, the red in my hair began to mellow a little. The gold came out. The freckles faded. And I realized that my wish had come true. I did look like her."

"She must have been stunning."

"Oh, my wish didn't have anything at all to do with beauty. I wanted to look like my mother so that I could remember her better. I felt it would bring her closer and somehow prove that I really had been a part of her once."

"You loved her a lot."

She sighed. "You know what's so strange? I can't figure this out, but it was only after I met you that I started being able to remember her. It began in Nairobi. Memories flooding in. And ever since, it's been the same. The one thing I remember most about her is her smile. She used to smile all the time—so happy and light. Her laughter hung around our house in all the corners. We lost it after she died." She paused and smoothed the napkin on her lap. "Do you know what, Rogan?"

"Tell me."

"This morning I was standing in front of the little mirror on the tree by the shower. I was brushing my hair just like I always do. Suddenly I realized I was smiling. Not just a little smile, but a great big ear-to-ear grin. It was my mother's smile. And I was wearing it."

"Fiona." He reached for her, but she put her hand on his shoulder to hold him back.

"You brought that smile to me, Rogan," she whispered, tears glistening in her eyes. "Thank you."

"But you're crying now.... Fiona, let me hold you."

"I can't, Rogan. Please." She crossed her arms over her stomach. "It hurt too much when you went away before. I can't go through that again."

"Was it just the loss of my body that you felt? Just the loss of the physical me?"

She shook her head. "No, of course not. It was you. You, Rogan. With your grand ideas, your boldness, your tenderness, your big hands holding that milk bottle for the baby elephants and your nose burned red by the sun. It was our talks in the night. It was the way you made me feel human for the first time in years. It was just you. All of you.''

"If it was all of me you wanted, then it's too late. It's going to hurt you again when I leave. It's going to hurt both of us. So let me hold you now. Please, Fiona. I've needed to touch you. I've been living in a nightmare without you.''

She came into his arms. The picnic went forgotten as they lay on the blanket, pressed close, mouths seeking. His hands slid through her hair, and a release of pent-up tension came from his chest in a deep, male sigh.

"I can't believe how good you feel," he said.

She buried her nose in the warm skin of his neck. As his hands stroked her back, she shut her eyes against the invasion of pain—the pain of knowing that this couldn't last forever. She'd felt too much loss in her life . . . loss that had never healed. She had been just like her injured elephants, outwardly whole and complete, but bearing inside a festering, life-threatening wound.

And Rogan, she now understood, was so much like her. They had each faced a childhood loss that had maimed them. How could they be so foolish as to invite a second loss into their lives? Perhaps a fatal one.

"I can't, Rogan," she whispered, feeling his hands on her neck, his lips against her ear. "I can't do this. You have to go away from me *now*.''

"Fiona." He drew her closer, feeling her own pain inside himself. But he couldn't obey. He couldn't make an uncertain future outweigh his present need for her. He slipped his hands beneath the hem of her shirt. She sucked in a breath and held it as his fingertips trailed upward.

"Oh, Rogan." The words came out in a rush of pleasure as his thumbs eased over the crests of her breasts. "You just don't know what that does to me.''

"Yes, I do." His touch hardened as her nipples went stiff with desire. He kissed her sweet neck, enjoying the arching pressure of her pelvis against his. Her long legs slid between and around his, bare skin against bare skin. It came to him at that moment that he would never again want any woman but this one. Pictures of her danced through his mind—pigtailed and freckled, long-legged and passionate,

gray haired and softened by time—and he knew he wanted
her.

"I should never have made love to you the first time, Rogan," she was moaning. "It was a mistake. I can't detach
myself now. I can't make myself hold back. And yet I don't
want to make the same mistake again. If we make love
again, the bond will be too much for me. The loss..."

"Fiona, listen to me. Listen."

The sound of gunfire was all she heard. Popping gunfire
that echoed through the ravines and along the valley. And
then the shrieks of elephants. Bellows of pain. Trumpets of
fear and panic.

"Rogan!" she screamed. She sat up, her eyes wide and
her nostrils flared.

"What is that? What's going on?"

"Poachers. Someone's shooting the elephants!"

It took two seconds for him to mobilize. She was yanked
to her feet. The Land Rover door was flung wide. She was
still crawling onto the seat when the vehicle leapt to life and
tore across the plain. Zebras scattered. Birds fluttered into
the air with screeches of alarm.

"Where's it coming from?" he shouted.

"There." She pointed to a dry riverbed and the stand of
acacias that lined it.

"God," he muttered. "God, please...please..."

The Land Rover flew over a mound of rocks and bot-
tomed out against the hard earth. Thorny scrub shrilled beneath the metal chassis. Tires bounced in and out of holes.
Dust flew.

"There they are. Oh, no!" Fiona covered her face as the
Land Rover slid in a half circle and came to a stop.

The machine-gun fire halted at the sound of the vehicle.
A half-dozen Africans scattered, their weapons slung over
their backs. The clearing fell silent for a moment before
erupting in panic again.

Rogan stared, frozen in his seat. "Margaret," he
mouthed.

Fiona opened her eyes. The venerable matriarch lay dead
on the ground, one tusk and half her face hacked away with
a buzz saw. A dozen bullet holes in her side streamed with

blood. The calves ran frantically around her, screaming and trumpeting. Mick stared at his mother's trunk, detached and limp on the ground near her.

Moira, three bullet wounds gushing, staggered across the clearing, bubbly foam dripping from her mouth. Megan, Mallory and Mitchell had vanished. Madeline was attempting to corner her baby, but the tiny creature couldn't be consoled. Matilda knelt on the ground. Her tusks were dug deeply into the dirt. She breathed in and out, wheezing with pain.

"Dear God in heaven help us," Rogan breathed.

Fiona couldn't move, immobilized with horror.

For a moment Rogan couldn't make his mind work. But then he saw a white tusk lying in the brush not far from Margaret's body. The poachers would be back.

He turned on the ignition and stomped the gas pedal to the floor. The Land Rover blasted out of the clearing and lifted into the air across the dry streambed. In moments it was barreling toward Fiona's camp.

"Nguyo!" Rogan shouted as he pulled the Land Rover up beside the kitchen. The African emerged through the cloud of red dust.

"Bwana?"

"Where's Sentero?"

"Not here, *bwana.*"

"Where the hell is he?"

"A message came for him. He went to the lodge at Lake Naivasha."

Rogan thumped his hand on the Land Rover's hood. "Okay, look. I want you to radio the game wardens. Poachers have slaughtered the M family over in..."

"D-5," Fiona whispered.

"Tell them D-5. Tell them to get the hell over there. I'm going after the poachers with my plane."

"Yes, *bwana.*"

Rogan slammed the door and started across the clearing at a dead run. Fiona came out of her trance. "Rogan!"

"Stay here. I'll be back."

"I'm going with you, Rogan." She flipped open the metal trunk and took out her rifle. Grabbing a box of bullets, she slid from the seat and ran after him.

In minutes the plane was lifting over the camp in a roar that bent the tops of the acacias and scattered the monkeys. Fiona gripped the rifle between her knees.

"Someone knew where they were," she said. "Someone had to know."

"Yeah, and I know who it was."

"Who?" She stared at him, her face white and her eyes wide with fear.

"Who's been keeping tabs on the elephants for months, Fiona? Who knows where they are every single day? Who has access to a radio? Who belongs to a tribe that thinks nothing of killing elephants?"

Her mouth dropped open. "Not Sentero."

"Damn right—Sentero."

"You can't mean that, Rogan. He would never . . ."

"Where is he right now, then? Off at the lodge? No way. He's probably out reconnoitering his troops after their massacre."

"No."

"Wasn't he supposed to stay in camp and feed the calves? Wasn't he supposed to work on the research while you went out in the field?"

"Yes, but Nguyo said he'd gotten a message."

"Fiona, try to look at this clearly. Who was the last person to spot Margaret and her family?"

She swallowed. "Sentero. But, Rogan, he cares for the elephants as much as I do. He's done so much work to ensure their future."

"Did he want you to keep the calves in camp?"

"Well, not really, but—"

"I'm telling you, Fiona—"

"He took his turn at the feedings after Moses ran off. Rogan, Sentero felt just like I do. The babies have to be saved, that's true—but their care threw our primary work into havoc. I resented them at first, too. You know that."

He brought the plane down over the treetops as they sped toward the acacia clearing. "You told me yourself, you felt someone was tracking the elephants."

She shook her head, her mouth dry and her lips parched. "It can't be Sentero. It just can't be. I couldn't stand it."

He glanced at her ashen face and realized that he should have kept his theories to himself. Her sense of betrayal was absolute. Devastating. Yet he felt certain the dark-eyed Maasai who showed so little empathy was the mastermind behind the systematic poaching in the Rift Valley Game Park. And the Elephant Research Project was the perfect cover.

"There!" She was pointing toward the clearing. "There they are! Oh, look at Moira. Look what they're doing to her. Rogan..."

He watched in horror as the men hacked the elephant's head with huge machetelike *panga*s and gas-powered saws. Blood reddened the dried grass. As the plane swooped over the clearing, the men turned their AK-47 machine guns to the sky. Flashes sparked from the barrels.

"They're shooting at us!" Fiona cried.

"Damn every last one of them to hell." Rogan pulled the plane into a climb. "We're going to keep them here until the wardens arrive. Get that rifle ready, I'm going in for another dip over the site."

"Rogan, this is only a .22! They'll shoot us down."

"Just have it handy, okay?"

For the next half hour the plane buzzed the clearing. When a few rounds from Fiona's .22 let the men on the ground know it was armed, they became more interested in taking cover than in firing back. The poachers attempted to leave with their heavy load of tusks, but Rogan and Fiona kept them safely corralled. The living elephants had vanished, and only the three gray bodies remained—Margaret, Moira and Matilda.

"We've got to find Moira's baby," Rogan said through clenched teeth as he herded a poacher back into the clearing by zooming straight at him and lifting only inches from his head. "When this is all over, we've got to get the calf to our camp. She was already weak, and this will kill her."

Fiona couldn't speak. Her thoughts spun dizzily with every swoop of the plane. Sentero...Margaret...blood...tusks...calves screaming in panic and terror...*panga*s hacking...saws buzzing...

"There," Rogan announced. "There come the game wardens. Good work, Nguyo. All right, Fiona. Here we go."

He circled the plane around the clearing while the wardens' vehicles pulled up. A swift gun battle ensued, but the poachers had used most of their ammunition on the elephants and Rogan's plane. As the scraggly men—hands on their heads—were herded into a group by the wardens, Rogan landed the plane on a strip of bare soil.

"Well done, Mr. McCullough," the beaming African warden greeted them, his hand extended warmly. "We've been after these chaps for months."

"They've killed three elephants," Fiona said.

"We have the tusks in possession. And we'll transport the poachers immediately to Nairobi for incarceration. They'll be punished, Dr. Thornton. You can be sure of it."

"I want to talk to them, Mr. Wambua. May I do that?"

"They've been disarmed. Go ahead." He turned to Rogan. "We'll need a report from you, sir."

"Of course." Rogan watched Fiona walk to where the poachers lay, stomachs flat on the ground and hands behind their backs as the game wardens handcuffed them. "But if you'll excuse me for a moment, I'd like to be with her."

"Yes."

Rogan followed Fiona to the men. They didn't look so fearsome, really. Just poor, dirty fellows with frightened eyes.

"Which of them is the leader?" Fiona asked one of the wardens. He translated the question into Kikamba, their native language.

There was a moment's silence, and then they all began to give the same name. The warden prodded a young man with the toe of his boot until he sat up. He stared at Fiona, terror written across his face, as she approached.

"I want you to ask this man something," she said to the warden. "Ask him the name of the person who told him where to find the elephants."

The man spoke rapidly. When the leader refused to answer, the warden gave him a swift kick in the stomach. Rogan watched Fiona's face, but it showed no emotion.

"Who is giving him the information about where to find the elephants?" she repeated. "Ask him again."

The warden spoke once more. When the man shook his head again, the warden clubbed him with a stick. Rogan slipped his arm around Fiona's shoulders.

"He won't speak unless he's beaten," she said softly. "It's the only way to make him talk."

"Let's just go find Sentero," he said. "We'll confront him."

"No, I want to hear it from this man. He knows the truth."

She turned away while the warden drubbed the man more fiercely. Finally crying out, he began to blabber.

"Who is it?" Fiona asked. "What is the name of the informant?"

The warden dropped the poacher onto his stomach once again. "He has given me the name, but . . ."

"Tell me. Please."

"The name of the man who betrayed the elephants is Clive Willetts. A pilot for Air-Tours Safaris."

Chapter 15

While Rogan flew the Air-Tours plane toward Nairobi, he answered questions for the chief game warden. Fiona couldn't hear their voices from her position in the rear lounge. The poachers lay roped and manacled on the floor in the plane's midsection. Their guards kept watch with rifles ready.

Fiona curled onto a seat and stared out the bubble-shaped blister window into the cloudless blue. It seemed to her that she was as separated from Rogan now as the earth from the sky. How could what they felt—simple human emotion—overcome the innumerable obstacles between them?

Rogan's employee was implicated in the poaching of elephants. There would surely be an investigation by the Kenyan government. And yet Fiona was the one who had given Clive all his information. Week after week she'd plotted the elephants' movements on the grid map for him. For his tourists. Clive could easily name her as a coconspirator. Then what?

Even if those issues were resolved somehow, she knew Rogan had already planned to sell Air-Tours. He'd told her he had an offer—a good one. He'd made plans to return to his position as head of McCullough Enterprises. It was only their telegram misunderstanding that had brought him back to her. And just that morning on the blanket he'd intimated that he would be leaving again.

No doubt with this new scandalous uproar in his life, Rogan would back away from Africa forever. He would probably sell or abandon the old house and give up his idea for the elephant orphanage. He wouldn't want to stay involved in something that only brought him pain and frustration. Why should he, after all? He was a success in every other area of his life. Why take on something doomed with problems?

And the elephants *were* doomed. Somehow deep inside her heart, Fiona sensed the elephants couldn't survive. Not in the wild. What chance did they have? Poachers, drought, disease or Maasai warriors would inevitably bring the species to extinction. Oh, she could fight for their lives. And she would. But Rogan had been right. What could one person do against such overwhelming odds?

The Burundi and Zimbabwe governments would continue to trade in poached ivory. Oriental carvers would keep creating their masterpieces. And collectors around the world would buy the piano keys, necklaces, earrings, bracelets, trinket boxes, statues and mounted tusks that could only mean more deaths, more slaughter, and, finally, the end.

She ground a tear into her cheek and bit her lower lip. It wasn't like her to see the negative in life, she realized. But what good could possibly come of all this?

Turning her head, she gazed at the miserable African men huddled on the floor. She could hardly hate the poachers. They were hungry. And men like Clive Willetts promised them untold riches in exchange for the tusks. But could she really hate Clive, either? He'd grown up in Kenya during the days when hunting was part of life. He couldn't see beyond the present, beyond the call of money paid to him by other men. And where did it all stop? Who, ultimately, was responsible?

She shut her eyes and rested her chin on her arm. Dear God, all she wanted was to stop feeling. She wanted her old self back—the woman who could turn away from a baby elephant being tormented by hyenas. The woman who dispassionately recorded elephant births and deaths alike. The woman who didn't speak, didn't laugh, didn't cry.

No. What she wanted was Rogan. She ached for him. And she knew her emptiness would take years to fill.

Clive Willetts was waiting in custody at the airport. A pair of ebony-skinned policemen, handsome in their gray uniforms and shiny black boots, marched him toward the emerging passengers. Fiona moved into the background, clenching her hands inside the pockets of her shorts, as Rogan strode across the bare concrete floor.

"What the hell is the meaning of this, Willetts?" he snapped.

"I can explain everything, sir."

"Give me the keys."

"Keys, sir?" The lanky blond man squinted in discomfort.

"The keys to the office. To the desk you keep locked up. I want every damn file you have. I want this out in the open. And you'd better not hesitate to hand over every scrap of information, Willetts, or I'll ruin your life. Permanently."

"Mr. McCullough, sir. I think I should be given the benefit of the doubt. You can't be certain—"

"I heard what the head man said, Willetts. He put the finger on *you*. I saw the bloody slaughter of the elephants. And you're going to pay. Now hand over that key."

He grabbed the slender brass key from Clive's hand as the policemen took their prisoner away. Marching blindly through the hangar, Rogan led other waiting police and the game wardens into the Air-Tours office. Fiona stood beside the plane, watching from a distance through the large glass window as he opened drawers, pulled out files, ransacked the place. He picked up the telephone and made call after call, speaking with such intensity that the others in the room stood back in silence and simply watched.

Finally the group of men emerged. They strode through the hangar toward waiting police cars. Rogan stopped beside Fiona.

"I've got to take care of this business," he said.

She nodded.

He glanced at the waiting officers, then his eyes returned to her. "I've been on the phone with Frankfurt and London. And I have messages waiting for me from New York. I'll have to sort everything out."

"Yes," she said. "I understand, Rogan." *I don't understand,* she wanted to cry. *Please, Rogan. Please don't let it all end like this.*

"I'm sorry, Fiona," he said. "I'm sorry about everything."

"No, please . . ."

He took her hand for a moment and squeezed tightly. Then he turned and walked away. She watched him go, his shoulders a little bent, as if suddenly he were carrying a weight that was too heavy. He spoke briefly to the limousine driver, then followed the policemen toward the waiting cars. As they sped away, she saw him turn and gaze at her. Then the squad car vanished around the corner of the hangar.

"Dr. Thornton." She lifted her eyes to find the limousine driver approaching. "Mr. McCullough has asked me to take you to the apartment."

She stood in silence for a moment, watching the trail of police cars disappear through the airport gate one by one. She supposed she could go to the apartment and wait for Rogan. But what would that bring? Only a longer goodbye. And she'd never been good at letting go.

"If you'll take me to a station," she said finally, "I'll ride the bus to Naivasha, and my assistant can pick me up there."

"But Mr. McCullough—"

"He'll understand."

The driver pondered a moment. "Yes, madam."

As she climbed into the long white car, she glanced at the Air-Tours airplane. Images of Rogan flooded her mind. His tanned arm waving as he approached with the first bottle of soy-based formula from Nairobi, his scowl as they droned around and around the scene of the massacre and finally his emptiness as he climbed from the aircraft that last time.

Rogan was a part of her now. She could read every nuance in his face. She could feel his feelings as clearly as she felt her own. And oh, it was going to be hard to let go of Rogan McCullough.

As each day passed without word from Rogan, Fiona knew her assumptions about the situation had been correct. She made a valiant effort to carry on with her normal work. Sentero's message the day of the slaughter had been from the veterinarian, who had arranged to arrive at the lodge in Naivasha and needed to be driven to the campsite.

The young African spent hours examining each of the three elephant calves. He pronounced them fit and growing at a normal rate. Later Fiona took him into the bush, where he helped her to locate Moira's newborn. The baby was near death by the time they found it and transported it to the camp. The rest of the elephants in the Rift Valley park, the vet assessed, were in as bad a condition as she'd suspected. He tried to prepare her for the inevitable deaths that would come.

The poaching, at least, had eased off to some extent. With the capture of Clive Willetts, the central organization in the valley lost its spur. Yet Fiona knew it would only be a matter of time before the small bands of poachers began to step up their work again. They would grow bold, realizing how poorly equipped the game wardens were. They had neither efficient Land Rovers nor modern weaponry. And so the slaughter would begin anew.

Mr. Ngozi with the wildlife federation drove to the camp one day and took a look at the four little elephants. By now Nguyo had practically given up cooking and spent most of his time herding the babies around, trying to keep them from uprooting the tents and the kitchen, and making a vain attempt to fill their huge tummies. The elephants adored him, of course, and his initial resentment had faded quickly under the loving caresses of rubbery gray trunks and moonstruck brown eyes.

"I have made a spice cake for you, *memsahib*," Nguyo said one evening as she sat beside the fire. "But it has fallen down in the middle like an old volcano."

The first smile in many days filtered across Fiona's face. Nguyo's cakes *never* fell. "It's all right," she said softly. "I'm sure your cake will taste as good as it always does."

He beamed. "The air feels different today. Windy. Perhaps that is the cause of my fallen cake. And, of course, with four elephants, I don't have much time in my kitchen."

"I know, Nguyo. And I thank you for all the help you've been."

"May I sit down, *memsahib?*"

She lifted her head. "Of course. Will you have some tea with me?"

The little man shook his head. It was not his custom to join her in the evenings. All the men knew Dr. Thornton liked to be alone to drink her tea and think.

But tonight Nguyo settled into the camp chair and crossed his strong dark hands one over the other.

"Perhaps you would like chicken tomorrow, Matalai Shamsi," he said.

She smiled again, knowing the name was a term of endearment. "Chicken would be wonderful. But you won't need to make much food now, with the vet and Mr. Ngozi both back in Nairobi."

"A casserole, then? With rice?"

"Wonderful. And a salad. Do we have lettuce?"

"No lettuce. I'll make a fruit salad."

For some reason Fiona found that her vision had blurred. The firelight had changed into bright sparkles, and Nguyo's face had blended away into the night altogether. She sniffed and tried to stop the trickle that started in the corner of her eye.

"A message came on the radio today," Nguyo said, his voice gentle. "Sentero has been approved for schooling in London."

"London?" She'd known the brilliant Maasai had been looking into several options for his doctoral work. But London. It seemed so far away.

"Perhaps you will find another assistant," Nguyo commented.

"I don't know. The elephants aren't doing well, and the funds are short, Nguyo. I may have to end the project here."

He regarded her. "You will stay, Matalai Shamsi."

"Maybe not."

"This is your home."

She nodded. "Yes. It is my home."

"Good night, Matalai Shamsi."

"Good night, Nguyo."

It was a long time before she left the fire.

Fiona lay in her tent, Sukari snoring against her stomach. She stroked his head, wondering whether other cats snored—or if she had the only one in the world with such a talent. A chill crept through the thin tent walls, so she pulled her blanket over her shoulders and snuggled deeper into the bedding. Shutting her eyes, she drifted for a while, memories playing through her mind, plans for the future darting in and out, sadness mingling with determination.

When a roar blasted over the tent roof, Sukari bolted onto her head, claws tangling in her hair. Adrenaline flooded her veins, and she sat upright. For a moment she was certain the deep growl had come from an airplane's engines. But a swift flash of lightning told her she'd been wrong.

It was thunder.

With sudden intensity the western sky filled with booming crashes and sheets of jagged light. Sukari crawled under the blanket and wound around Fiona's bare toes. A branch broke and smacked into the tent roof. Then the even patter of water droplets began to sprinkle across the canvas.

"Rain," Fiona breathed. "Rain!"

Raising her hands into the air, she lifted her head and breathed deeply. A familiar smell of damp musk filled her nostrils. The tap of raindrops increased into a drumming beat. The tent roof shook and began to seep. Water trickled onto her desk. Lightning hissed across the darkness. Thunder followed. Fiona sat immobile, head lifted, eyes shut and a smile spreading across her face.

"Rain!" she said again. "Thank you."

"Memsahib! Memsahib!"

It was Nguyo's voice. The ring of alarm sent a chill through her bones. She sprang out of bed and tore back the door flap. The little man took her wrist and began to pull.

"Nguyo—what is it? Is something wrong?"

"It is Sentero!" he said. "Come, *memsahib*."

Barefoot, she ran out into the driving rain. Nguyo dragged her across the clearing, past the hissing, smoky fire and down the slope toward the streambed. Her heartbeat in her breast sounded as loud as the roll of thunder across the plains. She could see nothing but white sheets of water. Mud sucked at her toes and splashed onto the hem of her nightgown.

"Nguyo!" she shouted over the roar. "What's wrong? Is it the babies?"

"No, *memsahib!*"

He said nothing more, only dragged her through the last stand of acacias and onto the stream bank. In the midst of a torrent of water sat the Land Rover, headlights faint against the rain and engine revving with a sick choking sound.

"Sentero!" she called. "What on earth—"

The Maasai's head emerged from the window. "The airplane!" He extended a long arm and pointed into the sky.

Amid the sheets of rain and the brilliant flashes of lightning, Fiona caught sight of a silver wing.

"It's the *bwana*," Sentero said. "I heard the plane fly over the camp, and I knew he would need light to land. But the Land Rover is trapped in the mud!"

Fiona gripped the edges of her soggy nightgown as she stared at the circling plane. *Rogan?* Rain streamed from the end of her nose and trickled through her parted lips. Her heart hung. Her toes sank into the mud.

"Nguyo, get Wilson!" Sentero shouted.

The sound of his voice brought Fiona back to reality. With the unspoken communication so familiar between them, she knew what must be done. As Sentero climbed out of the Land Rover and waded through the knee-deep water, Fiona waded in. She hefted herself into the seat and grabbed the wheel. In moments Sentero, Wilson and Nguyo had set their shoulders against the vehicle's metal frame.

"Moja!" Sentero shouted. *"Mbili! Tatu!"*

At the signal they began to push. Fiona stepped on the gas. The Land Rover slid forward, tires spewing water. Amid grunts and cheers and shouts, the crew eased the heavy car up the bank and onto firm ground. Fiona didn't wait for them. Blasting ahead, she aimed the Land Rover's headlights at the soggy airstrip and then set the brake.

As she slid out of the seat, her three companions joined her. They watched in frozen silence, arms linked, while the plane banked, lowered, skimmed over treetops. Lightning zapped passed one wing, making it shimmer and blaze. And still the plane came. Lower. Lower. Finally one wheel touched the ground. Then the other. The plane slid across the mud and came to a stop. The door flew open.

"Fiona!" Rogan's voice seemed to drown the thunder. His body emerged, dark as a shadow, running, arms spread.

She ran toward him, her wet white nightgown sticking to her legs. Her damp hair clung to her shoulders. Water streamed across her face. She blinked, not knowing whether tears or rain clouded her vision. Her feet slipped, but before she fell she was lifted up in arms as strong as the branches of the baobab and crushed against a chest as solid as the mountains of Africa.

"Rogan," she sobbed as he let her slide down his body to stand on her own two feet again.

"Fiona, why did you leave me?" He caught her hair in his fists and drew her head back. "Why did you leave me alone? I expected to see you again at the apartment in Nairobi. And then I found out you'd come back here, to your camp. Why, Fiona? Tell me why you left me."

"I didn't want to have to say goodbye to you again. You don't need me, Rogan. My way of life...the elephants...it's all been trouble for you. You don't need—"

"I *want* you, Fiona."

"But the poaching...and Clive...and your company..."

"I worked that out. I figured you knew I could. Damn it, Fiona." He took her shoulders and shook them, staring into her face with such emotion it was all she could do to meet his gaze. "I love you. Don't you realize that? It took me a hell of a long time, but I finally figured out that what I feel for you is stronger than anything else that's been trying to get in the way. Do you understand what I'm saying, Fiona? I'm telling you I love you. I'm telling you I want to marry you. I want to make this thing work. Forever.''

The onslaught of words numbed her. She stared into his face, trying to read his eyes. But the darkness made him no more visible than a wraith.

''Rogan,'' she whispered.

''Fiona, I've got to know how you feel. Don't tell me I misjudged what's been happening between us.''

''No.'' She tried to make herself breathe. ''Rogan...''

''Please, Fiona.''

''Rogan, I love you.''

He caught her in his arms again, his wet mouth crushing hers, their skin sliding together, hands tangling in damp hair, bodies pressed tightly. The African rain caressed their faces, a baptism of love, hope, promise.

Chapter 16

Bird-of-paradise blossoms stretched their orange-and-purple petals toward the sun as it slanted across the stone verandah of the old house. Pink frangipani flowers from a nearby tree scented the air with a heady sweet perfume. Red hibiscus flourished trumpets and silken tassels for the bees that hummed an evening tune. Crimson poinsettias nestled against a lace-curtained window, while the mauve, cream and white flowers of yesterday, today and tomorrow shrubs lined the stone walkway.

From inside the house drifted the melodic notes of a bamboo xylophone. In a moment Nguyo emerged on the verandah. Lifting one hand to his brow to shade his eyes from the low orange sunlight, he studied the distance. Near the water hole he saw the row of small gray bodies, heads lowered to drink. He counted. Twelve. Yes, good.

He turned to the airstrip beyond the steel fence and saw the safari plane lift slowly into the sky. The white faces of tourists pressed against glass windows, their eyes eager to catch one last glimpse of the little elephants.

A lone figure walked from the water hole toward the gate. Tall, dark haired, he was relaxed in a wrinkled khaki shirt and shorts, suede boots, tan socks. Three elephants saw the man's movement and bolted after him, ears flopping and wobbly trunks raised in alarm. He stopped, turned and bent to stroke their gray skin, his face softening into a gentle smile. In a moment three Africans clothed in the green uniform coats of the Rift Valley Elephant Preserve emerged from the brush to lead the calves back to the water hole.

As the man started up the long path to the stone house, a Land Rover burst over a hill. Bumping and lurching, it sped over long green grass, swerving to miss hidden ant bear holes. Nguyo saw the walking man's face break into a radiant grin as he quickened his steps toward the house.

"Rogan!" Fiona's long tanned arm emerged from the Land Rover window as she drove beneath an old baobab and put on the brakes. "Rogan, you'll never guess!"

Rogan was running now, his face alight. She leapt down from the Land Rover, her red-gold hair bouncing around her shoulders. In a moment he had caught her up in his arms and she was laughing—a sound that filled Nguyo's heart and silenced every other noise in the clearing.

"Oh, Rogan, you just won't believe this! Maggie seems to have adopted William and Amy!"

"You're kidding? Just like that?"

They were walking up the drive now, arm in arm. Nguyo watched them come, his eyes moving over the beloved forms of the woman whose hair shone like the sunrise and the man whose eyes were as blue as a rainwashed sky.

"I'm serious." Fiona stopped on the stone walk. One hand, fingers splayed, pressed against her chest as she spoke. "I was worried sick over Maggie, because she just wouldn't join any of the other families. It wasn't as though some of them didn't want her. She didn't want to be with them."

"Not even the Ms would take her?" Rogan couldn't imagine that the dwindled M family would reject the young female Fiona was trying to rehabilitate.

"I guess Mallory isn't feeling comfortable enough with her new position as leader. Every time Maggie tried to come near, she ran her off."

Nguyo cleared his throat and moved to the edge of the verandah. "Dinner is ready, *memsahib, bwana.*"

"Oh, Nguyo—you've got to hear this." Fiona took the man's arm and drew him into the group. "I was just telling Rogan about Maggie—you know, the half-grown female elephant we had here for a couple of months? Well, after the Ms rejected her, she grew really listless. But then Naikosiai and I decided to see what would happen if we put William and Amy with Maggie."

"She's old enough to look after them. And they were sure ready to try life in the bush," Rogan put in.

"When the three of them saw each other, it was probably the most intense greeting ceremony I've ever witnessed. Rumbling, flapping, backing into each other, fondling, the whole bit. And the next thing we knew, the three of them were wandering off together, happy as larks. Naikosiai and I followed them for two days and they stuck together the whole time."

"Where's Naikosiai, anyway?"

"I dropped him off at his village on the way home. He wanted to spend the weekend with his family. I didn't mind. He's done an excellent job filling in after Sentero. I never thought I'd get anyone as efficient, but he's tops."

"*Memsahib*, the roast will be growing cool," Nguyo added quietly.

"I'm famished," Fiona said, laughing. She leaned her head against Rogan's shoulder as he drew his arm around her, and they walked together into the cool depths of the house.

The parquet floor shone with a waxed gleam as they moved through the large foyer and into the dining room. There, deep maroon curtains blocked the remainder of the sunlight so that the room was bathed in the glow of the long candles burning on the white tablecloth.

"How were things at home while I was gone?" Fiona asked when Nguyo had served his sumptuous meal and they had eaten their fill.

Rogan leaned back in his chair and sipped his wine. "I missed you," he said.

"I missed you, too. I wish you could go with me next week."

"Maybe I will."

"Really?" Her heart lightened at the thought of her husband sleeping beside her in the old tent. The days she worked in the field were long ones, and they lacked some of their luster without him. Still, with Naikosiai working out so well, and the promised return of Sentero during the coming Christmas holiday, she had hopes that her research in the bush would taper off a little.

"You'll be so happy to see Maggie out there acting like a regular matriarch," she said. "In some ways she reminds me of Margaret. She's getting very bossy."

He smiled, but he noted the wistful tone in her voice. In the candlelight her hair had reddened. "Fiona," he began, touching a strand on her shoulder, "I want to talk to you about something that came up today."

"With the latest batch of tourists?"

He nodded. "A fellow by the name of Blundell was in the group. Dr. Henry Blundell."

"From Yale?"

"You've heard of him?"

"Of course. He's a brilliant biologist. I wish I'd known he was going to be here. I would have loved to have had the chance to talk to him."

"He was very impressed with the preserve. Said he'd never seen anything like it." He paused, then broached the subject he'd been weighing in his mind all day. "Fiona, Dr. Blundell would like to bring a group out here to study. Students and professionals."

"Great! They'd learn so much from the calves. I could tell them all about Maggie and how she's forming her own herd of orphans."

"How about *showing* them Maggie?" He watched her face for a reaction, but her eyes revealed nothing. "Dr. Blundell wants to work with you, Fiona. He'd like to take a few students—two or three at the most—out into the bush. He's proposing to work with you for a period of time. Take notes. Photograph the elephants. Compile your data for you. He thinks he could be of service to you, and his students would learn at the same time. Sort of a symbiotic relationship, he said."

He waited in silence, aware that this turn of events could bring on the first serious problem between them since their marriage three months before. The idea of people encroaching on Fiona's work had nearly prevented their relationship at the beginning—and he didn't want to endanger what they'd worked so hard to build. Yet he sensed Dr. Blundell's idea was a good one.

"So it would just be students," she said.

"And professors. People in your field."

She tucked a strand of hair behind one ear and turned her wineglass back and forth. "Well, there's something I've been wanting to talk to you about, too, Rogan."

"Okay."

She cleared her throat. "It has to do with babies."

"We can take on another seven or eight here, no problem. And, Fiona, I'm telling you, the people coming in here to see the babies are leaving with a new attitude. They're buying those T-shirts we had made up—Only Elephants Should Wear Ivory. They're buying bumper stickers for their cars back in the States. And most of them are donating. One fellow wrote out a check for five hundred bucks today. I feel like this thing is really going well."

"I'm glad. It's just that—"

"Every bit of that money is going back into saving the elephants, Fiona. And I don't mind taking on as many more babies as you find. I've got the workers to handle them. Most of the major international airlines have followed through on their promise to bring in the soy-based formula free of charge. I got a letter from the wildlife service today. Remember how I told you we're helping them purchase automatic rifles and helicopter gunships to fight poaching? They tell me it's working, Fiona."

She smiled and took his hand.

"The letter mentioned that ten or twelve years ago, Kenya had one hundred forty thousand elephants. A couple of years back there were maybe sixteen thousand left. But the killing is beginning to level off now. Some of that credit is being given to the funds that come from our project, Fiona. I think there's hope."

"Yes," she said. "There's hope again."

He studied her hazel eyes. "I haven't saved the world, honey. But I'm giving it my best shot."

"I love you, Rogan." She moistened her lips. "Now...about babies..."

"We're talking elephant babies here, right?"

"Human ones."

"Oh."

"I was wondering...well, if Dr. Blundell and his groups come out to work in the field...there might be a bit more spare time for me around here...and I've been thinking about babies...."

"Me too."

They looked at each other. His eyes wandered down her body, over the swell of her bosom beneath the blue T-shirt and along the curve of her hip. She drew her hand up his arm and let her fingers play beneath the hem of his shirt-sleeve.

"Care to dance, Mrs. McCullough?" he asked.

"There's no music."

"Does it matter?"

She rose into his arms, held there by the bond of their love.

In the silence of the African night, they drifted around the long dining table and out onto the verandah. The cool night air wrapped them in sweet perfume. The green grass nearby no longer wept, for within it the crickets began to hum, and across the distant savannah the elephants rumbled to one another—reassurances of companionship, of family, of tomorrow.

Lost in magic, Rogan and Fiona circled through the night, their dance of love a promise for the future as they drifted beneath the baobab tree and its rare white blossoms.

* * * * *

Author's Note

Although the Rift Valley Game Park, the Rift Valley Elephant Project and the Rift Valley Elephant Preserve are products of my imagination, I would like to thank the many organizations in Kenya and worldwide helping to preserve the African elephant, whose very real plight has been detailed in *Weeping Grass*. Among these organizations are the David Sheldrick Wildlife Trust, whose work with elephant orphans inspired this novel; the East African Wild Life Society; the African Wildlife Foundation; the Kenya Wildlife Service, and the World Wildlife Fund. Researchers whose work allowed me to portray elephant behavior with accuracy include Iain Douglas-Hamilton, Cynthia Moss, Joyce Poole, Katharine Payne and William Langbauer. My special thanks go to anthropologist Richard Leakey, whose efforts as director of the Kenya Wildlife Service have greatly reduced poaching. My deep appreciation and respect are accorded to the president of Kenya, Daniel arap Moi, whose ban on ivory took immense courage.

It is through the support of these people and organizations—and through our determination never to buy ivory—that the African elephant may have hope for survival.

From the popular author of the bestselling title
DUNCAN'S BRIDE (Intimate Moments #349)
comes the

LINDA HOWARD

COLLECTION

Two exquisite collector's editions that contain four of
Linda Howard's early passionate love stories. To add
these special volumes to your own library, be sure
to look for:

VOLUME ONE: *Midnight Rainbow*
                     Diamond Bay
                     (Available in March)

VOLUME TWO: *Heartbreaker*
                     White Lies
                     (Available in April)

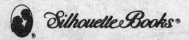
Silhouette Books®

SLH92

The spirit of motherhood is the spirit of love—and how better to capture that special feeling than in our short story collection...

To
Mother
with
Love
'92

Curtiss Ann Matlock
Carole Halston
Linda Shaw

Three glorious new stories that embody the very essence of family and romance are contained in this heartfelt tribute to Mother. Share in the joy by joining us and three of your favorite Silhouette authors for this celebration of motherhood and romance.

Available at your favorite retail outlet in May.

Silhouette Books®

SMD92

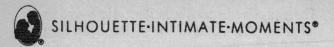

COMING NEXT MONTH

#429   NOW YOU SEE HIM . . .—Anne Stuart

She was his one weakness. The man who was known as
Michael Dowd knew this alluring woman could be his downfall—
and he didn't even trust her. But somehow Fancey Neeley had won
his heart, and for a man like Michael, that could be deadly.

#430   DEFYING GRAVITY—Rachel Lee

There was nothing Tim O'Shaughnessy didn't know about his
business partner, Liz Pennington—or so he thought. But when a
vandal attacked their company and threatened Liz, they were
thrown into constant company. Suddenly Tim realized that he still
had a lot to learn about her—and about love.

#431   L.A. MIDNIGHT—Rebecca Daniels

After a night of passion, Miles Richards couldn't understand why
Teresa Sandoval was avoiding him—especially because he needed
her help. She was the only one he could turn to now that he'd
become guardian for a troubled four-year-old. Could he convince
her to turn to him, as well?

#432   THE MATADOR—Barbara Faith

Five years ago, unable to stand watching her husband, Alejandro,
risk his life in the bullring, Megan Cervantes had taken their young
daughter and left him. But now he was injured and needed her
back. Would he ever believe that their love was worth more than the
price of glory?

AVAILABLE THIS MONTH:

"GET AWAY FROM IT ALL" SWEEPSTAKES

HERE'S HOW THE SWEEPSTAKES WORKS

NO PURCHASE NECESSARY

To enter each drawing, complete the appropriate Official Entry Form or a 3" by 5" index card by hand-printing your name, address and phone number and the trip destination that the entry is being submitted for (i.e., Caneel Bay, Canyon Ranch or London and the English Countryside) and mailing it to: Get Away From It All Sweepstakes, P.O. Box 1397, Buffalo, New York 14269-1397.

No responsibility is assumed for lost, late or misdirected mail. Entries must be sent separately with first class postage affixed, and be received by: 4/15/92 for the Caneel Bay Vacation Drawing, 5/15/92 for the Canyon Ranch Vacation Drawing and 6/15/92 for the London and the English Countryside Vacation Drawing. Sweepstakes is open to residents of the U.S. (except Puerto Rico) and Canada, 21 years of age or older as of 5/31/92.

For complete rules send a self-addressed, stamped (WA residents need not affix return postage) envelope to: Get Away From It All Sweepstakes, P.O. Box 4892, Blair, NE 68009.

© 1992 HARLEQUIN ENTERPRISES LTD.   SWP-RLS

"GET AWAY FROM IT ALL" SWEEPSTAKES

HERE'S HOW THE SWEEPSTAKES WORKS

NO PURCHASE NECESSARY

To enter each drawing, complete the appropriate Official Entry Form or a 3" by 5" index card by hand-printing your name, address and phone number and the trip destination that the entry is being submitted for (i.e., Caneel Bay, Canyon Ranch or London and the English Countryside) and mailing it to: Get Away From It All Sweepstakes, P.O. Box 1397, Buffalo, New York 14269-1397.

No responsibility is assumed for lost, late or misdirected mail. Entries must be sent separately with first class postage affixed, and be received by: 4/15/92 for the Caneel Bay Vacation Drawing, 5/15/92 for the Canyon Ranch Vacation Drawing and 6/15/92 for the London and the English Countryside Vacation Drawing. Sweepstakes is open to residents of the U.S. (except Puerto Rico) and Canada, 21 years of age or older as of 5/31/92.

For complete rules send a self-addressed, stamped (WA residents need not affix return postage) envelope to: Get Away From It All Sweepstakes, P.O. Box 4892, Blair, NE 68009.

© 1992 HARLEQUIN ENTERPRISES LTD.   SWP-RLS

"GET AWAY FROM IT ALL"

Brand-new Subscribers-Only Sweepstakes

OFFICIAL ENTRY FORM

This entry must be received by: April 15, 1992
This month's winner will be notified by: April 30, 1992
Trip must be taken between: May 31, 1992—May 31, 1993

YES, I want to win the Caneel Bay Plantation vacation for two. I understand the prize includes round-trip airfare and the two additional prizes revealed in the BONUS PRIZES insert.

Name _____

Address _____

City _____

State/Prov._____ Zip/Postal Code_____

Daytime phone number _____
(Area Code)

Return entries with invoice in envelope provided. Each book in this shipment has two entry coupons — and the more coupons you enter, the better your chances of winning!
© 1992 HARLEQUIN ENTERPRISES LTD. 1M-CPN

"GET AWAY FROM IT ALL"

Brand-new Subscribers-Only Sweepstakes

OFFICIAL ENTRY FORM

This entry must be received by: April 15, 1992
This month's winner will be notified by: April 30, 1992
Trip must be taken between: May 31, 1992—May 31, 1993

YES, I want to win the Caneel Bay Plantation vacation for two. I understand the prize includes round-trip airfare and the two additional prizes revealed in the BONUS PRIZES insert.

Name _____

Address _____

City _____

State/Prov._____ Zip/Postal Code_____

Daytime phone number _____
(Area Code)

Return entries with invoice in envelope provided. Each book in this shipment has two entry coupons — and the more coupons you enter, the better your chances of winning!
© 1992 HARLEQUIN ENTERPRISES LTD. 1M-CPN